Tease Publishing
Presents

LOVE'S IMMORTAL PANTHEON
anthology

TEASE PUBLISHING
www.teasepublishingllc.com

This is a work of fiction. Names, characters, places, and incidents are products of the author's imagination or are used fictitiously and are not to be construed as real. Any resemblance to actual events, locales, organizations, or persons, living or dead, is entirely coincidental.

A Tease Publishing Book/E book
Loves Immortal Pantheon
ISBN: 978-1-60767-025-4
Becoming Persephone Copyright© 2008 Dagmar Avery
Erato Copyright© 2008 Cat Johnson
Hephaestus Lays Down the Law Copyright© 2008 Tilly Greene
Seduction in Moonlight Copyright© 2008 Diana DeRicci
Dark Bond Copyright© 2008 Eliza Gayle
Pluto's Offering Copyright© 2008 Selena Illyria
The Spoils of War Copyright© 2008 Kayleigh Jamison
Cover Artist: Stella Price
Interior text design: Stacee Sierra

All rights reserved. No part of this book may be used or reproduced electronically or in print without written permission, except in the case of brief quotations embodied in reviews.
Tease Publishing LLC
www.teasepublishingllc.com
PO BOX 234
Swansboro, North Carolina 28584-0234

Tease and the T logo is © Tease Publishing LLC. All rights reserved.

BECOMING PERSEPHONE

Dagmar Avery

Drea felt his body before she heard his voice. The solid mass of him behind her, the smooth lines of his powerful thighs pressed against the backs of her legs, her ass, and the thick arousal riding high on the small of her back. His voice, of deep timbre, smoky and rich like her favorite claret, vibrated through her body.

"Beautiful night, is it not?"

She smirked and turned, looking him over with no small amount of amusement. Sexy? More so than should be possible, but when you're dealing with the 'gods', it was often so. And along with the sexy came the arrogance, something you couldn't get around when dealing with them either. He stood there in black leather pants, his straight black hair cut short in the back, choppy and long in the front, laying over the right side of his face, partially hiding one if his brilliant blue eyes. His skin, a glowing, stunning alabaster, seemed to soak up the moonlight on the terrace where they stood. No shirt to mar his beauty, though he was not without adornment.

His nipples were pierced through with a sooty mat black ring, and he had a tattoo, seemingly burned into the left side of his torso, a swirling mass of what seemed like undulating shadow.

Was this to be her lover tonight? This stunning vision of a man, who looked at her as if she were a snack? She allowed herself to indulge in the thought of what could possibly come to be by morning. The thoughts were more than agreeable. She licked her lips and cocked her head. While he wasn't the first she had met this evening, he was by far the most attractive. Zeus was pretty, but not her style, Hermes was sexy but blond, and Drea didn't care for blondes, and Hypnos, while dark and stunning, went sniffing after Tansy before she could even return his greeting to her. No, this one was perfect, exactly her type, and what was better, he seemed quite interested.

"It is. And who might you be?"

The man in front of her smirked and nodded. "Hades."

Hades? Well tales about his uber yumminess were true, if that was who he really was. "I'm Drea."

"Yes I know, the most stunning of the possible concubines."

Concubines? Well that was new.

Drea was there for a party, her and two other friends, Pander and Tansy. They had been invited while out walking around Athens, a young boy bringing them an invitation addressed to the three of them to attend an evening mixer in praise of Eros. They had laughed, and figured why not, after all who could say no to a party in praise of the love god, especially when they were in Greece for an anything goes kind of vacation?

Alone in the world except for each other, they had come to Greece to mourn the death of the only woman who had ever cared for them. Amalia was the closest thing they would ever have to a mother, and her death had jarred them all severely. Her will stated that there was provisions for the girls to go to Greece, celebrate life in her name, and enjoy the month they would be there. The will also provided a small amount of money for each, which stipulated that they spend it on luxuries and clothes as to prepare themselves for their adventure abroad. It was to be a grand adventure, and no expense spared. Drea, Tansy and Pander all went into it warily, as everything they had ever had was worked for, and hard, but when they received the money, and a letter each from Amalia, stating that their destinies would be realized in Greece, they collectively took the chance, and threw caution to the wind.

When they had arrived at the party by way of gondola, bringing them across a large glistening pond just on the outskirts of Athens, a woman dressed in a super sheer sheath informed them of the kind of party they were at, one where the males were all gods, and were looking for new companions. They were told that they had been invited because they possessed individually and collectively much of what each of the gods was looking for. Now, how they knew this was beyond any of them, but if these revelers wanted to roll play something this ornate, and include them in the decadence, who where they to say no?

"I suppose so, though why you think so is anyone's guess."

Hades looked her over with no amount of undisguised lust. His eyes traveled up her legs, and frowned as he met her mid thigh, where the tops of her thigh highs were peeking, the black lace with the blue ribbons weaved through. The look quickly fled as his gaze traveled up her body further, past the black satin pleated skirt, and the blue satin shirt, lingering at the upper breast that peeked out of the satin then resting on the pulse in her neck for a moment. When he reached her eyes, for he did look her dead on, he had a very satisfied smirk on his face, as if he had indeed bought something perfect for him.

"On the contrary, your attentions will be in demand tonight. I'm lucky to have them now. Let's hope the situation keeps." He offered his hand. "A dance I think?" he asked and smiled at her, making her body tighten in low places.

"Why not." She took his hand, letting the warmth of it seep into her pores and walked with him towards another room, one resonating with sound and darkness.

The music surrounded them, as her companion pulled her to him, placing his hands on her hips. They swayed, his body hard in front of her, hers yielding. The music took over and she soon turned and grinded her ass into his groin and bent over, coming up slowly, her dark raven hair around her head like a cloud as she arched.

His hands went to her hips again to steady her and then his right went to her hair and pulled her back, not violently, but enough to exert dominance over the situation. She whimpered, and heat pooled in the recesses of her body.

Hades tsked in her ear, and the sound made her shiver almost as much as his voice.

"Now pet, you're just teasing, and I don't do well with teasing. If you're serious, we should move to a more comfortable spot." He nibbled her neck. "I can't wait to get inside you."

Drea moaned at his attentions, and at the feel of his erection pressed against her once again. "Umm, and what makes you think you're going to?" she said and rolled her hips. "What makes you better than the rest around here tonight?"

"Come with me and find out."

Oh Lord did she want to come with him. Several times over the course of the evening if at all possible. Hades seemed like the kind of guy that could fulfill that fantasy ten times over, but she wasn't easy, and as much as her body was screaming for it, she would have to make him work for it. No matter what her vacation goals were, a hot guy hung like a Clydesdale wasn't going to get a piece of her after a five minute dance.

She rolled her hips once more, as if to prove her point, and then pulled away from him. He let go of her hair and she turned, smirking at him and walked further into the smoky room, intent on getting a game of chase out of it.

Bodies around her came in and out of view, almost as if they were coming into focus. What she saw in the darkness, in the driving resonance of the music, only proved to make her need for him and his touch greater.

Bodies writhed around her in various positions as she walked through the smoky darkness. Women danced around her. Men and women, groups of people, danced and moved as one, in various states of undress. They came close to her person, and she felt their soft lingering caresses as she walked passed and they reached out to her, beckoning her to join them. So many touches, fingers and bodies running over her arms, curving around her waist, cupping and pinching at her breasts... It all heightened her awareness of her surroundings.

She felt a longing, to join the unseen people, with their sudden advances, and the throaty moans she heard beyond her portion of the mist. They were not her pursuer though, and she had a game to play.

Then she was pulled from her path into what looked like a completely different room, but she had only moved a few feet into the smoky vapor. There were pillows, golden pillars and throws everywhere, and a man perched on them. She looked at who had grabbed her, and cocked her head. It was a woman, her skin painted opalescent silver, her lips dark as her nipples, which were completely uncovered, Drea looked at the man again, a stunning specimen of male beauty and smiled. He waved them on and the girl brought Drea's attention back to her and kissed her quickly.

Drea was startled at first, and then slipped into the kiss, letting the girl pull her closer. No, this wasn't the first time she had kissed a girl, but not knowing her made the action all the more wicked.

Before, it was something she experimented with in college, but this, this was sinful, and she reveled in the taste of her painted companion. She rubbed against her and the woman reached up and pinched her nipples through her shirt and Drea moaned.

Suddenly the man was behind her, his hands around her waist and his lips on her collarbone. She rolled her hips into both of them, enjoying the feeling of being the meat in the sandwich. It was then she heard the man's voice, a bit grating but no less beautiful then Hades.

"Little lamb, Orea just saw you and had to have you... and you respond to her quite well. Let us play..."

Drea wanted to, once again, but she felt the tug of something far off. Hades was searching for her, and if he caught her here, she wasn't sure how she knew but she was sure he would leave her to play with these two, and as much as the thought excited her, Hades catching her excited her much, much more.

She finished the kiss with the woman, Orea as the man called her and nipped her bottom lip. "Umm later. I'm in the middle of a game." She winked, and the girl let her go, a sexy pout on her lips.

She turned away from the man who smirked and

stepped aside, pointing towards a swirl of mist to his left. "Enjoy the hunt Drea, but make no mistake he will catch you."

Hades grinned as he felt her leave the room through the first portal, Bacchus and the Nymph. He waited 'til she turned them down, and then ambled through the mists.

He entered the room where Bacchus and Oread were necking and cleared his throat. Bacchus looked up and grinned.

"She's a fine one brother, and she resisted with us. First in how long?"

Hades growled. Bacchus and Oread, a mountain nymph, were always after his choice tail. It had been a long time since he lost his last concubine and had yet to find one that would be for him alone. He had heard the words she said to the nymph, but he didn't believe it. No, Drea was different, and she would be his next Persephone.

"Eat me you drunk fucker. Where did you send her?" He growled as the nymph went to her knees and nuzzled the wine god's groin. He didn't want to be around for much more of this. Bacchus wasn't his idea of a good time.

"What? You don't know?" Bacchus tsked and shook his head. "You think she could be your Persephone and you don't know where she is?"

Hades eyes flashed red, the flames that made up his domain coming to his aid. He squelched them, as he couldn't start a fight over a woman until that woman was his, as was the laws enacted during the Eros festival. Bacchus was a pain in the ass, but he wasn't a threat, not really.

"Get fucked man." Hades grumbled and moved past them toward the mists Drea went through.

"Already ahead of you. You're too testy these days H, you really need to get those pipes cleaned, and how. Stick around Orea will show you what I mean."

He ignored them and stepped through the mists, hot on Drea's trail.

Drea wasn't even sure she was still in the mansion anymore. Possibly a side garden, but this was ridiculous. How the hell she ever got outside was beyond her, but here she was. One minute she was in a room that doubled as a dance club and back room, the next she was in the equivalent of a harem with two oversexed people. Now she was in a moonlight garden, the breeze sweet on her face.

Everything here was hazy, as if it was kissed by the dream realms. All the edges were soft, and glowing, as if a hidden sun covered them all in shimmery glitter. A copse of elms stood to her left, thick and gnarled, to her right, oak and rowan, and dead in front of her, a garden thick and lush and green in the night. The ground was soft, the scent coming off it almost loamy, but her heels didn't sink into the earth. The scent of night blooming flowers wafted towards her, and it relaxed her, helped her to accept the possibility of the evening being what it was, something magical. She closed her eyes and inhaled, smiling to herself.

"You make it quite far when on your own." The deep voice to her left said and gave a chuckle.

Drea grinned and turned to see Hades leaning

against the trunk of one of the larger elms. Her nipples tightened, and she cocked her head. "This doesn't mean you caught me."

"I wasn't aware that we were playing hide and go seek or any kind of chase scenario, though I do love a good chase." He smirked and pushed off from the tree trunk, striding to her and stopping just shy of her trembling body.

He put out a hand, and traced the swell of her breast through her blouse and grinned as they both watched her nipples tightened further.

"You don't think this is really a chase? I never give anything up for free."

"Nor do I, though a little birdie told me you have been kissing girls."

Drea smirked and shook her head, stepping into his hand. She loved the feeling of his hands on her, and even though she wasn't ready to give in just yet, she didn't deny herself the luxury of his touch. "So what? You think you deserve a kiss as well? She took it, I just went along with it. And how did you find me so quickly?"

Hades shrugged. "I am Hades, you know."

She scoffed. "Right and those two I met before?"

"Bacchus and Oread, a mountain nymph."

"Ah, so everyone is playing a god tonight then, eh? And who am I to be?" she asked with a little interest.

"Simple. Persephone."

"As in your wife? Don't you already have one? Isn't that title already taken?"

"So full of questions aren't we? Well I will tell you, for a price."

"And that would be?"

"A kiss. Seeing as I deserve one anyway, because you gave that charm to the nymph already, so I'll be asking for two I think."

"A kiss for an answered question?"

"And a kiss because you seem so free with them."

Drea chuckled and shook her head. Kissing this man was high on her list of things to do, and quickly. "Why not? I mean a kiss is just a kiss."

"You haven't kissed me yet."

"So full of yourself aren't you? Very well, I accept the bargain. Now tell me how is it I could be Persephone?"

"Ah, that's far too big an answer for a lone kiss."

"I did agree to two you know."

"For other reasons. It will take more than a kiss to explain that to you. But I will answer a question."

She frowned. "Fine. How did you find me so quickly?"

"I told you. I. Am. Hades. Now, about that kiss."

He didn't wait for her to respond, but pulled her closer to him and claimed her lips, slipping his tongue between them. Drea moaned and wrapped her body around him, kissing him with much more passion then she kissed the nymph with. She rubbed against him, showing him she was interested, but teasing him still. When they finally ended up at the end of this chase, both of them were going to be ravenous, and that was her intention.

Drea was never one for the boring courtships of the everyday man. She craved creativity and wild experiences, and this could very well be one of them, even if she had to help the god roll play along.

Hades reached up and thumbed her nipple through her shirt, making her whimper, and broke the kiss with a grin. "So? We going to keep going with this chase, or do you want me to take you against that tree there?"

She shivered, thinking she would like nothing better than to do that, but pulled away and shook her head. She turned and saw the opening to a hedge maze that wasn't there before and then turned back to him. "Time to give chase once again."

She winked and tore off into the hedge maze, quickly being enveloped in the scents of the night and something sweeter, almost sugary. Drea ran through the maze, her feet seemingly guided on their own. She could hear Hades behind her, His deep chuckle coming to her on the breeze. He was enjoying their little game almost as much as she was. She inhaled and sighed and the deeper she got into the maze the thicker the mists got. Once just tendrils, they now almost obscured her vision.

She walked forward, hoping to hell she didn't walk into a hedge and came through the dense vapor on the other side, and walked into what looked like the reception room of the mansion. She looked about, still bewildered and noticed that it was a room in the mansion, and went to the bar to grab herself a drink. Running from her sexy god did make a girl thirsty.

The bartender, a hunky piece of a man with penetrating blue eyes close to Hades' winked at her and handed her a pink drink that smelled suspiciously like the sugary scent she caught in the maze. She took a sip and shuddered. The taste was heavenly.

"Excuse me, but what did you just give me?"

The bartender turned and smiled. "It's called ambrosia."

Of course it was. She shook her head. *Keeping with the theme with everything, aren't they?* She thought to herself and scanned the room for either Pander or Tansy. She hadn't seen either since they'd arrived and moved about to mingle, but then again when they went out partying that was nothing new. It was every woman for herself at these things, and the one who went home alone lost. Still, she wasn't as free with herself as her friends, and she knew they were probably having an adventure not unlike her own.

"All alone?" a deep voice to her right said close to her ear.

She turned to see another beautiful man, with sandy hair and deep brown eyes smiling at her. Sexy, but not her type. "No, I'm not alone, I'm being hunted."

He smirked. "Ah, well, then you haven't been caught yet have you?"

She shook her head and eyed him up. He was tall, sexy and from the look of the front of his pants, very well endowed. She looked at his face and the very masculine look that graced it made her giggle. "And who are you today?"

"As with every day, I'm Priapus, and you are?"

"Drea."

"The third of the new concubines."

She laughed. They were all really into this roll-play thing weren't they? "I suppose."

"So tell me, would you like a massage?"

Her eyebrow shot up and she shook her head. Drea knew that she was sexy and attractive, but this lot of men and women coming on to her out of nowhere was insane. "I don't even know you."

"You could. It could be quite pleasurable."

"Probably, but I'm not interested." No, not when she had her pierced hottie out there looking for her. He was probably getting close, and she didn't want to linger longer then she had to. If he caught her this early the game would be lost.

"No and why not?"

She grinned, took another sip of her drink and then placed it down on the bar. "Because, I told you I'm being hunted. Excuse me." She pushed off from the bar without a backwards glance and went towards a door that seemed to lead further into the house.

Hades came around from behind the bar and pulled the glamour from his person, becoming the god he was once more and ceased to be the bartender she received the drink from.

Priapus grinned at him and gave him a stiff half bow. "She is ripe for you, and she drank the elixir. You sure you want her around?"

"She turned you down, what do you think?" Hades sneered.

"She isn't my type anyway. Why do you think I didn't whip it out and show it to her?"

"Because you knew I would have intervened."

"Oh what's the matter Hades, can't do with any competition?"

Hades scoffed. "Competition? Brother I wouldn't go near any woman that you had first. There's a reason why you're always the clean-up crew."

"Fucker."

"Exactly." He smirked and followed after Drea. She had passed up on Priapus, and Hades was convinced she was ready for him.

She passed through the door and into another trail of vapor, stumbling through quickly into a bedroom, done in blue, black and silver. She was close to accepting the whole gods thing, especially with being dumped in different places every time she walked through a door. There wasn't a chance that this place was a damn funhouse and while she could have accepted that in the beginning, going from inside to an outside garden, and then back again while in the garden...she wasn't ruling anything out anymore.

The room was spacious, even cavernous, the focus of the room the large freestanding fireplace and the large bed a few feet from it. The bed itself was made of a very dark wood, and the walls were a dark grey, almost black, and everything was edged in sapphire, and it glittered just like the jewel.

Just whom the hell do I get to meet now? She thought and sighed. She wished she had brought her drink with her; her pallet was starting to crave the sweet taste and texture of the concoction.

She walked to the bed, the shiny material catching her eye. She passed her hand over it and smiled. Silk. Sumptuous. Sexy, and very soft. Wherever she was, it was a sin waiting to happen.

"So you finally found your way to my bedroom I see."

She turned and saw Hades standing behind her, drink in hand, the top button of his leather pants undone. As he stepped closer the fireplace came to life, bathing the room in a flickering glow. Everything softened, the light sconces on the wall darkened, and she saw him in the half-light of the fire and smiled.

His smile matched hers and he bowed. "Post time Drea."

"And what does that mean?" she said as she walked around the room.

"Well we are here, it's where I planned to take you earlier this evening, but you had to play didn't you?"

"I wanted you to chase me. I told you I don't give it up that easy."

"I never thought you were easy. So? What now?"

"You could tell me how it is I could be Persephone you know."

"I could, but I told you before, I give nothing for free."

"So what do you want?" As if she didn't know.

"You. In that bed. Naked. Sweaty. Satisfied. Forever. Not a bad bargain is it?"

No, it didn't sound bad at all. "You do talk a big game you know that?"

He chuckled. "Only because you have thwarted every attempt I have made to prove it to you. So do we have a deal?"

Drea moved toward and then sat back on the bed and leaned back on her hands, shaking out her hair. She had her legs crossed, though the skirt she wore, a pleated satin mini, hid nothing, least of all the garters she was wearing. She looked down and frowned, knowing full well she didn't put garters on. She looked up at him and he laughed. Hades had added them to her outfit, as if by magic.

"I thought they would suit you. They do."

"How the hell did you do that?"

"Hell indeed. Or a semblance of it. I am Hades you know. And try as you might to ignore it, I am a god, and you are sitting very pretty on my bed."

Drea grinned and uncrossed her legs. "So, say you are a god..."

"I did say I was pet."

She moved her left leg so that the heel was on the edge of the bed, her knee in the air. She knew he could see up the skirt just a little, and she was glad that he was indeed looking with very hungry eyes. "So, you going to tell me?"

"So, you going to fuck me?"

She grinned and leaned back a bit more, her hands going to her flat stomach and caressed the exposed skin between her skirt and the partially lifted blouse. "Thinking about it."

He was on his knees between her splayed legs in less than the space of a heartbeat. She looked down at him with a smirk and slipped her hand slowly up her torso, over her breast and to her neck. Her efforts were gifted by a growl from the man kneeling before her.

He took her right leg, the one that was hanging still and placed the heel of her shoe on his leather clad thigh and bent, trailing his lips up her leg from just below her knee.

She shuddered at the contact, felt the resulting tremors of his fingers as they slipped up the nylon beneath his lips. His mouth reached mid thigh as his fingers reached her knee and he caressed her there as he looked up at her, a lustful sparkle in his bright blue eyes.

"Really thinking about it. But I want the answer to the question."

"You'll get it." He grabbed her around the waist and pulled her forward, a sexy grin gracing his lips. He turned his head and placed a searing kiss on the inside of her thigh, then nipped at her and she gasped. The man knew seduction that was for damn sure.

She shook softly in his grasp. His lascivious look promised so much. She waited, praying he wouldn't tease her much longer. He dragged his hands from the skin around her waist and found the thick lace garters, pulling her closer by them and settled his arms around her thighs. She whimpered, knowing full well he was doing it on purpose, that he knew that all this anticipation was making her wilder and wetter by the second. A scant touch of his hot breath on her flesh and she would come for him, and he would know just how much he affected her. She didn't care. Let him know. Let him play his games, she was enjoying the torture.

Seeming to read her mind he moved closer to her soaked panties and groaned. One second he was smiling at her, the next he was nuzzling the wet scrap of silk and tugging at it with his mouth. He made quick work of it, and the warm air of the room hit her flesh and she quivered. She was closer now, and she looked down to see her skirt pushed up and the magical garters the only thing still on.

"Well aren't you pretty?" he said and kissed her sopping pussy, his tongue snaking out to tease her more.

Drea exploded.

Her vision hazed, and she arched, pulling at the bedclothes she panted, moaning under the onslaught of him tipping the velvet. He was relentless in his attentions, moaning as she did, proving to her he enjoyed it as much as she did. His tongue was magic, caressing every place she wanted, dipping inside her to make her writhe more, as if he knew what to do and when, instinctually.

As she was cresting the next plateau of orgasm she cried out and shuddered, her body shaking. He pulled away and then kissed her again, sending jolts of pleasure racing through her again. "Stunning. Perfect. You taste like heaven pet."

She looked down to him and licked her lips trying to catch her breath. "You think?"

"Umm, I know." He licked another line up her and

sucked hard on her clit, his eyes on hers as he did.

She cried out and came again, arching once more. He slipped two fingers into her and chuckled. "So ready for my cock aren't you?" he said more to himself then to her and pulled back, coming off his knees to crawl up her body.

She watched him as he did, and licked her lips as he settled fully on the bed over her. She raised her head and captured his lips with her own, tasting herself as her tongue slipped into his mouth.

In a flurry of hands and kisses Hades had her clothes off her in mere seconds, and she lay there, clad only in the garter and stockings he put her in. Drea grinned.

"And you still have those fetching pants on."

"So I do." He kissed her again and she nipped his bottom lip.

"Tell me."

"What was it you wanted to know again?"

"How could I be Persephone?"

He nuzzled her neck and then reared up, unzipping the pants and slipping them off his hips, showing her that he didn't wear underwear, and he was more than ready for her. His cock stood straight and proud curved ever so slightly up towards his body.

Dear God, the man was beyond perfect. "Umm, that is quite a sight but it's not going to deter me."

"Nor should it. I was merely getting comfortable. As for how you could be Persephone, it's just a name." He was completely at ease with his nudity, and she smirked.

"Huh? So if you're really Hades, then Persephone is your wife in mythology."

Hades grinned and settled on his side, his tattoo

visible, as it appeared to move in an undulating manner. "You said it. Mythology. In truth, Persephone is the name of my consort. She is the light to my darkness." He kissed her hard and she arched into him as he moved over her. "And you're my Persephone."

"Who the hell said I was looking for a boyfriend?" she asked as she wrapped her legs around his waist.

"You think I would pursue you for a one night stand? Not a chance." He rolled his hips and slipped into her wetness, and she arched, calling his name. "You're mine now Drea...and I couldn't have picked better."

Hades looked down into the face of the woman that had all but agreed to be his consort for all time and his chest ached. He had been watching Drea since she came to Greece and all signs pointed to her being the one to take over a position that had long been vacant, his lover and companion.

She felt like heaven quivering around his shaft, her body hugging tight around him. He placed both hands on the small of her back and arched her, so that he got deeper inside her, and she gasped, licking her lips as her eyes closed.

"That's it Drea, enjoy what I can do for you, what I will always do for you."

She moaned and shivered as she kissed him, completely lost to the moment. Watching her in her pleasure was a mind-altering experience.

She came for him again and he grinned as she panted, and flipped them both over, so she rode him, her nylon-covered legs hugging his hips. The sensation was an erotic caress and he grinned up at her.

"What's with the look?" she purred and leaned down while his hands circled her tiny waist.

"Your stunning astride me, I think I'll have you in this position more often," he said and let his hands travel up her torso to her breasts, his fingertips leaving little trails of ghostly fire in their wake. She purred at the feeling, arching into his hands as they grasped her soft breasts and flicked at the hard peaks of her nipples.

She was so responsive, and only to him. "It pleases me that you turned down Bacchus and Priapus... It further proves my point."

"Ummm, point?" she asked as she began to ride him hard, her hair wild about her head.

"That you belong with me. You're beautiful like this."

She shuddered and looked down at him, her body coming to another precipice of pleasure as she moved on him, as he pleasured her with his hands and cock.

When she came this time he followed her over, his right hand on her stomach just below her belly button, his left on her breast, pinching her nipple between his thumb and forefinger. She cried out, and he called her name as magic spilled across them.

They were enveloped in a thick cloud of sparks and sparkles, and as the air cleared Hades grinned and pulled his hand away from her stomach. There, made of magic and desire, was a delicate scrolling tattoo that moved much like the one that lived on the left side of his torso, the one that marked him with his power. He watched as she looked down at it, with undisguised awe and surprise playing across her face.

"What the hell?" she murmured.

"Hell indeed. I told you, you're my Persephone."

"I didn't agree to this..."

"The hell you didn't. If you weren't ready for this to be your fate the mark wouldn't have appeared. Deep down, you already accepted this as where your destiny lies. Admit it to yourself Drea, and we can move on."

Her eyes glittered with defiance and he smiled.

"Love, don't act like this isn't what you want. You love the idea of being mine, and I know you can't wait to see the world I have to show you."

"Why me?"

She didn't deny what he stated. "Because. You and your friends are a very special type of mortal. You were destined to be the mate of a god. You have no family to tie you to the mortal world, you aren't pillars of society, and above all, you are overly sexual and crave the unknown. You belong with me, here in this world. You are mine, now and always."

Drea blinked and then looked over the man that she still sat astride, his body quiet but still inside her. He was right, Pander and Tansy were all she had in the world, three orphans that found each other and, even now in their late twenties, had never had a serious or steady man in their lives. They had been raised by a kind woman that had always told them they were special. Maybe she was right.

Hades felt right, and she looked down into his blue eyes, which were now glowing with an unearthly light and nodded.

He was right. She did want this, did want a place to belong. Hades was offering her everything she had ever wanted since her childhood, though for how long was the question.

"And how long does this last?"

"Forever Drea, You aren't like the rest... you were made to be Persephone."

"And just how do you think that's going to happen. Call me what you want, say that this is my destiny, but in the end I'm still mortal."

"That's not entirely true. Immortality is already slowly creeping through your veins. It would have been faster, and more apparent, but Priapus didn't leave enough time for you to finish your drink." His grin was wide as his hands stroked over her skin yet again.

Of course. The ambrosia. Looked like the bartender wasn't kidding when he handed it to her. "So you're telling me that sweet tasting drink was the fabled ambrosia? Seriously?"

"Indeed. And if you weren't meant to be a consort of the gods, you wouldn't have been able to drink it. But you did, and you crave it now don't you?"

She did. Drea licked her lips and nodded and he motioned to the side table where his drink sat. "Be my guest, that is, of course if you want to stay."

She looked at the cup, then back to him. "And what about Tansy? And Pander?"

"What about them?" he asked as his hands once again found her waist and he flipped them over so they were both lying on their side. She propped herself up on her elbow and he followed suit.

"What is to become of them? If I agree to be yours, and not leave you, what happens to them?"

Hades shook the hair out of his eye and ran his free hand up her side, his fingertips ghosting over her flesh, making her shudder. His touch was intoxicating.

"That's up to them. They will be pursued, and given a choice. Before the end of the festival they will have found their destiny's as well."

Drea nodded. "And I wouldn't have to be without them?"

"Well you will hardly see them every minute of every day, but yes, you will still have their friendship and their love. Always."

Drea grinned. A devastatingly handsome god, her best friends and a torrid and interesting new life with immortality to boot. Who could ask for anything more? "Hand me the ambrosia will you?"

Hades kissed her sweetly, nipping her bottom lip, and grinned. "You sure?"

"You just handed me the keys to the kingdom, Hades. My friends, a virile lover and an eternity of pleasure."

"And what of love?" he asked.

She smirked. Love indeed. She could love him, would, she knew. "Oh I think that's a safe bet. In the old stories, Persephone loved you with everything she had in her, even when apart from you half the year."

"Well yes, but unlike the stories of old, that will not happen."

"No? You're telling me we aren't to be in love or split up half the year?"

"The half the year thing. Old wife's tale. Trust me love, we won't be parted."

On those words she smiled and sat up taking the cup from his hands and drank deeply of the sweet liquid, relishing its texture and flavor. She felt a warmth flow through her, infusing her with a very pleasant version of pins and needles and gasped as her body came alive, along with the swirling mark of her consort. The tattoo caressed her, stroked the fire that was slowly building inside her and she looked at Hades, who watched her with knowing eyes.

"I can feel your arousal...and your mortality slipping away." He kissed her and pulled her close once more, his magnificent cock thick and begging attention against her lower belly. She giggled as she felt him twitch, felt his tattoo pulse as she reached up and tugged sweetly on his nipple ring. He growled and lifted her leg, sliding himself along her slick pussy, coating himself in her wetness. They moaned in unison and then she sobbed, and looked into his eyes as he entered her.

Yes, she did think she would enjoy becoming Persephone, and being her for always.

ERATO

Cat Johnson

Chapter One

The heat thrown from the fire crackling in the hearth nearly overwhelmed him, adding to the sheen of sweat already bathing his body. In spite of the high temperature, a shiver stemming from pure pleasure ran down his spine.

A tangle of limbs so complex Erato couldn't tell where his body ended and the next person's began, writhed as one on the large, soft, down pillows covering the white marble floor. The trickling of the waterfall filling the pool just a few feet from the group was barely audible over the mingled symphony of many bodies taking pleasure. With so many various moans, sighs and cries, Erato couldn't be sure who made which sound. What he did know was that he was close to coming, the sensations assaulting all parts of his body was too much for his resolve.

A nearly feral groan, loud and deep, rose from within Erato's chest.

He tensed every muscle as he attempted to fend off his impending orgasm, refusing to be the first among them to lose control. He felt the female beneath his hands and mouth begin to shake and took that as an indication that she, too, was close. Redoubling his efforts, he switched from tongue to teeth, scraping them against her swollen clit as he slid two fingers inside her slick channel. She laced her fingers through his curls, pulling his mouth tighter against her honey-sweet cunt as she trembled. Erato's fingers found just the right spot inside her and worked it with expertise gained over centuries of practice and experimentation, hoping to send her tumbling to completion before she tore the hair completely out of his head.

While the woman beneath his mouth clenched and squirmed from his ministrations, the second female between his legs clasped his erection tighter within her hot, talented mouth. She began to move faster, up and down his length, just as he felt an oil-slicked finger deftly probe his hole, and then slowly breach him, sliding into his ass and causing him to gasp. He squeezed tightly both his eyes and his muscles against the invasion, knowing this final assault on his body would be the end of him. In spite of his efforts, the determined digit penetrated deeper and hit the sweet spot inside him.

That was it. Erato knew he was done. Giving in, he relaxed his muscles and felt a second finger invade him. He rocked back, forcing them deeper, riding both the fingers and a wave of pleasure as he let the sensations overwhelm him. Thrusting his cock further into the throat engulfing him, he shuddered and shot all he had into her.

Erato's own cry was muffled by the thighs clasped tightly around his head as the female he pleasured with his mouth shattered, too. He rode both his own and her orgasm until neither one of them could take anymore.

Bonelessly rolling away from the two women, he saw more participants had at one point joined them, unnoticed by Erato until now. Neck deep in the pool of water nearby two men grunted, front to back, obviously enjoying each other. Closer by, a nude male moved in and buried his cock deep between the thighs of the woman who'd had Erato in her mouth just seconds before.

Spent and exhausted, but not opposed to enjoying a bit of voyeurism, Erato watched as the man rammed himself deep into the female while lifting her hips high off the ground. She began to shudder and scratch first at his arms, then at the clenched muscles of his ass, leaving long, raised, reddened welts as her nails dug into his formerly perfect skin. That had Erato dipping his fingers into one of the many bowls of oil scattered around the floor and stroking himself as he watched.

A newcomer arrived, his eyes brightening as he observed the scene. He dropped the cloth towel covering him and knelt on a pillow behind the man on the floor. The new arrival dipped his fingers into the oil, lubricating his not inconsiderably sized erection until it glistened. As Erato continued to observe, the new man slid three well-oiled fingers, one by one, into the ass of the man on his knees who had now paused his thrusting into the girl beneath him to give the latecomer easier access.

Erato leaned back on the pillow, stroking himself and watching as the newcomer, having stretched the man before him to his satisfaction, removed his fingers and replaced them with the head of his cock. A visible shudder ran through the recipient of his attentions, whose eyes squeezed shut with a blissful look on his face. Once completely filled by the cock, he resumed thrusting into the female as the male behind him matched the rhythm, the three moving in an erotic dance.

As the three-way coupling became more frenzied, and then finally completed with a series of grunts and groans, Erato found himself hard as steel and completely aroused once again. His gaze roamed to the girl still recovering from the orgasm he'd provided her with, using his oral skills just moments before. She'd been touching herself as she watched the threesome through heavily lidded eyes, as entranced as Erato had been.

As he crawled back between her thighs, the two men who had coupled in the pool had since left the water and now lounged lazily atop chaise lounges covered by white fluffy towels. While observing the scene with twin amused looks on their faces, they accepted the wine and plump grapes fed to them by servant girls.

Erato did his best to ignore the pair, whom he'd never liked, as he concentrated on the female beneath him. Lifting one of her knees, he wrapped it around his own narrow waist, poised to thrust his erection into her just as a figure standing in the doorway cleared his throat tactfully.

"Yes?" Erato bit out. Annoyed at the interruption but not letting it stop him, he pushed inside the female below him.

"Your presence is being requested."

The look he shot the messenger would have most likely killed the man, had Erato been endowed with that particular power like some of the others in the room were. "I'm a bit occupied at the moment."

His mind still on the tantalizing lovemaking he'd just witnessed, Erato considered flipping the female over and indulging in her sweet ass until he was once again rudely interrupted.

"And what message would you have me deliver to Aphrodite as to why you cannot attend her summons?" The messenger dropped the goddess' name casually, as if he didn't realize it would garner Erato's complete attention, even as the head of Erato's cock breached the warm, wet folds that promised so much pleasure.

The summons would have to be from one of the gods and not just any goddess either, but Aphrodite. A command from anyone else, save perhaps Zeus himself, and Erato would have ignored it until after he'd satisfied himself, however the look on the face of the messenger echoed Erato's thoughts exactly...when Aphrodite was unhappy, everyone on Mt. Olympus suffered. And if she knew he didn't fly directly to her side because he was taking pleasure with another woman, a *mortal* woman no less, the waves of her displeasure would spread through Thessaly and beyond. To ignore her now could cost him a millennium of agony. A few moments of mindless rutting, even with a mortal female whose pussy tasted of honey and who craved his every touch, was not worth that.

Erato thrust into her one last time, and then regretfully withdrew, taking solace in the fact that the girl beneath him looked saddened he must leave. Unfortunately, the feeling was short lived. As Erato arranged his toga, letting the white fabric drape over his arm, the two males from the pool fell, grinning, upon the abandoned female's body. He watched with overwhelming regret as one lay on his back and lowered her onto his cock and the other, after oiling himself, entered her from behind while shooting Erato a look of triumph.

Already under their spell, the body of the mortal female bowed in pleasure as she was doubly penetrated by the two demigods. *Who both had a superiority complex to rival Zeus in spite of their half human parentage*, Erato thought silently.

So with the departure of Erato, a mere lowly muse, no longer an issue for anyone in the room except himself, he left the bathing chamber, its inhabitants and its pleasures behind and made his way down the long corridor to face Aphrodite. The gods only knew what that meeting would bring.

Chapter Two

Aphrodite's chamber was, of course, the best in the palace next to that of Zeus. She had her own pool for bathing and didn't need to share the common rooms like the lowlier beings, such as Erato did. Though as evidenced by his recent activities, sharing did have its benefits.

At that thought, Erato smothered the feeling of regret at having lost his mortal tidbit to the cocky half gods in the bathing chamber. More than likely the two bastards (and they were that, both literally and figuratively) would bespell her so she'd never want another except for them.

It wasn't fair. Erato had discovered her down below when he'd traveled to Thessaly in search of new mortal literature for his library. He'd brought her up the mountain specifically for his own enjoyment and now *they* had her.

It made him angry enough to spit fire, but Erato had more important things to worry about at the moment, such as Aphrodite, seated regally before him on her pearl and shell encrusted throne, attended by the usual entourage.

A shiver of both desire and fear ran through Erato's body from simply being in this room and surrounded by Aphrodite's familiar instruments of pleasure and pain. The oversized bed sat in the corner with its leather restraints permanently attached to metal rings drilled into both the abalone-inlaid head and footboards. An assortment of whips hung on the wall, and nearby stood the leather-clad, masked whip bearer whose massive arm muscles rivaled even those of Aphrodite's blacksmith husband, Hephaestus.

Aphrodite's taste ran to the dark side. It aroused her to watch the red welts the whip-man caused to rise on her lovers before she stepped in and soothed their pain with the nearly unbearable pleasure that only she could provide.

Erato eyes landed on a particular whip, the one with the phallus-shaped, mother-of-pearl inlaid handle. That was the one Aphrodite loved best. She liked to personally dip the handle into her private stock of herbal oil and use it on her lovers as they knelt, facedown, with hands bound. Just the scent of oil and rosemary could arouse him now, no matter where he was or what he was doing.

If her lover followed her orders, he would be treated to many more of Aphrodite's pleasures. However, if Aphrodite was not pleased, there were consequences. She didn't require that the whip bearer use only whips on her lovers. When she demanded punishment, the masked man was allowed to enjoy free reign with the subject, all while Aphrodite watched.

Erato had only displeased Aphrodite once. He never let it happen again. Remembering every moment in vivid detail, his gaze went uncontrollably to the whip bearer. Erato shivered even as he grew harder.

The room reeked of the herbal oil today and Erato wondered absently who had been the most recent recipient of Aphrodite's attentions. Who was it that now, more than likely, lay limp and unconscious in his own chamber, awaiting a visit from the healer?

Aphrodite was not a gentle lover, nor did she let up until she had loved the subject of her affections to exhaustion, and at times, near death for the mortals, both men and women.

Torn between his fear of her and his body's automatic desire for the Goddess of Love, most beautiful of all the gods on Mt. Olympus, and the pleasures she could provide, Erato clasped his hands in front of his rising erection and waited for her to address him.

"Erato! Good, you're here. You may approach." Aphrodite stretched her long, lovely, alabaster arms out to him and he stepped forward, letting her clasp each of his hands.

"Thank you, my goddess." He lowered himself to sit on the stairs at her feet; relieved her mood seemed exceptionally good today. Whoever she'd just bedded must have pleased her well.

She sighed and gazed down at him, her face displaying a mix of emotions. "Erato, Erato, Erato... My faithful muse. My loyal lover."

Uh, oh. This was starting to not sound so good.

Aphrodite continued, "I've been told that you, above any other, have the most experience with the mortals living below us. And because of this, though you have served me well, now I must part with you."

He tried to control the panic in his voice. "Why, my goddess?" Was he to be banished from Mt. Olympus, or worse, turned into a tree or a flower for all eternity just because he enjoyed the literature, and customs, and physical favors of mortals too much? It had happened before to others, better than he, who had crossed the gods. But he hadn't meant to do anything wrong. Nowadays, Erato only traveled to the mortal realm about once every fifty mortal years. He would never purposely anger the gods, well at least not the big ones, anyway.

Eros entered the chamber through the private doorway behind the throne and Erato had a glimmer of hope. Eros, Erato's closest friend and Aphrodite's most faithful attendant, would never let anything happen to him. Eros, of all those on Mt. Olympus, could surely persuade the goddess to change her mind.

Aphrodite of course noticed immediately that Erato's attention was no longer solely trained upon her, and turned her head to seek the source of his distraction. "Ah, Eros, darling. Come. I was just telling Erato my plan."

Eros was privy to her plan? What could that mean? Erato tried—and failed—to keep his breathing steady as he waited to hear his fate.

The handsome Eros, his quiver full of arrows as golden as his perfect locks of hair, settled himself beside Aphrodite's right knee, letting her take hold of his hand. He aimed a brilliantly dazzling smile at Erato, causing the muse to once again flip flop in his opinion as to whether his fate would be favorable or not.

"So, as I was saying my lovely Erato, your familiarity with the mortals is what makes you perfect for this assignment, and though I am loathe to part with you for even a short time, I must, for you are the best suited for the task at hand."

Erato cleared the frog from his throat and steeled his nerves. "If I may, my perfect goddess, what is this task of which you speak?"

Aphrodite ran one nail down Eros' sculpted arm. "Tell him, my golden one."

Eros shot Erato another grin full of mischief. "It's

simple, my friend. You go down below, locate one particular female, and let her fall in love with you."

Erato frowned. It sounded simple enough, deceptively so. Mortals were extremely susceptible to those who resided on Mt. Olympus, which was one reason why once a mortal entered the palace of the gods, they never willingly left.

One look into his eyes and the female would be his. One night in his bed and she would never want to part with him. But still, why him? "And why have I been chosen...specifically?"

Aphrodite looked proud of herself as she explained. "It may be required that you live among the mortals for some time. Mortal time, of course, is nothing for one of us, but still, any of the others would stand out among the commoners. You, however, with your strange preoccupation with those living below, will know how to blend in."

Aphrodite thought he and he alone could blend in with the commoners? Erato wasn't sure whether to take that as a compliment or an insult. So he collected mortal literature. He was the Muse of Poetry, for Zeus' sake. It was his job to be familiar with mortal writers.

Compliment or not, Erato said, "Thank you, goddess. And will Eros assist me with one of his arrows and his ever true aim to make the female fall in love with me?"

Now Eros' involvement in the plan made more sense, since love was the goal. All that needed to be done was for Eros to shoot the female with one of his golden tipped arrows and she would be irretrievably in love with whomever she saw next.

"My arrow will not be necessary, my friend. She will fall in love with you as certainly as the sun rises and sets. What female could ever resist you? But I will be nearby. Do not fear." Eros treated Erato to his cherubic smirk once more.

Erato nodded, not sure he was relieved by Eros' assurance. "All right. When am I to leave?"

Aphrodite smiled. "Immediately, but treat me to one last kiss, Erato, before I lose you to the mortals."

Erato rose at Aphrodite's command, in more ways than one, and touched his lips to hers. Her mouth tasted of the sea and the familiar tang caused a tide of memories of all they'd shared to flood his mind. A moan of pure desire rose from Erato's chest and he had to stop himself from pressing his body against hers, a presumption that would surely earn him more pain than pleasure.

The chamber around him began to swirl into an indecipherable tangle of sensations. Erato still smelled the scent of rosemary oil lingering in the room, his body still ached with wanting what pleasures it knew the goddess could provide, he still tasted the salty sea in her mouth, but things were no longer clear...

Dizzy and barely able to think, Erato heard Eros giggle and then everything went blank.

Chapter Three

Acantha chopped the fresh rosemary with a deftness that came with countless hours of on the job practice. She should be good at her job. What else did she have to do besides work? It wasn't like she had a boyfriend or anything.

That thought had her throwing the herb into the pan of heated oil with an audible *hmmph* and far more force than was necessary, causing both her sous chef and one of the prep guys to shoot her an interested look.

"Problem?" Greg asked while popping a tray of tenderloin under the broiler to brown for that night's Beef Wellington dinner special.

Yeah. You're gay and I'm horny! Acantha thought to herself. "No." *Nothing new, anyhow.*

Scrubbing a large pot with gusto, Pablo grinned wickedly. "Jefe needs some pene, I think."

Acantha knew enough Spanish to raise a brow at Pablo's unfortunately true assessment of his boss' situation. She did need some penis, but she didn't need her prep guy to know that. Meanwhile, Pablo's wife was pregnant with their, what was it, fifth child? It was more than obvious Mrs. Pablo was getting plenty of pene.

"Jefe is just fine on her own and does not need a man to make her happy, but thank you, Pablo," Acantha informed him.

Pablo mumbled a word that translated roughly to

"rabbit" and Greg nearly choked before recovering his composure.

Jeez! Did everyone know about that mail delivery from the online sex shop? What the hell good was shipping a person's very embarrassing vibrator order in a plain brown box if everyone in the world guessed that's what was in there? Anyway, she didn't end up ordering *The Jack Rabbit.* She'd opted for another model. That reminded her; she needed to pick up more batteries. Maybe she should switch to rechargeable. It did seem better for the environment.

Environmentally friendly masturbation. The thought had Acantha rolling her eyes at herself.

Before she had time to feel worse about her whole situation and sink further into self-wallowing, the back door flung open. Her busboy, Julio, flew in spewing a string of rapid Spanish that far outstretched Acantha's ability to translate, but judging by Pablo's expression as he followed Julio back out through the door, it was something urgent.

Acantha flipped off the burner beneath her pan of oil and rosemary and ran into the alley after them, only to stop dead at what appeared to be—*oh my God*—a dead body leaned up against the restaurant's dumpster.

Greg flew out the door and skidded to a stop, echoing her thoughts. "Oh my God! Is he..."

Good question. Glancing at the three men one by one, it was more than obvious that none of them were going to find out.

Chickens. She let out a sigh. "I'll check."

Gathering her courage, Acantha took one tentative step forward, and then another, until she was directly in front of the man. He looked good for being dead. In fact, he was downright gorgeous with his dark brown curls and muscular chest that showed through his white cotton button-down shirt.

"Check for a pulse," Greg suggested from a very safe distance away.

Easy for him to say.

"All right." Swallowing hard, Acantha kept her feet as far away from the man as possible, while leaning over and placing one finger lightly against the side of his neck—which is when his eyes flew open wide.

He screamed. She screamed. Julio, Pablo and Greg all screamed, and Acantha lost her balance, landing head first in the man's lap.

Two large hands took a firm grip on her arms and raised her face from his crotch until she was staring directly into a pair of eyes as green as the ocean.

"Are you all right?" the nameless hunk asked.

"Um." Words escaped her for a moment, and then sanity returned somewhat. "I'm fine. Are *you* all right? You were unconscious against my dumpster."

Still holding her, not that she was complaining about that, the man frowned and swiveled his head, taking in his surroundings as if for the first time. "I feel all right. Where am I?"

"You're behind *The Acanthus Tree.*"

His frown deepened as he glanced at the brick wall near him. "I don't see any tree."

Acantha shook her head and pointed to the name embroidered on her chef's jacket. "It's the name of my restaurant. You're behind my restaurant. My name's Acantha."

He shook his head. "I...I don't know my name."

"Maybe you have some identification in your pants?" *Among other things.*

"Um, why don't we take this conversation inside

instead of holding it out here amid the garbage?" Greg suggested.

Acantha remembered for the first time since gazing into the pool of the stranger's eyes that they were not alone. "Of course. Let's all get inside."

Flustered, Acantha straightened, and she and the man helped each other up, all the while never breaking eye contact with each other.

"Dios mio. Here we go again." She heard the comment unhappily muttered under Pablo's breath and shot him a look. Hadn't he just said she needed a man? Or at least a penis? This gorgeous surprise in the alley could easily fill the need for both things.

While maintaining a strong hold on one hard bicep, Acantha was about to lead the stranger through the kitchen door when Greg decided to suddenly be helpful. "Pablo, Julio, you two take this gentleman inside and get him a chair and a glass of water, or hell, a scotch might be better."

The two nodded and Acantha was pushed out of the way. As she rushed to follow, Greg's hand on her arm stopped her.

She turned to him. "What?"

Greg shook his head. "Don't."

"Don't what?"

"Don't fall head over heels for a stranger you found in an alley. Please, Acantha."

She had kind of landed head over heels, but still. "Don't be ridiculous! I'm not falling..."

"Yeah, you are. I've seen it too many times before. Tomorrow morning you'll come down from your apartment upstairs glowing and all happy while he sleeps the morning away in your bed. In a week you'll be totally in love with him and planning your future. That part will last maybe a month before he starts pulling away and finally dumps you and breaks your heart, hopefully before he lets you run up a fortune in expensive gifts for him on your credit card."

She lowered her eyes. "That only happened once."

"Jeez, Acantha. It's like you've got your name on some sucker list that all the bad men in the world have access to. And you fall for them each and every time."

"I do not!"

"You do. Look, I'm your friend. I care about you. I won't stand around and watch as you do it again, with a man you found in the alley no less!"

"He's just a man who needs a little help."

"He's a stranger who you know nothing about but who you were practically drooling over. Tell me you aren't attracted to him."

"Tell me you don't think he's gorgeous too!" she challenged.

Greg tore at his hair. "Acantha, he was unconscious in the alley!"

"He could easily have been a customer coming in to make a reservation and on the way he was mugged. And now I am going inside to make sure he is all right. I suggest you finish those Wellingtons for tonight."

Greg's eyes opened wide. He set his jaw angrily. "Yes, boss."

Acantha watched his stiffened back disappear through the door. It was bad enough when the other guys called her boss in Spanish, but to have Greg, her friend, say it like that in anger made her feel absolutely horrible. She'd worry more about it later, but for now, she did have a nameless, possible mugging victim to deal with.

She found him seated with his hands clasped tightly in his lap in the corner of the kitchen, a glass of water and a glass of scotch untouched on the prep counter near him. Acantha squatted down to be eyelevel and found his face flushed. "Are you okay? Are you feeling worse? Should I call an ambulance?"

He shook his head. "No. I'm...it's just... What is that smell?"

Acantha sniffed the air and found the typical kitchen smells. Nothing foul or particularly odorous. She shook her head, not knowing what he meant.

"It's like some sort of herb," he suggested, looking agitated.

"Oh. You must mean the rosemary. I was cooking with it right before we found you. Does it bother you? Would you like to move into the dining room?"

"No!" Avoiding eye contact, he shook his head as if to reinforce his answer to her suggestion.

"Okay. Are you sure you're all right? I really think maybe I should call..."

"I'm fine. It's just...embarrassing."

"What is? Being unconscious in my alley? Believe me, that is nothing to be ashamed of."

He shook his gorgeous dark head again. "No, not that. I seem to be..." He finally looked up at her now, pain clear in his eyes as he said, "aroused."

It took a second or two before understanding dawned and, as if they had a will of their own, Acantha's eyes dropped immediately to his hands in his lap as he vainly tried to conceal the outline of one impressive erection.

Shit, Greg was right. She was drooling, literally. Acantha swallowed. "Um, maybe it's a symptom of a concussion."

He shook his head one more time. "I don't know. I apologize."

"No, no don't. Really. It's fine. I'm fine with it. We're both adults here. It's natural. Good really. I mean it shows you aren't that hurt, right?" Jeez. She was babbling and on top of it, Acantha was pretty sure she had wet panties just from imagining this aroused man between her legs.

He nodded, dropping his eyes again.

"Um, so. Did you find anything in your pants." She scurried to correct herself. "Identification, I meant. Of course. Not anything else... Do you have a wallet?"

Acantha's gaze shot quickly behind her to see all three men working more quietly than ever, most likely while straining to hear every word.

The man glanced at her and hesitated before standing and reaching in his back pocket, which only put the part of him she was craving eyelevel with her, outlined to perfection by tight gabardine. He quickly pulled out a leather wallet, thrust it at her, then sat again and covered his lap once more.

She opened it and found an impressive amount of cash. There went Greg's theory that the stranger was some con man trying to get her money. Unfortunately, there also went her excuse that he'd been mugged. No thief would leave a wallet full of cash on an unconscious man.

There were no credit cards in the leather slits where they would normally be, however, there was one white business card. She pulled it out and read it. "*Erato—Poet.* Is that you?"

As her heart did a little flip, Acantha flipped the card over, looking for more. All she found in tiny lettering was *Eros Printing*. Hmm. She'd never heard of them.

The man before her tilted his head slightly. "Erato..." The name flowed from his tongue naturally, with just the hint of an accent. "That does seem very familiar. It feels…right."

"That's great! Maybe you only use your last name. It might be your pen name or something. It sounds Greek. Maybe you're of Greek heritage" It would explain the dreamy, dark curls and the eyes the color of the Aegean Sea. Greek, gorgeous, and he was a poet! *Wow.* How romantic. "Anyway, look! We're learning more about you by the minute."

"Yes." He nodded half-heartedly, still looking uncomfortable. "I think maybe I should move to the other room, if you don't mind."

"Of course." Acantha jumped up. "Let me help you up."

"I'm fine. Really." His face turned a deeper shade of embarrassment and, knowing the source, Acantha couldn't help but let her gaze drop one more time.

Damn. Had he gotten bigger? She'd spent so much time with her vibrator, she had started to fear that no living man would be able to live up to its size, as well as its gyrating shaft and two-speed vibrating clit appendage. But this man, Erato the poet, may be up for the challenge.

She caught the glance Greg shot her as she opened the door to the dining room for Erato and frowned. Greg had his share of men, so why was he trying to ruin her fun? "The smells are getting to him so we're going to the dining room," she quickly explained to the men in the kitchen.

"Sure." Greg raised a brow cockily. "Should I finish off your Rosemary Potatoes, boss?"

Acantha ignored both the "boss" comment and the judgmental tone of his voice. "Yes. Thank you."

Out in the dining room, Erato seemed to visibly relax.

"Better?" she asked.

He smiled and the beauty of it nearly knocked her off her feet. "Yes, thank you. Much better."

"Um..." She momentarily forgot what she'd been about to say until he stopped flashing his gorgeousness at her and raised one brow expectantly, waiting for her to finish her thought. "Oh, yeah. I was thinking we could look your name up on my computer. Maybe we can find more information, like an address."

"Can you do that?" He seemed a bit surprised. Maybe instead of working on a computer, he was one of those poets who still wrote by hand. She pictured him with a fancy sterling silver pen and a leather-bound notebook, sitting outside in a park, sipping a latte amid the doves.

Damn, she was ready to drop her polyester chef pants for him right there in the dining room over that image.

"Yeah, sure I can. We just have to go upstairs. That's where my computer is."

She imagined an angel with the face of Greg sitting on her shoulder saying, *Acantha. You know you can carry your laptop down here.* Meanwhile, a devil with Pablo's face sat on the other shoulder prodding her with his pitchfork while saying, *Go upstairs, Jefe. You need a nice big pene.*

Acantha realized Erato was waiting for her to lead the way upstairs and her decision was made. Besides, just because they were going up to her apartment to research his name on her computer, didn't mean they'd jump into bed. Though for some inexplicable reason, she wanted nothing more. Strange. Perhaps the rosemary was having the same effect on her.

That herb seemed to be one powerful aphrodisiac. *Hmm. Who knew*?

Chapter Four

His mind was a blank.

No, that wasn't true. He knew some things, like how to speak English and that the scent of rosemary made him want to rut like a stag... That the name Erato seemed right, as if it belonged to him... That the petite, voluptuous, dark-haired woman with the honey-colored eyes whose curvy ass swayed temptingly up the stairs in front of him was exactly the type of female he preferred best. But the important things—his past, where he came from, where he was going when he ended up in the alley behind this tempting nymph's restaurant—that was all missing, as if someone had selectively erased parts of his mind.

He had been found unconscious and had partial memory loss. Maybe he did receive a blow on the head. It would explain a lot of things but didn't solve the problem that he had nowhere to go.

Maybe Acantha's idea would work. "Do you really think you can find where I live?"

She stopped in front of a door at the top of the stairs and turned to look down at him. "I think so. It's worth a try, anyway."

Erato nodded, longing to see what was beneath the hideously ugly black and white pants she wore. He was sure what treasures lay beneath far surpassed the exterior wrapping. "Yes, it is always worth trying."

Acantha opened the door and they entered a

sunny room filled with nothing more than a few pieces of furniture, one of which happened to be one large bed in the corner. She sat at a desk and began tapping her fingers. He walked up behind her and his mind supplied the word he sought. "This is your *computer*."

Acantha nodded without looking up at him as she concentrated on the words that appeared before her. "Yeah. If you don't have a private phone number, you should be listed in the white pages. And hopefully, you're a famous poet and you'll come up in a search."

Many minutes and a lot of hmming, huffing and sighing later, Acantha finally turned to look at him and he was once again struck by how he was drawn into the depths of her eyes. "Anything?"

She pursed her lips and shook her head. "No. I'm so sorry. But maybe it will all just come back to you with time."

"Time." Erato laughed. Where in the world would he go in the meantime to wait for his memory to reappear as mysteriously as it had left him? "I do thank you for your assistance, though."

He took her fingertips in his and dropped his head to plant a kiss of gratitude and farewell on her delicate hand, when the scent assaulted him again, making him dizzy and once again hard as marble. His whole body tensed in response.

"What's wrong?"

Erato knew he needed to drop her hand and step away, but he couldn't. He swallowed the lump of desire from his throat but still his voice came out husky and low. "Your hand. You reek of rosemary."

Her eyes opened wide with realization. "Oh! I'm sorry. I was chopping it. The oils are still on my hands."

Erato nodded, mortified, yet still unable to release

her hand. He held it near enough that he could still smell the herb, like it was a drug he couldn't get enough of.

She bit her lower lip in the most sensual affectation he'd ever seen. "Why do you think that happens to you?"

"I don't know. I suppose something in my past has made me associate rosemary with...um...sex." His body remembered it, so why didn't his mind? All he was certain of were the tingles that shot through the base of his spine and spread. He'd give anything to relieve his ache.

Acantha made no move to disengage her hand from his, and instead added her other one to it. "I don't know about that, because it's affecting me, too."

He suddenly was aware of every one of her quickened, shallow breaths. She leaned slightly closer and he saw the dilation of her pupils as he whispered her name, "Acantha."

"I don't usually act like this, Erato, not with strangers, but I can't seem to help myself around you. It's like..."

She shook her head, at a loss for words, so he completed her thought for her. "It's like we are drawn to each other as the moth is drawn to the flame."

Acantha drew in a shaky breath. "Wow. You are a poet."

Erato brought her hands up to touch his lips and inhaled deeply. "By the gods, I want you."

A small sound of longing escaped her throat as he dropped her hands and his mouth crushed against hers. His tongue parted her lips and he tasted honey and sunshine.

She pulled away long enough to say, "Take me, Erato. Please. I don't know what's wrong with me but

I can't wait another moment."

His own willingness shocked him as he scooped her up and threw her onto the bed. Her pants only survived because the elastic waist allowed both pants and undergarment to be yanked down her legs. The white cotton jacket she wore was another story. He gripped the two sides and tore, sending knotted cloth buttons flying.

Her breasts spilled out of the lace of her bra. He shoved the scrap of fabric aside and feasted upon the peak of one nipple while his pelvis pressed against hers, gyrating.

"Erato. Your pants," she gasped.

It was only then that he realized he was clothed. He rolled to the side and frantically pushed at the waistband of the trousers, to no avail.

"Wait. The belt." Acantha sat up and leaned over him, her hands working quickly at the leather strap around his waist. His nostrils flared as a memory assaulted him. *Leather. Sweat. Rosemary. Fear. Pain. Sex. Pleasure.* Yet he couldn't see who it was, or where the memory was from.

He didn't care. Erato needed this woman. She unfastened his pants and pushed them down his legs. He kicked them and his shoes to the ground and rolled between her legs with a groan. Smelling her arousal, seeing her glistening in anticipation of him, he could wait no longer.

Raising her leg and wrapping it around him, he plunged his full length into her with one stroke. She gasped and he pulled all the way back and plunged in again, withdrew and then repeated the action, his rhythm echoed as the bed banged against the wall.

As he rocked into her, he spoke. "I'm going to taste every inch of you, all night long."

"Yes," she shuddered.

He looped her other leg around his waist and thrust deeper. "I want to feel your mouth on me."

Her eyes looked unfocused as she nodded. "Yes."

He reached and grabbed one of her hands, bringing it to his nose and breathing in the erotic scent once more. "And I want you to go downstairs and bring back rosemary and a bottle of oil."

Her eyes widened, but she nodded. "Yes."

He nodded also, satisfied that by morning they would have shared everything a man and a woman could share, possibly more than once.

At that thought, the tingling in his spine increased, shooting sparks of sensation straight through to his bowels. Erato adjusted his angle of entry and increased his speed. Acantha's body bowed, wracked with the power of the orgasm Erato could feel radiating from her into him.

As Acantha's muscles milked him, her teeth sunk into the flesh of his chest. Erato groaned with pleasure at the pain. "Yes. Bite me. Harder."

Acantha opened her mouth wider and bit down again, harder, and Erato shot into her with an animalistic roar. Breathless, he finally let his motion slow, and then stop.

Acantha's eyes drifted shut as she moaned and wiggled beneath him. "Mmmm. You're still hard."

As Erato cupped Acantha's face in both hands, her lids opened and her beguiling eyes stared into his. "Acantha, I haven't gotten nearly enough of you yet. It may take me a millennium to get enough."

With a moan, she stretched her arm out toward the table next to the bed.

"What are you doing, my lovely?"

"I need to call downstairs."

"Now?" Erato frowned.

She tangled one hand in his curls and pulled him in for a rough kiss before she continued. "I need to tell them I won't be in to work tonight...and ask them to bring up some rosemary and oil."

Erato smiled.

Chapter Five

Acantha lay in her bed, eyes closed, waiting for the feeling of regret to hit. It didn't. How could that be? She'd had a night of insane sex with a man she barely knew and yet she felt...serene.

Then she opened her eyes, turned her head, and faced an empty pillow, and that feeling shattered into a million little pieces. Her heart pounding, Acantha jumped from beneath the covers, realized she was very naked, and grabbed her robe.

Maybe he was in the bathroom.

Hanging on to that hope she gave the door a tentative shove. It swung open and revealed nothing but the empty space.

Acantha's eyes shut as she gripped the doorframe to prevent from swaying. Greg had been right. She was stupid. Always had been, always would be. Bracing herself, she opened her eyes and dared to look at her desk. The laptop was there. That was something anyway. Her purse was still locked in the desk drawer downstairs in the restaurant office so that was safe.

Shoving her feet into slippers, Acantha let out a puff of air. At least all Erato had managed to steal was a small piece of her heart, and she had plenty of experience healing her own broken heart.

The phone on the desk rang and Acantha jumped on it—*apparently vain hope was the last thing to die.*

Hand shaking, she raised the receiver to her ear.

"Acantha? Oh, thank God! It's Greg. I was worried

about you when you didn't call me this morning. Are you okay?"

She frowned. "Yeah, I'm fine. Sorry, but when did you ask me to call you?"

The sex had been absolutely out of this world, but she didn't think it had given her amnesia. The word *amnesia* reminded her of Erato. The memory loss was probably all an act on his part, she realized sadly. Acantha's stomach twisted to the point she feared she might vomit, if there were anything in her stomach besides acid at this point.

"When I left the giant note that said *Call Me* on the coffee maker in the kitchen after I closed the restaurant last night."

"Ah. That's why. I haven't been downstairs yet. I just got out of bed actually."

Acantha could hear the shock in Greg's silence. "You just got up? It's after noon, Acantha. Oh, wait... Is he still there?"

"No. He's not." She glanced at the tangled bed with a sigh and rolled her eyes at her own repeated stupidity for once again opening her heart to the wrong man.

"That's it. I'm coming over."

"No, Greg, don't be silly. It's Monday. It's your only day off this week. I'm fine." Besides, she wasn't up for the "I told you so" speech, which would surely come the moment Greg stopped being concerned and started getting righteous.

Silence again, then finally Greg said, "Okay. But I am only a phone call away."

"I know, and I appreciate that and you, more than you can imagine." Sad the only man in her life she could count on was in her employ.

Greg hesitated a beat. "Can I ask you something?"

~58~

"Sure." She didn't have anything else to do, so why not?

"Rosemary and a bottle of oil? I know you weren't eating french bread up there in your bed, so I have to ask... Was he as good as he looked?"

Acantha laughed. "Yeah. Better. Why?"

"Just wondering how long it will take you to get over this one."

Acantha knew the answer to that herself. *A long time.*

Hanging up with Greg after more assurances that she would call if she needed him, Acantha headed downstairs for some much needed coffee, maybe some of her signature Chocolate Lava Cake too. Desperate times called for desperate measures.

Wallowing in self-pity and in a caffeine-deprived haze, Acantha stumbled into the kitchen and was faced with a sight so beautiful it nearly caused her knees to buckle.

A barefoot and shirtless Erato stood by the cutting board. Wearing only the ass-hugging black pants he'd arrived in the day before, he arranged sliced fruit and chocolate truffles on a plate. An open bottle of champagne and two filled glasses sat on the counter nearby.

Erato turned and sent her a heart-twisting smile as radiant as the noonday sun before he breathed one word, "Acantha," and she found herself crossing the kitchen and settling into his open arms.

He tasted of strawberries, chocolate and champagne when his mouth covered hers. Pressing closer, she felt sparks shoot through her body. Breathless, she pulled her mouth away before she either passed out, or hopped right up on the counter and spread her legs for him—he had that effect on her.

Erato's face became intensely serious. "I have bad news."

Acantha heart skipped a beat. "What?"

"Apparently, I can't cook. I nearly exploded the kitchen trying to work the stove and that contraption over there that I think brews coffee was just beyond me. Oh, and someone wants you to call them. There was a note." His face lit once again with a luminous smile. "But I did discover I love fruit, chocolate and that sparkling wine."

Acantha laughed until the tears of relief blurred her eyes. "It's okay. I can cook for us."

He squeezed her tighter. "One of the many things to love about you."

Acantha' heart jumped into her throat and the word slipped out unbidden. "Love?"

Erato tilted his head to the side. "Acantha, you fill my heart. Even being this small distance from you the past hour was nearly unbearable. I almost woke you just to gaze into the brilliancy of your eyes. If that is not love, then I don't know what love is. In fact, I think until yesterday, until you, I could not comprehend the meaning of the word love."

"No man has ever said anything like that to me before," she choked.

"Then all the men you have known have been fools." Erato took her face in his hands and leaned so close she could see the flecks of gold in his emerald eyes. "I love you, Acantha."

She laughed tearfully. "And I love you, Erato."

An unseen force knocked Acantha away from him and off her feet, and as she felt her head strike the floor she was aware of a brilliant flash of light, and then nothing more.

Chapter Six

In his chamber, Erato sat and gazed into the mirror as the serving girl fastened the myrtle and rose wreath upon his head. Erato glanced angrily again at the parchment invitation—nay, summons—he'd found slid under his door. *Formal attire.* He scowled at the thought.

Erato's only desire at the moment was to storm into Aphrodite's chamber and demand she return his memory. Not that he could actually demand anything of the goddess. To do so would risk his life. He could try to cajole her into revealing something about his recent assignment in the mortal realm, but instead, he sat here, preparing for Zeus' pointless assembly.

He'd awoken that morning in his own bed, exhausted and confused and without an ounce of memory save the last few moments he'd spent in Aphrodite's chamber when her kiss had stolen his mind. Erato only knew he had actually traveled to the mortal realm and back because he'd awoken with his legs covered in the clothing of a commoner.

Standing, he let out an angry huff of annoyance as the girl handed him his lyre, the final touch to his ensemble.

"Have I angered you, my lord?" Her tiny body trembled beneath his gaze.

Poor thing. He shouldn't take his annoyance at Aphrodite out on the unfortunate servant. "No, you haven't. You may leave."

She nodded and practically ran from the room as Erato shook his head at himself for frightening her. With a sigh, he made his way out the door and down the long, wide hallway to the assembly. The sooner this was done, the sooner he'd hopefully have some answers.

His hopes for an explanation increased when Eros, splendidly outfitted in the Great Hall, greeted Erato warmly. "Hello, my good friend. You are looking no worse the wear after your journey."

Erato raised a brow. "Yes, about my journey. I'd love to know more about it."

Eros giggled as only he could. "Ah, Erato. Details are not important. What is, is that you were an overwhelming success, and in far less time than we'd anticipated. Aphrodite will reward you well, I am sure."

The cherub grinned mischievously as Erato rolled his eyes thinking how he'd rather have his memory back than any other *reward* Aphrodite might give.

Erato's gaze roamed the rapidly filling hall, biding his time until this would be over and he could request an audience with Aphrodite, when his eyes stopped on one particular female. "Eros. Who is that nymph? She seems familiar."

"Who? Her?"

Erato followed Eros' line of sight, then glanced down at his friend and noted the strange look on Eros' face. "Yes, her. Who is she?"

Eros visibly swallowed. "Acantha."

Erato frowned, trying to bring forth a memory that hovered at the edge of his mind. "Acantha. Ah, yes. Now I remember."

"You do?" Eros squeaked out the question and Erato once again looked at him more closely over this strange behavior.

"Yes, of course I do. Sister of Acanthus. She's the nymph that Apollo was in love with for a while, isn't she? She's hasn't been around. Whatever happened to her?"

Eros' continence changed once again, looking almost relieved. "Yes, of course you'd remember her. It was quite the scandal back then. She rebuffed his advances and in the process, left a scratch on his precious face..."

If Erato remembered correctly, it was more like attempted rape than an *advance*, but he let Eros continue uninterrupted.

"...and as punishment, she was banished by that vain bastard Apollo," Eros finished with a scowl.

Erato nodded. He remembered Acantha's fate now. He'd threaten to turn her into a tree but instead doomed her to live in the mortal realm but never be loved. There was no love lost between Eros and Apollo, either. Not since Apollo had insulted Eros' skill as an archer, and Eros retaliated by making Apollo fall in love with Daphne while at the same time making sure Daphne feared and hated Apollo in return. That had been a mess.

Erato found his eyes inexplicably drawn back to Acantha, who gazed serenely around the assembled group until her eyes met his, and then it was as if a lightning bolt sent a blast of ions straight through him. It had been a long time since a female, even a nymph, had that effect upon him. "Hmm."

"Hmm, what?" Eros was back to looking at him oddly again.

"Hmm, I think I'll make time to find Acantha later. To welcome her back." *Perhaps while she was on her back,* he added, suddenly feeling amorous.

Eros raised a brow. "I think you should attend Aphrodite later. As I said, she will want to see you."

Erato's anger toward Aphrodite replaced any fantasies Acantha had inspired. "Yes, and you can be sure I want to see her as well."

* * *

Erato entered Aphrodite's chamber by Eros' side and was shocked when the goddess herself rose from her throne and stepped forward, her arms extended.

"Erato. My favorite. You have surpassed all my expectations!" Aphrodite grabbed both of his hands warmly. "What can I give to you as reward? What is your heart's desire?"

Now was his chance, and Erato jumped at it. "My goddess, I thank you for your generosity. There is one thing I desire above all else. I would like my memories of the time I spent in the mortal realm returned to me."

She smiled and for one short moment, Erato hoped she would grant his request. He was wrong.

"Ah, my muse. That is the one thing I cannot grant. But I know your desires well, and I will fulfill every last one of them." The goddess turned from Erato to address the others in the room. "Whip bearer. Bring me my special oil. The rest of you may leave me."

Eros smirked knowingly before bowing and exiting, along with the others in the room.

Erato felt his body react with an ache of longing in his bowels and a tingle in his spine as the bearer returned with the pot of oil, setting it on the table and awaiting further instructions. Her eyes never leaving Erato, Aphrodite addressed the masked whip bearer. "You may go, my loyal man. Today I will handle things personally."

Erato swallowed hard as she took the lyre from his grasp and laid it on the table next to the oil. "Perhaps later you will pleasure me with a song, Erato."

"I could play for you now, my goddess," he suggested, unsure why he wished to delay what he'd always anticipated before.

She raised a perfect brow then laughed. "Hmm. I wonder if you can play for me while I play with you. It would be an interesting experiment I think. Don't you?"

That wasn't quite what he had in mind, but his cock began to rise anyway, no matter what his mind thought.

"Whatever my goddess desires."

"Oh, Erato." She ran a hand down the front of his toga, stopping at the obviously swelling bulge between his legs. "You are always so responsive. Now, go to the wall and choose, my muse."

Erato drew in a shuddering breath as he stepped to the wall of whips. She'd told him to choose, but he knew her favorite, and to choose any other would be a gross folly on his part. He reached up with a trembling hand and took down the whip with the mother of pearl handle then turned back to see the goddess smile.

Aphrodite removed the lid, then lifted the pot of uncovered oil and carried it to Erato. When she was just steps from him the scent of rosemary hit him like a physical blow and memories flooded his brain.

A pair of golden eyes. Hands that smelled of rosemary. A body that tasted as sweet as honey. A woman writhing beneath him.

Acantha.

It had been Acantha Erato had been sent to the

mortal realm to find after Apollo banished her there to suffer an eternity of unrequited love. The pieces all began to fall into place. Aphrodite hated Apollo as much as her favorite Eros did. Going behind Apollo's back to bring Acantha back was sure to anger Apollo, and that was exactly what Aphrodite and Eros wanted. Erato had been a pawn in yet another game of the gods. But Erato could play with the best of them.

His mind reeled with the knowledge, just as his desire for Aphrodite waned to nothing. "My goddess, I fear I have picked up a mortal ailment from my journey."

Her eyes opened wide. "How is that possible?"

"I am not a god, just a lowly muse. I guess I am more susceptible than one as mighty as yourself. But it is clearly evident, I am ailing." Erato laid the whip on the bed and used both hands to gather the lower edge of his toga, raising it to show Aphrodite a sight she had probably never seen in all of her years, the cock of a man who was not aroused by her beauty. It lay shriveled, barely visible amid a nest of dark curls and Erato had never been more pleased with its performance.

In front of him, Aphrodite sputtered, then turned her face away from the sight. "Yes, Erato. It is clear you have contracted some horrible ailment from the commoners. I only hope it is not irreversible."

"My hope as well, goddess. May I be dismissed to seek the council of a healer?"

Still obviously horrified, she nodded and dismissed him with a flick of her wrist. "Yes, of course."

Erato would have laughed at the look on the face he'd once considered beautiful above all others, but he was too angry with Aphrodite and too anxious to get to Acantha's side.

Would Acantha remember him?

He bowed to the goddess and left the chamber at a near sprint, heading down the hallway to the nymphs' wing of the palace when a horrible thought nearly dropped him in his tracks.

Erato spun in his sandals and instead headed for Eros' favorite haunt, the Archery Range. Erato spied the golden head as the god took aim at a target so far away Erato's own eyes could barely make out its circular colors.

He spun the young man by the shoulder and came face to face with a tiny arrow.

"Erato! You nearly got yourself shot! What were you thinking?"

"Did you shoot me, Eros?"

"I almost did!"

"No, I mean while I was in the mortal realm. Did you shoot me with one of your little golden arrows so I'd fall in love with Acantha?" Erato spat out in disgust.

Eros' eyes opened wide. "You remember?"

"Yes, I remember, but I haven't told anyone *yet*. I bet Apollo would be very interested in knowing how you and Aphrodite interfered in his affairs. Zeus, also."

Eros opened his mouth to speak, and Erato silenced him with a raised hand. "This can remain our little secret, Eros, not even Aphrodite need know I remember *if* you tell me the truth now. Did your arrow make me fall in love with Acantha in the mortal realm?"

Erato prayed with everything in him as he awaited Eros' answer.

"I admit the plan was to let her fall naturally in

love with you first, which we knew she would, and then shoot you so you'd fall in love with her." Erato let out a foul curse and had the overwhelming urge to break the golden boy's neck when Eros' quickly continued, "But I didn't have to, Erato. You fell in love with her all on your own."

Erato grabbed Eros' toga and growled, "The truth? I swear, Eros, if you are lying..."

"It's the truth, Erato. I swear to you. I was going to give you a mortal week and then shoot you, but you told her you loved her after one mortal day. That ended Acantha's banishment, so we brought you immediately back to Mt. Olympus."

He released his grip on Eros and laughed. Erato loved Acantha, without Eros' interference, and it had only taken one mortal day. The whole thing was incredible. Amazing.

"I have to go."

"What are you going to do?" Eros called after him.

Erato turned. "See if she remembers me."

"She won't," Eros shouted at his retreating back.

Erato yelled, "We'll see!"

Chapter Seven

"Acantha."

She turned at the sound of her name as the man who'd spoken it entered the nymphs' bathing chamber. Acantha dipped quickly beneath the water to hide her nudity, glancing around for something with which to cover herself.

The equally nude nymph seated on the edge of the pool laughed. "You've been gone from Mt. Olympus too long, Acantha. You've become modest in your time away."

Acantha noticed the nymph stared boldly at the male muse who'd entered the room. The same muse she'd seen starring at her in the Great Hall during Zeus' assembly. He knew her name and now he sought her out. *Why?*

"May I speak with you in private, Acantha," the muse asked, almost begged.

Acantha glanced helplessly at the female on the edge of the pool, hoping she wouldn't leave her alone with the stranger, even though there was something slightly familiar about him.

The muse too looked to the nymph, who rose and sauntered shamelessly up to him, running one hand suggestively down the front of his toga. "Erato. I'll be waiting for you when you're done with that one."

Erato. As the nymph left them alone, the name she'd spoken tugged at Acantha's memory, stirring strange feelings within her.

"Acantha," he said again.

"I'm sorry. I don't know you, though you seem to know me."

He waded down the stairs of the pool, still fully clothed, and Acantha took a step back.

His face showed pain at her retreat. "Please do not fear me. I would never force myself on you. I promise."

"I don't remember you," she said, pleading.

"I know." His voice was gentle as he took another step forward. She forced herself to not take one back. He took yet another and stood directly in front of her now, taking a sprig of herb from within the fold of his toga. He crushed the needles between his fingers, then held them to her nose. "Breathe."

The scent had her leaning inexplicably toward him, wanting him as much as she feared him. Confused, Acantha raised her eyes to his and something stirred within her. "I used to know you."

He nodded. "Yes."

A flash of naked limbs, slick oil, and cries of passion hit her like a blow. She touched her fingertips to her head.

"There are images. You and I, we..." She blushed at the memory.

He smiled knowingly. "Yes."

Acantha shook her head, frustrated. "I can't remember anymore."

He took another step forward until his chest brushed hers. He leaned his head down, his lips hovering near hers. "May I?"

Bespelled, she nodded, suddenly not caring if he dropped his toga and took her right there in the pool.

His lips touched hers gently at first, then became more demanding before his mouth released her so he could speak.

"Remember, Acantha." His hands roamed down her back as his tongue ran over her throat. "Please, remember."

She felt his body, hard against hers through the wet cloth. He crushed the rosemary stem until there was nothing left but a bare twig, and then held his fingers up to her nose as he said, "Please remember, Acantha. I love you. I can't live an eternity without you."

He loved her? She inhaled again and suddenly it was all clear as day. How she'd fallen into the sea of his eyes the first time she'd seen them. All the things they'd done. Every word he'd said.

Acantha breathed out the name of her love. "Erato."

His eyes opened wide. "You remember me?"

Acantha nodded, a smile on her lips. "Yes, and I remember I love you."

She was swept up into his arms and spun through the water, all while being kissed like she'd never been kissed before, until they came to a stop against the wall of the pool. Then Erato's face became serious, the desire written clearly there.

Her arms around his neck, she clasped her legs behind his back and felt him press against her. "Erato, my love. Now. Please, love me now."

"Yes. Now and for forever, my Acantha," he whispered. "You are mine, and only mine."

"Yes, yours," she echoed. "Forever."

HEPHAESTUS LAYS DOWN THE LAW

Tilly Greene

Chapter One

"Hey, Hephaestus, how's it hanging?"

"Hermes."

Pounding on a molten piece of metal, Hephaestus didn't bother to look up at the other man. Even though Hermes was family, he was annoying, and obviously up to no good. They had the same father, but different mothers. Not surprising knowing who their sire was. Zeus was the ultimate horn-dog and rarely had an offer for sex turned down by anything with a heartbeat.

"This place is hot as Hades and filthy too."

Out of the corner of his eye, he watched Hermes walk around his workshop, wiping the sweat off his pretty face. Even though they were both members of the elite pantheon of twelve Greek gods and goddesses who resided on Mount Olympus, Hephaestus didn't trust his brother, not one bit. The other man was very clever and appeared to be full of purpose, and this worried him.

Silence usually made others uncomfortable and encouraged them to rush to their point, so he said nothing. He waited for the other man to get on with the reason for his visit while he kept beating on the hot steel. As expected, it didn't take long for Hermes to start dancing around his reason for being there.

"Looks like you're working hard."

"Unlike you, I'm always hard at work." Hephaestus still didn't look at the other man. He didn't want the distraction his brother's walking around his workshop presented, and tried to make that perfectly clear. Keeping his grip on the tongs holding the red hot material steady and sure was necessary when working around fire. He understood how volatile a tool it was to work with and had learned to be very respectful of its power.

"Asshole," Hermes gave him the insult as he moved a little closer to him.

"No thanks. Your ass, while rather feminine looking, is not for me." The annoyance in his brother's voice almost made him smile.

"Ha ha, you are such a jerk which makes it so much easier for me to pass on some information you're not going to like."

"Fine, what is this horrible news?"

"Only that your wife is once again rolling around naked on a hillside with someone other than you. Everyone knows how much she loves young, virile, and pretty men to fulfill her sexual needs. Obviously something, or more likely someone, is lacking in the passion department."

"You've delivered your message, now leave."

"Ahhh, is the big, lame, blacksmith upset? You shouldn't be. She'll never leave you. She's simply looking for something better, more satisfying. It is common knowledge the woman needs to constantly be adored and pleasured, not pawed over by a sweaty beast or worse, ignored."

"Leave, or I'll bust your winged shoes. I made them and know how to make them useless with one stroke from my stick."

"So violent, what would our daddy say?"

Hephaestus made a move toward the smaller man. It wasn't a quick or agile motion. It could be because he had one severely twisted leg that made his gait hobbled. He wouldn't actually hurt his brother, but he wasn't above using his size and power to scare someone when necessary. This moment called for a little intimidation in order to regain his peace. If he hadn't been so upset by the news, he would've smiled at how easily the simple move worked on menacing his brother.

Hermes threw up his hands in defeat.

"I'm going," the younger man called out as he quickly made his way out of his workshop. "You could've asked for help, old man. I'd be more than happy to explain how to satisfy a woman until she climaxed with delight and not faked it out of fear or disgust."

Upset over Hermes's parting shot, he fiercely thrust the metal he was working on back in the midst of the burning coals, causing embers to fly wildly in the air. Knowing the forge was not the place to be when unsettled, he tried not to think about what he'd just been told. Only he found it difficult not to be upset.

There was never a doubt for him, that while he may have won her hand in marriage, ultimately it was an arranged union. She hadn't handed him her heart and that hurt, but this was a lack of respect Aphrodite was showing him, and he'd had enough.

Hephaestus made an effort to calm himself down. It wouldn't do him any good to lose his temper and end up ruining his current project. Later he'd figure out what to do about his wife's wandering eye, meanwhile, he'd work.

Turning the glowing rod in the coals, he looked it over, and pulled it out to start working on the once again malleable steel. Zeus, his father, was always in need of quality thunderbolts and he was the man who was charged with keeping him supplied. He swung the mallet up and started beating the heated metal into a thin, narrow jagged length, ending in a sharp point.

The field he chose to toil in was extremely hot, with multiple fire pits burning around the forge, but there was much more to it than that. A good blacksmith had to be patient and skillful in bringing the best out of raw materials. Fire was his best instrument to manipulate the rigid steel. It helped him mold the hard substance into whatever shape he wanted. It was a dangerous job he did and wanted it no other way. The challenge of producing superior products through tough labor while viewed by many as being physically imperfect, appealed to him. Hephaestus constantly used everything inside him to prove he could do anything anyone else could, no matter what he looked like.

For long periods of time he worked over a roaring fire. There were certain limitations in what he did, and because he didn't like being uncomfortable while there in the forge, he chose to wear only a heavy leather apron to protect his flesh from flying sparks and out of control flames. Sweat covering his bare body became both his nemesis and a lure. The down side was the slickness made it difficult to hold onto whatever he was working on. On the other side, the physical labor his work required had made his body well-muscled.

In the beginning of their relationship, he often caught his wife watching him work with lust in her gaze. These incidents had usually led to wild sex games they both enjoyed. Now, she only stopped by the forge not to admire his fit physique, but to apologize for fucking another man.

It was all so infuriating. Why did she do this to him? Didn't she find him appealing anymore? It certainly seemed as if she liked him well enough whenever they were together, although that wasn't nearly as often as he'd like. Up until now, he hadn't thought about being unhappy in his marriage. Despite his misshapen leg that caused others to cringe, she'd married him, and freely came to his bed where there was always pleasure for them both. Surely these weren't the actions of someone who didn't enjoy what they had together.

With one last hit, he'd finished making the thunderbolt shape, and plunged it into a vat of cold water. Steam and a sizzling hiss filled the air around him. This final step would set its unique character before he added the fire element. Later it would be up to his three assistants to insert the thunder, lightning, and intensity, bringing them together in each piece of metal, becoming a perfect thunderbolt for Zeus to throw.

Hephaestus saw nothing wrong with being a calm, good natured, type of person. Anger didn't get him anywhere. Besides, he was too big and powerful to allow rage to rule his emotions. Someone with his strength could easily hurt another, permanently. While he made things that killed and maimed, he wouldn't do it personally.

Since his difficult childhood, he focused on keeping his emotions in check. Up until now, it had been easy for him to do. Without any warning, the grip he had on his more volatile feelings started to loosen. He grabbed his stick, used it to knock a stool out of his way, and started pacing the workshop. Circling pits full of roaring fires and lengths of various raw materials, he knew they were ready to be changed into something useful, except his mind was firmly settled on his wife, Aphrodite.

This was the last straw in their relationship. No longer would he stand by while she played these games. Not with him. He was tired of them and how they made him feel, useless and lacking in the sex department. From the first incident between her and a mortal man of all things, having sex by some river, he'd put up with her extramarital activities.

Well, no longer.

Deep down, it hurt when she snuck off to find her pleasure with someone other than him, her husband. In their short married life, he'd put up with her affairs with gods, warriors, even mortals, but enough was enough. This was the last time she snuck out on him and he did nothing in return. It was time he took his wife in hand and settled what was between them, once and for all. This latest incident put an end to his patience. Things were going to change for them or they'd no longer be a couple.

Stopping in the center of his forge, Hephaestus looked around and saw nothing, although one very important thought flooded through his mind. No, he couldn't easily cast his wife away. He'd fight to hold onto her before allowing that to happen.

A decision to do something was one thing, now he needed to figure out what he had to do to ensure she looked no further than him for her pleasure.

Aphrodite was certainly stunning and sexy. Without any effort, she inspired his cock to rise whenever he saw her, despite not being blinded to her faults. She was beautiful, but she was also extremely selfish, fickle, and at times, cruel. If he could somehow reach into her heart, there may be a chance for them to have a future together. Otherwise he will have no choice but to do the unthinkable and leave her.

Not wanting any further delays, Hephaestus believed there was only one person he could talk to about all this. One man who would help him ensure his plan to regain his wife's attention was successful. Without any further delays, he left his men hard at work in the forge and made his way along the ridge of Mount Olympus to the big temple at the highest peak.

There wasn't anyone who knew women and how they thought about sex better than Zeus. His reputation as a ladies' man was well-earned, and like it or not, his father, the King of Gods, was someone who would give him some guidance in this problem with Aphrodite.

Carefully he maneuvered up the stairs leading to the main temple as possibilities of various things he could do came to mind. No matter what path he chose to follow, he had to remember a secret side to his wife. She enjoyed sex, all forms of it, so it would be best if he formed a plan around that. The brain and talking was the best avenue for communicating between couples, but she understood the body and what it expressed even more. No, he definitely wouldn't throw anything out that might appeal to her naturally sensual side.

"Hello Zeus."
"Hephaestus. Did you bring more thunderbolts for me? I'm running low and there are some seriously

stupid mortals who are pissing me off. There's a handful that deserve them to be sent up their asses, but I'm holding that punishment off for when I'm finished with their nonsense."

"I'm working on them and should have a dozen ready for you later."

"Good, good."

"Actually, I've come for another reason."

"What do you need, son."

"I want to talk to you about something important and personal."

"Personal, you say?"

"Yes." Hephaestus didn't elaborate too much. One of the first lessons he'd learned about how to handle being in the big temple was that it was best not to talk too freely with so many people hanging around. For some, it was their life's work to listen for news, and spread it at will, whether it was true or not.

With his eyes locked on his father's, he made sure not to squirm or shift around. Any sign of discomfort would bring the older man to the point of demanding immediate answers and he'd prefer to have this conversation in private. It was bad enough his ego regularly took a bashing by his wife's actions. He didn't need to make it any worse by talking about it before whoever happened to be present.

Thankfully his father didn't query the request, simply demanded privacy.

"Everyone out. Now. My son wants to talk with me." There was a mad scramble of various deities, nymphs, lesser gods and immortals scurrying out of the throne room. When Zeus voiced a command, it behooved everyone to follow it without question, and quickly.

"Would you like some ambrosia?" Hephaestus asked his father, knowing it always helped put the other man into a better mood if he had a fresh glass of the special elixir. With a nod from the powerful man who ruled the heavens, as well as the universe, he walked over to a sideboard, and poured them each a cup brimming with the food for the immortals.

Once they both had a full glass, and the room was completely cleared of everyone except them, he did the one thing he never wanted to do. He opened his heart to his sire. It was one of the most difficult things he ever had to do. Admitting to having any kind of problem was bad. Having to tell his father the details and ask for his guidance was even harder. Inhaling deeply, he let the air out, and jumped into the deep end.

"It's about Aphrodite."

"I hate to say it, but I'm not surprised she's giving you problems. That is one goddess who is very high strung and needs an unlimited amount of undivided attention. Personally, you've lasted longer than I could. So tell me, what's the problem?"

"Up until now, I haven't been all that bothered by her finding satisfaction elsewhere. Today, when I was told she was out with someone else, having sex where anyone could see them, I became angry."

"Son, I'm shocked. You don't get upset about anything."

"I know it, but this news irritated me. Besides her insulting my prowess by seeking satisfaction elsewhere, my pleasure is not being seen to as often it should, nor in the manner I enjoy. I've decided she either starts being my regular bedmate, dangling from my cuffs or I'll leave her. I'm sure it won't be difficult to find another bedmate that would be more than happy to take her place."

"Wow, no one walks away from Aphrodite."

"Well, I will if she doesn't do right by me."

"Have you talked to her about this ultimatum?"

"No, not yet. It's all come about today and I wanted to talk to you first."

"Do you want me to talk you out of taking such a hard line with the notoriously beautiful and very intelligent goddess?"

"Actually, no. What I'd like is to discuss my plan of how to do this and to have your support while I see it through to its natural conclusion."

"You have some ideas to make it come about in your favor?"

"I believe so."

"I want you to succeed. Let's hear them and I'll give you any advice I have."

"So you'll support me?"

"Absolutely! I stand behind you, no matter what. You've never had it easy up here on Mount Olympus, especially with Hera, but that's in the past. I'm here for you, son."

"I'm honored, Zeus."

"Yeah, yeah, just make sure you don't ever call me Dad." The older man shivered and Hephaestus almost laughed because the disgust he felt over the title was obvious. "Now, tell me what you're going to do. I can help because I know her better than just about anyone else."

Sometime later, after a great deal of help from his father, Hephaestus was pleased as he made his way back to the forge. He had a solid plan to bring his wife to his side for good and was ready to get started.

There was plenty to get done while he waited for her to stop by his workshop.

Aphrodite may not realize that she followed the same pattern after each of her indiscretions, but she did. Despite the forge being her least favorite place, it was where she went to see him after she'd had sex with someone else. To his way of thinking, this made it the perfect place for him to lay down his laws in order for their marriage to go on. If all went well, he'd never have to listen to her apologize for going off with another man again. If it didn't, then at least he'll know he gave it his all to make it work.

Chapter Two

If he went by her past behavior, it won't be long before she walked through the door on the arm of her latest conquest.

With help from his loyal assistants, the Cyclopes Brontes, Steropes and Arges, his plan was ready for whenever Aphrodite decided to make an appearance. Meanwhile he worked creating more thunderbolts for Zeus.

Hephaestus geared up for whatever happened. He'd seen to it that the workshop and his private quarters had been prepared for any eventuality. To his way of thinking, his wife was notoriously stubborn and didn't like to be told what to do, so he had to be prepared for her to make things difficult. To help his quest to bring her firmly to his side be successful, he'd also crafted a few personal items to use. Jewels were pretty, but not always useful or fun, so preferred receiving elaborate sex toys instead.

If nothing else was gained by the quest he was about to undertake, then at least they'd both experience a great deal of pleasure before going their separate ways. No animosity, hurt, or angry feelings would help either one. Whatever happened between them, they still had to maintain their positions on Mount Olympus. He'd promised his father he'd ensure neither of them brought their feelings into the throne room, good or bad.

His unique physical appearance, added with the fact he needed a stick to walk, encouraged Hephaestus to believe many people underestimated him and what he was capable of. Like him, she wasn't big on confrontations, so he expected her to say anything to get out of a difficult position. It was going to take discipline of mind to determine when she was lying, because he expected her to.

Just because he knew what she was capable of, didn't mean any of this was going to be easier to deal with.

Well, her free reign over him and their sex life was officially over. It was long past time he toughened up and took this part of his life in hand. Before he walked away from this woman, he had to put in the sweat and labor to make it work. At the end of all this, he did want them to be together, but he also wanted what he deserved. Respect, happiness, and yes, love. Whether he found them with Aphrodite was up to her, although he certainly hoped it was possible.

No one really knew that Hephaestus cared about the names he was called. Repulsive, flawed, lame, beastlike, were often voiced behind his back and sometimes to his face. He wouldn't believe them, at least tried not to. There were a few times when he felt insecure and these horrible taunts made him second guess his decisions and actions. He knew it didn't do any good when he did that, so tried very hard to deny them a place in his head and heart.

This all started when Hera, Queen of Gods, his own mother, had thrown him from the top of Mount Olympus into the sea to make his own way through life, if he survived at all. A long time ago he'd come to terms with what had happened back then. He'd turned that ugly start around and made them respect him and his skills, including his mother.

Now, in spite of that horrible beginning, he had an immense amount of power as one of the twelve Olympians. With titles like God of the Forge and Master of Fire, he was revered by mortals and immortals alike. However, he made sure not to abuse his power over others or dwell on past hurts. For him, it was a waste of time. He was ready to look forward and that could be done with his wife at his side, or not.

Putting all that was happening in his life to the side, he moved over to his desk to start drafting a special set of crowns for Castor and Pollux. The twins had recently been granted special compensation to leave the sky and search for their true mates. This was a really big deal for them and he believed they would be successful in this difficult quest. If they were both able to find mates and the ladies proclaimed their true love for them in return, then the two men would be pulled from the constellations to be with their partners on Mount Olympus. Leda, the Queen of Sparta and their mother, was very excited to possibly have her sons be granted immortality. In fact, she'd wasted no time in coming to him with a request for something extraordinary for the ladies to wear when they arrived.

Making notes beside the sketches he'd send to her for approval, he wrote of various materials and stones he suggested using. He also explained how he thought bringing in the stars and planets into the final pieces would personalize them for the men.

Before he was able to finish the notations, Hephaestus heard a couple of guests moving across the forge's rough floors. Apparently his wife had arrived, but how they went on from this point, was going to follow his rules, not hers.

Even though he could sense her standing in front of his desk, he continued working on the drawings until he was finished. It didn't take all that long, and yet he could hear her sighing heavily, shifting from foot to foot. For him, it didn't matter if she was put out by not instantly gaining his notice. Aphrodite expected to be the center of attention wherever she was. She would continue to be in his mission to bring her to admit her love for him, although maybe not in the way she expected.

He found it interesting that, no matter how impatient she was to gain his attention, she didn't interrupt him while working. After he completed what he needed to and packaged the drawings with a personal letter for the Queen, he looked up at his wife and her current lover.

"Aphrodite."

"Hello Heph. Hard at work I see."

"Always, darling."

"Yes, I know." The beauty looked disgruntled and briefly he thought maybe this was her problem with him. His dedication to work and fulfilling his obligations as a Greek god in a sensible manner did take up a great deal of his time. Especially if there was a war going on and new weapons were needed. It could be one of the reasons why she acted out and did outrageous things to gain his attention. Until now, he hadn't thought of their problem in this way. She had as many, if not more obligations as a goddess, but he would definitely delve more deeply into the concept before he finished doing everything he could to bring her back into his life.

"Tell me, wife, how was your day? You bestow copious amounts of love and beauty all over the fine citizens of Greece?"

"Actually, I spent today with this delightful man."

"Boy. If you spent the day fucking him, then he's nothing but a pretty boy."

"Oh."

"You can't be surprised, Phria. I've met enough of your playthings to be able to figure out what you lust after."

"Well, yes, um..."

"Don't know what to say? That's all right. I suggest you tell your current partner to leave my forge before I lose my temper, and mar his perfect body."

When she still didn't do anything other than look at him with her mouth inelegantly opened, something she'd never knowingly do, he figured he was on the right track to victory. He'd stepped away from his usual pat responses to her extra marital activities. It may have been mean to threaten the callow youth, but it actually felt pretty good when he saw the fear on his flawless face.

Hephaestus looked closely at the scrawny but pretty boy. For him there was no understanding why she would want someone that looked feminine and girlish, not when she could have him, a real man, riding between her thighs. This man's cock was most likely no bigger than his largest finger, a little bit of nothing. It couldn't possibly satisfy her desires.

Under his focused gaze, Hephaestus saw her lover start to shake in his skin, and was even more disgusted. Surely she didn't think someone like this was appealing.

In the end, all it took to get the other guy to leave was for him to stand up, collect his stick, and begin walking around his desk.

"Stop, don't hurt me. I'm leaving!"

The lack of a backbone was revolting, he thought as he watched the young man run from the forge. He couldn't stop himself from, for the first time, voicing his disappointment in her actions.

"You sell yourself short by taking someone like that into your body."

"Now Heph, you know me."

"I thought I did, but what I just saw from that boy looked more like a complete lack of respect for you. You're a smart woman, and that means you know you deserve better than that weak-kneed youth."

"Really? And I suppose you're the ideal person for me."

"Maybe, but it doesn't matter what I think, it's for you to figure out."

"Aren't you in a deep and thoughtful mood," she stated with a hint of confusion in her voice.

"No, no more than usual. I care for you, Phria, and don't see any sign of you loving yourself in these actions."

"Of course I love myself. I'm the Goddess of Love and Beauty. Everyone wants me and wants to be me. There is no one more loved or able to love than me."

There was no kind or gentle answer he could offer in response to her claim, so he kept his mouth shut.

"I take it you want to apologize for the mess your fucking around caused me?"

"What mess? I had sex with someone else while you were hard at work. No harm, no foul."

"There is, but we'll discuss the details later," he whispered as he moved to stand in front of her.

Hephaestus stood with his arms crossed over his chest, his legs spread wide for balance and the big stick he used for walking hanging from his fist. The stance was chosen to ensure she understood he was not happy with what she'd done. For the first time ever, he was putting himself in position to not just be a participant in their marriage, but the one in charge. "Shall we go into the other room and relax with a glass of ambrosia?"

"Are you going to bathe first?" An adorable wrinkle spread across her nose.

"Why, are you bothered by someone who spends their time working?" It was obvious she was, but he didn't care. This was who he was, a man who enjoyed physical labor, and she either accepted him, or not.

"No, but you're all sweaty."

"So what? I've labored hard today and am not ashamed for doing that. However, right now I want to sit down with my wife and unwind. Besides, I have a surprise for you and don't want to miss your expression upon seeing it."

"A surprise? For me? Really? How exciting!" Aphrodite clapped her hands and started dancing with excitement.

"Of course it's for you. I enjoy making things that make you smile." While it was easy to turn his wife's head with baubles and pretty trinkets, the one he was leading her to was going to be pleasurable for both of them. Hopefully it would eventually lead to her proclaiming her heart in his favor. He may be an eternal optimist, but didn't care if there was a chance it was true.

"You're so creative. Everything you've made for me is simply divine."

"Thank you. That's very thoughtful of you to say, especially since you can't stand to sit near me after I've spent a great deal of time crafting your gift with my own hands."

"Yes, well..."

"It's all right, darling. I know I'm not pretty or perfect to look at, but don't make the mistake of misjudging me. I can still bring you multiple orgasms and make you scream out with passion. Not bad for a lame beast."

"Stop it! I hate it when you put yourself down or let others go unpunished for doing it. I happen to think you're sweet, creative, and very handsome."

"Really?" The conviction behind her claim surprised him. Of course he knew she found him appealing, or at least enough to have sex with him, but he still had to wonder if it was his appearance that caused her to turn to others.

"Yes, really. One of the reasons I married you was your ability to turn me inside out with a single look from those golden eyes."

"Then why, if I turn you on, do you go to others for sex?"

"I don't know. It doesn't matter anyway, because I always come back to you." Her answer was flippant and didn't answer the question. Hephaestus knew it couldn't have been settled that quickly, so continued.

"But it matters to me, Phria." They walked into their private quarters and Hephaestus turned to watch her face as she found an elaborate and fussy throne he'd made just for her. Of course he'd added a few special things just for him, but that was for later.

"Ooo, Heph, it is incredible!" He was entranced by her delicate hands stroking over various shells, pieces of coral, and other treasures from the sea he'd used to decorate the chair. He could almost believe it was his body she was touching.

"Have a seat, check it out firsthand, and see how it suits you." Aphrodite settled her delightful backside onto the blue cushion. She squirmed around a bit, as if she couldn't find any comfort.

"Everything all right?"

"Not quite."

"Well that isn't good. Maybe your toga is getting bunched up. Why don't you take it off and try the throne naked." The silky sheer sheath, gathered at one shoulder, floated to the ground, and with a flick from her fingers pooled around her feet. His next breath stuck in his throat, she was simply stunning.

Her beautiful curves tempted him to run his hands over them all and treasure their sensuous feel. Plump pink lips tempted his own to kiss them, full breasts with hard red tips made his fingers twitch with a need to touch them, and the pussy she kept bare taunted him to fill it with his hard cock. However, before he did that, there were words of love and devotion he needed to hear first.

"Is that better?" Walking over to the bar, he poured them both a cup of ambrosia. They'd both need the energy it offered immortals.

"This throne is divine. Do I look good sitting in it?" She asked her question while looking at him with a smile on her lips and intensity in her blue eyes he couldn't quite put his finger on. Possibly she had her own idea for what this evening would produce, but so did he. And he intended to come out the victor.

"Of course you do, Phria. As stunning and sumptuous as the day you stepped from the sea."

"That was quite a day. From such a horrific act as Ouranos having his penis cut from his body and tossed into the sea, the epitome of beauty was created in me."

"You are beautiful."

"But?"

Hephaestus hadn't realized the tone of his voice had implied there was a *but* tacked onto the end of his compliment. Of course, it could be she was reading into his tone that there was more he wanted to discuss. Honestly, he just wanted to get his hands on her body. She understood that emotion better than any words.

"And I'm still confused as to why you seek out others. You've offered up plenty of excuses, but nothing with any real substance to it."

"You know I hate to be called shallow."

"I didn't say that."

"Yes, you did."

"I'm sorry you believe that, because I don't think you are." It was the truth. He, of all people, knew exactly how smart she was. Didn't she have most immortals and mortals' alike running around doing anything to please her? Hephaestus noticed she'd just about finished her ambrosia and was relaxed into the comfort of the throne. Exactly the sign he'd been looking for to get started on his quest for complete fulfillment and her truthful claim of love.

As he took the cup from her relaxed hand, he turned to place it on the bar beside his own and started letting his mind take control of the throne. In a few seconds, he was pleased by the sensual squeal slipping from her lips.

"What was that? Did you add something special for my pleasure?"

"You know I'm all for ensuring you are pleased and your passions satisfied."

"Seriously?"

"Of course. You see, I wouldn't be so upset if you were honest and told me about wanting another. Especially if it gets you off. Shoot, maybe we should bring others into our marriage. You can have some immature, pretty boy, take you, and I can have a mature, voluptuous woman satisfy me. How does that sound to you, Aphrodite?" It was a risk for him to make such a claim, but he was willing to go that far in order to be able to assert she was his.

"I-I..."

"What? Not sure about fucking someone else with me in the same room? Trust me, darling, I can handle it. It's the secrets that I can't stand."

"But—"

"We've always been open about what we both desire sexually, I say we expand our playbook and see what else we may enjoy. What about you, Phria? Do you fancy watching another woman suck on this?"

Chapter Three

Tossing his stick to the ground, he laughed at her little scream, and then proceeded to strip off his leather apron, dropping it on the floor as well. With her pretty gaze coasting over him, he started to stroke his semi-hard shaft.

Oh yes, he definitely had her attention. Aphrodite stared at his cock with lust burning hot in her eyes. Hephaestus had hoped she'd deny his offering to bring other people into their marriage. If she did, then they could get busy loving each other. Only she hadn't, and he was prepared to go to the next level to get her to admit he was the only man for her.

"Brontes, Steropes and Arges, boys, go wash up and then come back here," he called out to his assistants. "My wife's ready for your undivided attention."

"No! Don't call for them!"

"Why not? They'll be able to satisfy you better than the stupid boys you chase."

"They're—"

"What? Ugly? They may each have a single eye, but they're all very well-endowed in the dick department, so they won't disappoint you. Besides, I hear they know how to wield it to the satisfaction of their partners, so why not try them out. You want to come, right?"

"Yes, but not by them."

"Well, I know you aren't opposed to entertaining more than one partner and they are all young, so I can only determine your denial is based on their appearances. The Cyclopes in my workshop are all strong men, demi-gods, and yet they aren't pretty enough for you."

"Stop it, Heph, just stop it. I know what you're trying to do and I find it offensive. Your damaged leg doesn't define who you are. You are a thoughtful, creative, handsome god that everyone adores. When we're together, do I not stroke my hands over your entire body? Don't I massage your twisted limb to try and ease the pain you suffer? My being with other men..."

Aphrodite trailed off as a naked woman came into their private quarters and knelt in front of Hephaestus. During their earlier conversation, Zeus had recommended this particular woman because of her skills in pleasuring a man. As a dedicated maenad, she wasn't particular about the men she chose to bed down with, but she was careful when not in a frenzied state. Cyra was pretty, with a perfectly proportioned figure, and young, everything his wife chose in a partner.

Without a word passing between them, the newcomer took hold of his hard-on and moved until her mouth covered the crown. The pleasure was instant, immense, and threatened to take him over. The last time he and Aphrodite had sex seemed an eternity away.

The woman currently sucking delightfully on his cock was the first one he allowed to touch him since he'd married. He wasn't entirely sure what went to his head quicker. The fact it was happening in front of his wife and she wasn't saying anything to stop it or that his needs were being more than sufficiently taken care of. Either way he was enjoying himself and didn't want to stop. This caused a slight pause in his seeking release. While there was pleasure racing through him and it was enjoyable, having someone else touch him with the intention of arousing him even further felt wrong.

As long as he had a wife, he wanted her to do this for him.

Unable to deny the delicious pull on his rod from her mouth, Hephaestus placed his hands on Cyra's head to hold her still, except it didn't matter. As long as she had his shaft in her mouth, she would find a way to pleasure him. There'd been a moment where he'd forgotten maenads had the ability, like all immortals, to change enough so they could handle unique genitalia of gods and other lesser immortals.

Desperate to get back on track toward victory, he searched for some way to refocus on his mission. From beneath lowered lids, he discovered his wife still hadn't said anything about having another woman take him in such a passionate and personal manner. However, things weren't looking so dire, because he believed she was starting to look angry, maybe even jealous.

That was all he needed to slow his lust for climaxing back down to a pace where he wanted his pleasure to be. Now he could continue on with his plan of having his wife all for himself. There was a small bit of sadness when he accepted that, if they weren't meant to be a couple, then being set free to find his pleasures wherever that may be was preferable. In fact, if he had to choose another bed mate now, it would definitely be this woman.

Thankfully he didn't have to make that decision. Hephaestus was still solidly set on bringing his wife to his side.

The throne he'd created had a few special treats he believed would engage Phria in a way that he was sure would lead them to the truth he sought. As he'd been engaged with Cyra, his special powers had sent delicate ribbons of gold curling from the legs of the chair to wrapped around her and the chair, ensuring she couldn't move any of her limbs without his permission.

While he watched her closely so he wouldn't miss a thing, he set the next phase of his plan in motion. As the seat beneath her shifted, he saw her eyes grow large, and then they looked up, locking with his. Earlier he'd made a duplicate of his cock and balls out of gold and configured it in such a way within the unique throne, that it could be imbedded in her pussy while she sat on it.

Hephaestus knew he was a large man, in every way, but especially what he possessed between his legs. Since his first time with a woman, he was concerned he'd harm a partner, be they immortal or not. In order to be careful with his partners, he never hurried the act of putting himself inside their pussy. This was the first time he used this particular faux rod and didn't want anything to go wrong. With this in his mind, he ensured the special toy moved cautiously between his wife's lower lips and into her moist, heated channel.

Although he couldn't feel it personally, he knew the replica cock, polished to a high shine, slid easily within her tight clasp. Slowly the shaft moved inside her, and then he pulled it out a little, only to return again. Eventually, without laying a finger on her, his wife was completely filled with him. Suddenly she screamed out and had what looked to be real anger flashing in her eyes when the golden tool stopped moving.

Phria was truly stunning with her lust demanding satisfaction. No intelligible words had passed her lips, but he was sure they were coming. A faux cock was fun, but it undoubtedly lacked the unique things that were only offered by a real breathing man connected to the rod. Because that wasn't possible here, he'd designed an extra element to replace the usual throbbing she liked. What he'd done was add a series of mini pellets that were charged and lodged them in a reservoir inside the tip. The charge and being enclosed made sure they clanged against the edges and driving her needs wild.

It looked like this was a good move for him to have made, because his wife hadn't stopped crying out with passion. He knew her well enough to expect the begging for a release to start soon.

With all that was happening and the pleasure filling him up, Hephaestus almost forgot what he was actually doing. Apparently his hold on Cyra's head had loosened enough so she could take even more of his cock into her mouth. He was hard as steel pipe and a few short moments away from coming. A release for either him or Aphrodite wasn't going to happen until they'd agreed on where they were headed. Either together or apart, he needed to know.

"Darling, tell me, do you like seeing another woman pleasure me?" He helped Cyra stand in front of him and set out to ensure she found some pleasure in this game he played with his wife. Of course they'd spoken earlier and she'd been in agreement with what he intended to do, but he was thoughtful, and didn't want to leave her feeling unappreciated or unsatisfied by his mission. "Do you get turned on by how hot she makes me?"

With his fingers playing with the pretty maenad's pointed nipples, he looked at his wife while waiting for an answer.

"Not particularly."

"Why not?"

"It's not right that there's no pleasure for me while you are well taken care of."

"But you have a cock inside you, while there's nothing filling her here." He slid a hand down and cupped her bare pussy, ripping a moan of pleasure from Cyra's lips. Hephaestus leaned down and kissed her neck before continuing to talk with his wife. "By the way, technically I am inside you. See, the rod your divine cleft is gripping so tightly, is an exact duplicate of mine. I know exactly how full you are."

"It's not the same. You're touching her, bringing her even more pleasure with your hands and body, and I have none."

"You're feeling no passion, no need for more loving?" Using the power of his position as an Olympian god, he slipped the golden cock from her pussy, and then slowly pushed it back in, causing Aphrodite to quiver with need.

"How about now?"

"Yes, but it isn't the same as when it's you fucking me."

"You say you enjoy my way of loving you, but instead of being with me, you've been out fucking around. In fact, it looks like you prefer anyone other than me to have you, so I'll ask again. Why do you prefer others over me?"

"I don't."

"You keep saying that, only your actions don't match up." Fed up with Phria's lies and half-truths, Hephaestus turned the other woman around until she was face to face with him and pressed his lips to hers. The kiss was mutual, carnal, and wonderful. When her arms wrapped around his waist and she held him tightly, he felt wanted.

At the start of their marriage, he remembered how his wife had wanted him. He didn't know what happened, although it was apparent for her the spark of desire was no longer a part of their relationship.

It was intoxicating for him to be wanted so intensely. He felt his cock thicken even further and was surprised. Women turned him on, that was no revelation, but it had been a long time since he actually wanted to have sex with someone other than Aphrodite. There was no doubt his body wanted Cyra, but he wasn't too sure where his mind stood on the issue.

Letting their kiss continue uncontrolled ended up being the final straw on his desire. He was intrigued by how she was trying to climb him like one would a tree. The pleasure he felt was taken even further by the force of need he felt coming from her. How she responded to him was so seductive, he helped bring her closer by putting his hands under her soft ass while her arms and legs embraced him.

They kissed with their lips and tongues, each trying to gain more of the other. Even though he knew she hadn't been to a bacchanalia before coming to his forge, she still tasted like wine. Like the wild sexuality, he expected this from a nymph often associated with Dionysus. She moaned and the sound trickled down his spine, down his ass, and up to his cock and balls. Hard pebbled nipples stabbed into his chest and he could feel the honey gathering in her pussy. This was real and powerful passion. His wife had once wanted him this deeply.

Thinking of Aphrodite pushed the pleasure back long enough for him to look to where she sat in the throne he'd built for her. It wasn't that he had forgotten she was there in the room with them because that wasn't possible. He'd simply been lured away from dealing with their problems by the passion he experienced.

The sadness in her eyes had him immediately pulling away from the other woman's kiss, but it was the tears tracking over Aphrodite's cheeks that had him putting Cyra aside, and stumbling toward his wife. He didn't stop until he was kneeling in front of her. With hands on her knees, he spoke to her in a quiet voice.

"What is it, darling? Why are you crying?"

"It hurts."

"What does? Seeing me with another woman?" Finally, he was making progress in solving their troubles.

"Yes! I love you so much, Heph, and have tried everything I could think of to get you to really see me, and you don't."

"I see you, Phria."

"Not what's far below the surface, because that's where what truly matters to me is held close, and carefully protected."

"Tell me what's really bothering you."

"It isn't easy to talk about."

"Try me. I promise to listen and not pass judgment."

"I know you will, it's just so hard to, well, speak about flaws."

"Flaws? You don't have any flaws, darling."

"Yes, Heph, I do. I know it may sound selfish, but I want to be more important to you than your work."

"My duties as God of the Forge and Master of Fire or specifically what I do here in the workshop?"

"I understand your duties as an immortal. What bothers me is whatever it is you do here, in this dirty workshop. Time and time again, I've come in second place to this filthy place. That alone isn't something I accept easily. For goodness sakes, I'm the Goddess of Love and Beauty. You, my husband, above all others, should fall to your knees whenever I'm around, except you don't. You keep working, creating magical items for whomever asks, and I am left without you."

"Is that why you go with other men? To be with someone who would pay you the attention you need to maintain your position? Or is it something else, something more personal, like a need to climax?" They were making progress, but weren't quite there yet.

"No, you are way off base. An orgasm isn't everything, although when they come from you they are very special because of my feelings for you. No, I went with those men to get a rise out of you. Stupid, I know, but I wanted you to feel so much for me that you'd actually get upset at another touching me."

"Of course I'm angry!"

"Then why didn't you do something about it?"

"Because I figured you wanted them more than me. They were young, I'm not. They were pretty and perfect, which is definitely not me."

"Would you stop talking down about yourself? I happen to think you're perfect and wouldn't want to be married to anyone else."

"Really? I mean technically we have an arranged marriage." Hephaestus hated to remind her of this, but it was true. The beautiful Aphrodite wouldn't have looked at him as anything other than another member of the powerful Greek pantheon if circumstances hadn't become so desperate.

"No we don't. You asked me out and we were able to get to know each other outside of our positions on Mount Olympus."

"Phria, I only had the guts to approach you because Zeus suggested we get together to try and keep the peace amongst the immortals. Didn't he have the same discussion with you?"

"No, he didn't, nor would he ever have dared interfere with my love life. You and I married for love." Fine. As far as he was concerned if she said so, and he definitely did, then he'd leave it at that.

Chapter Four

"You're right. If I promise to be a more attentive husband, will you stop sleeping around?" Were the problems they'd suffered really all his fault? Had he been ignoring Phria to such an extent that she saw no other way to gain his attention? It was a horrible discovery and one he would ensure never happened again.

"Are you going to make out with anyone again, either in front of me or behind my back?" The whispered question, he believed, said more about how she felt about what happened than she was willing to say.

"No, I've been true to you throughout our marriage and will continue on this path. While Cyra was able to tempt me because of my problem accepting your half-truths, no answers, and outright lies for why you slept around, it's you I want. I mean it, Phria, don't stray again. While I don't tend to get angry, hearing about you with other men brought me closer to the point of losing my temper than I've ever been before. Knowing my size and strength, I might cause some serious damage to someone else, and that wouldn't sit well with me."

"I won't be with anyone except you. Now, while I was upset watching you with the lovely maenad, I feel bad for her because you've left her beautiful body quivering with need. You know maenads constantly need their passionate desires fed or they're susceptible to losing their minds. I understand it's very difficult for them to be left unsatisfied. So, while I don't want you to touch her again, I must know that you're going to do something about the condition she's in."

Hephaestus looked over his shoulder to where he'd left Cyra. She was lying on her back, with her hands covering her breasts and her legs pressing tightly together. The maenad was valiantly trying to ignore the pleasure racing through her body, but it was impossible for her to do so. He felt horrible for thinking only of himself when he'd instigated and then built upon their pleasurable play. There was no doubt about it, he had to do something.

A movement he vaguely saw from the corner of his eye had him shifting his attention to the doorway. His assistants, Brontes, Steropes, and Arges, must've been standing there since he called them in to help ease his wife's needs.

The three men were naked and very aroused. Seeing their sturdy hard-ons bouncing in the air, he had to wonder if the maenad would want one or possibly all of them.

"Excuse me for just a moment, darling. I have an idea of how to ease Cyra's plight, but need to discuss it with her first."

"No touching, Heph."

"Only as a concerned friend, nothing more."

"Okay, but I'm watching you."

"Don't worry. I'll make sure you know how much I'm thinking of you."

"Wait, what does that mean?" Hephaestus stood up and couldn't help but laugh. His wife was making valiant attempts to release herself from the throne, only he still had plans for her in that particular seat.

They may have proclaimed their hearts to each other, but he was far from finished laying down his law for their marriage. Before he could do that, he needed to help the lovely maenad. The least he could do after all she'd done for him was to ensure she received fulfillment, if that was what she wanted.

He believed she'd been with at least one Cyclopes before, so didn't think she had any prejudices against having them as a sexual partner. Bacchanalia's were wild, with a variety of species having sex with whoever touched them. This meant he didn't see her having any problems being with his men, but needed to discuss it with her first. She could want something different when not under the frenzied and wild spell that surrounded maenads when worshipping Dionysus.

With faltering steps, Hephaestus made it to where he'd left his stick without falling over. He picked it up and walked to Cyra's side. Kneeling wasn't easy for him, but he did it again to put himself more on level with her. Gently he moved the blonde hair that had fallen across her face. Once he could see her clearly, he was able to determine that, while she was definitely feeling very needy and had tasted of wine, it was clear she wasn't under any others' control.

"My beautiful maenad, I want to thank you for your help in regaining my wife. I greatly appreciate your willingness to throw yourself so completely into my embrace. Whether it repulsed you or not, you did such a convincing job, Phria believed you were ready to lay down with me."

"I would have sex with you, Hephaestus, gladly. You offered such incredible truthfulness in your passion, something I've never experienced while not at a bacchanalia. I only wish you'd followed through and taken me."

"I'm sorry. While I think you're very stunning and was tempted to taste a new brand of pleasure with you, being faithful to my wife is the path I choose follow."

"Don't worry, that's completely understandable. She is the Goddess of Love and Beauty, after all."

"You're a very thoughtful woman, Cyra. You're help was greatly appreciated and because I've left you in a difficult position, I thought I might make a suggestion to ease your most pressing sexual needs. I believe it's something that, in the end, would please you more than I ever could."

"Are you being serious?"

"Absolutely." He helped her sit up and immediately felt his wife's temper flare. As promised, he didn't forget she was there in the room, and went about reminding her that he was a very creative person.

The throne slowly and with care to keep the golden cock lodged inside her, shifted, twisted, and turned until it was no longer a chair. In a short amount of time, the glorious gold framework was locked to the wall and had Aphrodite standing on her own two feet. What had been armrests, now held her confined hands above her head, and the chair's legs, kept her limbs spread wide and tied in that position. There was a little movement from the golden ribbons, but they were there to keep her in a position for his pleasure.

Hephaestus didn't need to look at her to know she loved what happened to the throne, he could hear her delightful cooing found only with a newly discovered pleasure. To push her even further along the road to climax, he pulled the faux rod out, and then let it slowly glide back into her pussy.

Wanting to get back to her in a hurry, he confided to Cyra what could be hers, if she wanted. "Over there are my three assistants. They are good Cyclopes, strong, and driven to please."

"Driven to please?" The wicked grin on her face told him she knew exactly what he meant. They were a boisterous species that strived to be the best at everything. Yes, they were definitely driven to please and a maenad took quite a bit of passionate play to be thoroughly satisfied.

"That's right. They are willing to go to any level for fulfillment, but only to the point their partner wishes to go."

"Have they ever shared the same woman? I mean, I know Cyclopes can be very protective and covetous for those they have sex with. They will even go so far as to declare one as their mate. There was one woman I heard of who shortly after accepting the attentions from a Cyclopes, was removed from society entirely, and never seen or heard from again. That's pretty serious and I'm not sure how these guys are when it comes to casual sex partners."

"I couldn't tell you how they'd react, although I know all three are unmated." He knew his assistants well, but not about their sexual preferences. Well, other than they always chose women as partners, which was in the plus column for this match.

"What about pain? I know there are some groups who find that type of sex play more appealing than any other."

"Again, I'm not sure. I've never heard any of them mention it. But, if it would make you feel more comfortable, you can entertain them here, and I'll stay to ensure nothing you don't want comes about."

"Seriously? You'd really stay here in case I needed help?"

"Yes, of course I would, because I want you to find nothing except pleasure with whomever you're with. Be it one or all three of them, it is your desire we're looking to satisfy, and I'm sure they'd be happy to follow your rules."

"I've been with a Cyclopes before and found him to be a wonderful sexual partner, but I don't think I could pick one of those three over the others. They are a group that wears their feelings close to the surface. It would hurt me to push two of them aside in order to seek my pleasure."

"Okay, would you be put off by being with all three of them?"

"Now that's an interesting idea. I've never been the center of attention of a group not under the influence before. I'm finding the idea of it very intriguing. However, I'll only say yes if they are truly interested in being with me. I'm not into being a pity fuck for anyone."

"Trust me, Cyra. I can't imagine that ever happening and especially not right now." With an awkward movement, he stood up, and explained what he'd do. "I'll go talk with them and see what they're thinking. Although I think the engorged state of their hard-ons and the intense look in their eyes pretty much says it all. If they show an interest in you, then I'll delve further into you choosing not just one of them."

"Thank you, Hephaestus. You truly are a gentle god."

"If things were different, don't doubt I'd have chased you for a chance to enjoy your voluptuous body."

"Anytime you want."

He laughed, shook his head, and made his way over to his three assistants.

"So boys, do you see anything interesting?" Of course they did, Hephaestus told himself. Not one of them looked away from the sexy maenad when he walked up and that was unusual.

"We all do, boss. She's stunning and that's the problem. We aren't sure how to go about picking the one who should go over there and offer to ease her needs." Brontes was the leader of the trio when it came to speaking. He was the one responsible for adding thunder to the bolts, which left his voice deep and rumbling, or in sharp cracks. It all depended on his mood.

"Cyra, that's her name. She's a maenad who, right now, isn't under the influence of anything. No wine, no enchantment from Dionysus, nothing except her own unsatisfied needs."

"Chaos abound! That's her natural passion we see controlling her beautifully lush form?" Steropes rarely talked because when he did it came out in a rapid pattern that was sometimes not understandable. Obviously the man who was filled with lightning was too excited by the woman to not ask what came to his mind.

"Yes, that's all her."

"You've made this even more difficult for us."

Their heads turned toward each other and all he could hear was grumbling. Cyclopes weren't deep thinkers or individualists, but they were very careful. Their society had more of a pack mentality, which

Hephaestus figured was at the root of their current problem. When a decision had been made, they each kept their large, single eye, focused on her, while Arges, the one responsible for the bolt's intensity, spoke to him. "We think you should pick one of us to have the honor to try and woo her."

"Just out of curiosity, have you boys ever played any games together?"

"What do you mean? We do everything together."

"I'm asking if the three of you have ever shared a woman sexually, at one time."

"Really? This is possible?"

"I take it that is a no." He didn't know whether to be happy or not. One thing he did know about his assistants was that they were adventurous, wanted to experience everything other societies did.

"No, wait, I mean yes, but we'd love to try it. Wouldn't we guys?" Brontes was quick to clarify their position on being open to making their potential session with the maenad a quartet.

"This sounds like the answer to our problem and also a great deal of fun for everyone."

"I'm game, if they are." In short order, they'd all piped up and Hephaestus had his decision.

"Well, that young lady over there is intrigued by the idea as long as no one is hurt, physically or mentally. If you want this then listen closely to what I'm about to say. Be gentle, thoughtful, and thoroughly cherish her, and you just might have the best sex you've ever had, or will have." He honestly didn't think there was a mean bone in them, but needed to be sure they were all in the same place.

"Boss, we're so honored by this offer."

"Just make sure you stop whatever you're doing if she says *no*. This is very important, because without her being able to trust you'll let go of her if she needs it, then nothing will happen for any of you." Hephaestus was proud of how they were approaching this new idea and hoped it worked out well for them all. So many turn from the Cyclopes in fear when there is no need for this. They aren't mean unless they or those they love are attacked.

"Yes, yes, we hear what you're saying. We'll be calm and listen to her, follow her every wish."

"Fine, but I promised to remain in the room to act as a safety net."

"Good, we like knowing you'll be here to keep us from entirely losing our heads." Arges let him know they wouldn't feel insulted by his remaining while they indulged their lust. It wasn't to watch them, but to be sure they all played fairly.

Hephaestus made one last suggestion to help get the ball rolling on this odd coupling.

"Do you want to follow me and I'll introduce you to Cyra?"

"Please, I think that will help ease our nerves." Steropes piped up, but the other two were nodding their approval of what he said.

"Okay, let's go."

As a group, they walked over to the sexy woman eager for a release, and he set out to make the introductions. He didn't mean to be rude, but as soon as he gave the beautiful maenad the names of her potential partners, he made his way back to a dangling, voluptuous, Aphrodite.

"You've been a very wicked man, Heph. I'm hanging here, with your faux rod inside me, and left starved for your real throbbing flesh. I demand you take me to our bed and have your way with me."

"I will, Phria, just not yet."

"Why not? I must have you inside me or I'll dry up and wither away until nothing remains but a shell."

"Soon, darling, I swear. First I must make sure everything works out for those four over there. I promised Cyra that nothing would happen to her that she didn't want."

"If you could be hurt in any way, then I would find a way to do it right now! Have you already forgotten to make me your priority?" She was hysterical, almost screaming at him, which is something she never did.

"No, I haven't forgotten anything." To make sure she knew how aware he was of what was going on within her body, he once again brought the golden cock to a standstill inside her pussy.

"That isn't fair." Her head fell forward in apparent despair, leaving her long blonde hair spilling over her face.

"Nothing is fair right now, but we'll make due until we can be on our own."

"Hephaestus, I want—"

"Enough is enough, Aphrodite!" He shouted over his wife, something he never did, but his patience with her was at an end. Struggling to find a calmer tone, he continued because he had to get things settled. "I would've waited until we were alone, but apparently you won't let it be. So here it is in a nutshell. It's now my turn to make the rules for us to live by."

"What do you mean?" She looked at him with a glint of surprise in her pretty blue eyes.

"I mean that from this point on, I say what we're going to do, when and where we'll do it, and most importantly of all, how we'll do it. And this isn't just about sex either. It's about our every waking moment together."

"Oh," she uttered quietly while not so much as blinking her big blue eyes. It wasn't fear that made her stand completely still, but something else he'd never seen before.

"Is that all you have to say?" After finally telling her how their relationship would move forward with him in complete control, Hephaestus expected more of a response from her. It took some time, but eventually she started explaining her position, and he felt it was the truth.

"To be honest, I find it very sexy when you act all controlling and powerful. Usually you're very sweet and accommodating, which is lovely, but I think I like how you take over and tell me how it's going to be even better."

"Fine, because this is how it's going to be between us from now on. I'm finished listening to your complaining and endless demands. I love you more than anything, but I won't stop working at the forge because you don't like it here. Nor will I stop being concerned for others and doing what I can to ensure they're safe, if not happy. That's me and you'll have to find a way to live with it."

As soon as he said the words out loud, he remembered Cyra, and turned to see how they were all doing. Only he was stunned by what he found to look away. In the short span of time he'd been talking with his wife, they'd started their erotic play. Since there were no clothes to be discarded by any of them, it was bound to go quickly, he just hadn't anticipated it being this fast.

"Do you see that, Heph? Do you see what they're doing? I'd say her moans are showing how much pleasure she's getting from their undivided attention."

Truth was, while he didn't consider himself a prude, he didn't think he could ever participate in group sex, especially not with his wife. Despite it not being his thing to do, it was apparently not true when it came to watching others.

"Did you hear that?" Aphrodite whispered, but never looked away from the pile of naked bodies. "Someone in that writhing pile of naked bodies sounds like an immortal that was denied ambrosia for a long time. They sound hungry and desperate for something. My, oh my, this is an incredible fucking session."

"I don't know about you, darling, but watching this is seriously turning me on."

"I'm in the same position, although it may be a little more serious than the one you're in. You see, you had me climbing the ladder to climax from this naughty faux rod. And, I know you said no more demands, so I'm not going to make any on you. However, you should know that unless you do something about it, watching them go at it will tip me over the edge without any further help from you."

Chapter Five

"Oh really?" Phria's claim was very serious and he found it extremely odd that she'd made it at all. She'd managed to divert his attention away from the amorous quartet playing before them and back to her. What she was suggesting went against everything they, as Olympian God and Goddess, believed in. To choose solitary pleasure over that found with a willing partner was considered blasphemous. Of course there were times when nobody was around to help ease a need, but that wasn't the case right now for his wife. "You'd actually ignore the rules and seek your own peak instead of basking under the attention I offer?"

"Yes, but it isn't an easy decision to make, especially not in my current frame of mind. What those four over there are doing is really exciting and you're not relieving any of my pressing desires."

"And what about that replica cock buried inside your pussy?" For the first time since it entered her body, he reached out and manually pleasured her. He took hold of the golden balls resting at the base of the faux rod and took control of its movements. "Isn't it fucking you? Making you shiver with need, completely filling you, and promising you an incredible climax?"

"Personally, I love this particular toy, and yes, I feel everything you've mentioned. However, nothing will ever be as satisfying as your very real shaft stuffed inside my cleft, pounding with passion in and out of my body. And, I'll say it again. I need to come, Heph, and you're not doing anything to help me achieve a release."

Hephaestus was torn about what to do next. He'd promised Cyra that he'd stay in the room as her guardian, but he wanted his wife, very badly. She was ripe and eager for his attentions. There was no way he could disappoint the lusty maenad, but neither did he wish to deny his wife her pleasure either. Unfortunately, it wasn't as easy a choice to make as it should be. There were problems that he needed to think through before going any further and possessing her in this room.

There were few rules for them to follow as a part of the Greek pantheon. Zeus was a fairly easy taskmaster and didn't like any restrictions, so wasn't comfortable putting them onto others. However, one thing the King of Gods strongly recommended was that the twelve gods and goddesses that were the Olympians should never make love to each other in front of mortal or lower levels of immortals.

When two powerful beings came together, it was such a special coupling that there was usually residual affects filling the space around them. The aura that lingered didn't simply dissipate. Instead, it hung around, and looked for a place to land, which usually turned out to be whoever was the weakest in the room.

Despite needing to think this through, his mind was made up for him when he heard a long moan from his wife. Consequences be damned, he had to have her. No longer was there any will left in him to deny either of them their ultimate pleasure found only in each other. He'd willingly accept whatever price Zeus demanded from him for the pleasure of being inside his wife, in a way that he wanted to be, while lesser species were in the room.

"Fine, my beautiful goddess, we'll fuck, but we'll do it my way."

"I don't care how you take me, Heph, as long as I find my release before I age for lack of loving." The way she tugged on the golden ribbons that held her arms securely above her head was how he'd imagined her reacting to being confined. Bondage was his thing, but he'd always held off playing such games with Aphrodite because of who she was. Well, unless she balked, he wasn't going back to the plain way of loving her again.

"Do you like how I've restricted your movements?" Shifting the faux rod in and out of her pussy, he could feel how tightly she clung to it. Lust was not her problem, being patient to let the need swell to unimagined levels before exploding was.

"Yes! Now please—"

"Patience, darling, the best fruit is discovered after a thorough search."

"I'm begging you, please take me." The Goddess of Love and Beauty never needed to plead for anything and yet his cock grew even harder hearing her do this. Of course he'd do what she asked, he couldn't deny her anything. But after she came, he'd take great delight in building her needs right back up, even higher than they were now, and watch her tumbling into a another climax.

"Shhh, here you go, Phria, here you go." Slowly, he pulled out the golden cock by its balls, and then stepped so close to her, they were touching. Temptation was how her smooth, silky, skin felt resting against his own hard and haired body. They were opposites in many ways, but he was sure they'd been created for pleasing each other.

Once their gazes locked together, he dropped his stick and gripped her full hips, before carefully sliding his shaft into her pussy. When he was fully embedded inside her, he took a deep breath and gloried in finding his way through her divine body. He was further pleased by the deep breath she took and held until there was no more space for his cock to fill. Buried in her luscious depth was sweet, but he'd promised her relief.

It took only a few strokes from his engorged shaft for him to realize exactly how close she was to coming. Phria was very tight and slick with excitement. She hadn't been lying earlier when she claimed to be on the verge of an orgasm. Only a couple more thrusts and his wife screamed, while her slit shattered around him. He held still, thriving on feeling her release. It was a matter of pride for him to be able to withstand her delicious pulsating clasp as she came and have the strength to continue holding his own off.

The grip she had over his cock started to ease. Hephaestus lowered his head and lightly pressed his lips against hers. Between gentle bussing kisses, he whispered of the enjoyment he found in her climax.

When her body came off its high and became boneless over his cock, he reminded her they weren't finished. Far from it. Steadily, he pulled his rod out and then thrust back in, driving a long low pitched groan from Phria. She lifted her head to look at him and her mouth dropped open when he again, powerfully moved his rod in and out of her pussy. In no time at all, her passionate body was revived and ready to tackle the next level. Her needs were already rising higher than before.

He could feel her stiff nipples pushing into his chest. Hephaestus was tempted to take one in his mouth and feast on the tender treat, but didn't want to pull his shaft from her in order to do it. That was one of the down sides to being so much bigger than her. Otherwise it was empowering to be large and strong next to her small and delicate form. In spite of his obvious disfigurements, his physique ensured everyone knew she had a protector who was capable of taking on anyone, and winning.

Right here and now, with his shaft buried inside her while she looked at him with love and need in her eyes, was his idea of bliss. He thought he could handle hearing anything she said and be able to take it in stride. Only that wasn't true, he wasn't prepared for what she told him as he continued lacing soft kisses on her plump lips.

"You should know I'm nothing without you inside me. I feel like an empty shell of a goddess. I beg you Heph, don't ever leave me, or I'll become a beautiful but vacant body without a purpose."

The total honesty of how empty she felt without him went straight to his heart. There was no exaggeration in her claim. She really did care for him, as much as he felt for her. They were completely, totally, devoted to each other. He would not waste another day being bothered by her past behavior. For him, it was over and done with. From now on, it was all about them, together. Gently he bit her lip, pulling on the lower fold in order to bring her focus back to him.

"I'll always be inside you."

"My heart and body?"

"Yes, I'll always keep you filled with my love."

Without any further delays, Hephaestus pulled his cock out, only to push it right back in. Fast and hard he fucked, taking her right along with him. They didn't say anything to each other that mattered or needed to be remembered later, they simply rejoiced in being together.

Holding her pressed against the wall, he allowed his god-like power to release her limbs from the golden ribbons. Because he wasn't completely steady without his stick, he carefully shifted her legs until they were both draped over his arms. He pressed his hands against the wall on either side of her waist for balance. Then he returned to his intent to bring them both to the cusp of climaxing.

Again and again, he retreated and returned to her tight slit. There was nothing except the most erotic and loving joy circling around them when they were together. This was the start of the aura that built from coupling immortals. He knew it had been there before, but nowhere near as intense as it was this time.

When they were so close to coming and neither one of them could breathe, he covered her mouth with his own. His lips opened hers and they shared air between them. They were one, the aura of mutual pleasure and acceptance surrounded them, and the ultimate claim to satisfaction, broke around and inside them. Hephaestus and Aphrodite shared their orgasms with each other and then luxuriated in the dance of true love that filled their hearts.

Pure pleasure encapsulated them, engulfing their individual powers, and they were reproduced as one, this time a single claim locking them together. Love and everything the important concept encompassed tied their powers to each other.

They were lost within the other's body and the emotions they created with their bodies, but reality quickly crashed around them, ripping them away from enjoying the aftermath of their spent passion.

Clanging and banging erupted behind them. Looking over his shoulder didn't reveal anything, but he recognized the sounds as coming from his workshop. It was unheard of that anyone would dare invade his forge without his permission. Immediately he was furious that someone would disrespect him so severely, not to mention disrupt his time with Aphrodite.

Completely out of character, he was ready to send whoever was in there straight to Hades. The only reason he could think of for these types of thoughts was that his power must still be merged with his wife's. Hephaestus reluctantly pulled away from his delightful wife, and went to investigate. Grabbing up his stick, he made his way into the other room as quickly as he could manage.

What he found robbed him of his irritation and speech.

Despite his promise to protect the maenad, he'd actually forgotten all about the quartet. He was concerned for what might have happened to them because he and Phria had made love with them close by. Thankfully, his quick glance told him they were all physically intact, but their appearance said nothing about what was going on inside their minds.

With a more thorough glance, he found Cyra looked to be healthy and whole, if not still in need of satisfaction, but that was not what worried him. No, that feeling was reserved for finding her standing naked before the main fire, while the men continued their passionate pursuits from her body. That wasn't good, but what made the entire situation even worse was that none of them seemed to care about the shower of embers floating around them. They weren't wearing any of the usual protective gear and he knew his men would never be so careless with another, much less a woman, unless they weren't right in their minds.

"What's going on here?" The tone of his voice was quiet but demanded answers. He didn't want to startle any of them and cause more problems, but wanted them to be sure he was not to be ignored.

"We're building a leash, boss." Steropes told him what they were doing. Hephaestus was greatly impressed that he did so without slowing his fucking down. He stood behind her, while it looked like Brontes was in front on his knees licking her pussy, and Arges' hands were busy teasing her nipples. Seeing the three of them together, once again excited him, although he wasn't sure how she managed to hold the tongs with some sort of red hot material steady, but she did.

"A what?" He hadn't really caught the rapid words of the Cyclopes' explanation. The reason why was right there before him, he'd been too caught up in what was happening between the four of them.

"A leash, like the one we helped make for Hades to control Cerberus, only this one will have one collar and three leads." It was Arges who gave him the details while he moved to the side of the pit and started pounding the metal she held into the shape they wanted.

"Why are you doing this now?" Hephaestus decided now wasn't the time to mention the leash they'd made for the three headed dog, the one who ensured those who crossed the river Styx never left, was special. It had needed to be created out of the strong material, because the animal was dangerous. The woman they were thinking of putting a collar on wasn't remotely difficult. In fact, the wildest she would ever get would be when denied sex. Hephaestus thought the three Cyclopes could handle that without any restraints.

"Our lovely mate promised to stay with us, but when we told her it meant she'd never leave our cave, she balked, and then came up with this idea."

"Isn't she clever?" Brontes called out from his position between her legs.

His and Aphrodite's passion had definitely exploded over this quartet, but as long as they weren't harming anyone or themselves, then he'd discuss this collaring thing with them later. Who knows, he thought as he made his way back to his wife. Maybe they were actually meant to be together. Making their relationship into a quartet fed into both the pack mentality of the Cyclopes and ensured there was a ready cock always present for the maenad.

It was interesting how the group was putting down roots together at the same time he and his wife had solidified their love for each other. Something, for a brief moment, he had started to doubt was possible. How wrong he'd been.

Obviously anything was possible when on Mount Olympus.

PLUTO'S OFFERING

Selena Illyira

Chapter One

Buzz. Buzz. Buzz.

Iriana rolled over and hit the stop button on her alarm clock, sighing in relief as the shrill buzzing sound became silent. Keeping her eyes closed she rolled back onto her stomach and promptly fell asleep.

Ring. Ring. Ring.

Groaning Iriana rolled over again, keeping her eyes closed she reached blindly for the phone. "Hello?"

"Where the hell are you? You were supposed to be here an hour ago. The bride is freaking out." Her best friend and assistant Corrina hissed.

Groaning Iriana opened her eyes and turned her head. The clock clearly read 10:20 A.M. "Shit."

She sat up quickly and ran a hand through her hair. "I'll be there ASAP, just give me a few minutes to get it together."

"Hurry up, if I have to hear, 'It's my day, I'm the bride.' One more time I will be going to jail for sticking my foot up that pretentious heifer's ass." The line went dead and Iriana shook her head and let out a heavy sigh. "Today is going to be a long day."

She showered quickly, pulling her long, dark brown hair back into a low ponytail. Dressed in her favorite red suit that hugged her curves perfectly, she checked her appearance in the full length mirror.

Brushing off some lint from the smooth cotton fabric she smiled at her reflection and slid on her sunglasses. "Time to work my magic."

Turning, she left her apartment and headed for the bank of elevators on her floor. Tapping her foot with impatience she glanced toward the panel of floor to ceiling windows on either side of the hallway. The sun shone brightly in the sky, large puffy white clouds floated against the robin's egg blue sky. Smiling she felt a sense of calm. The wedding she was heading to was outdoors, no rain meant a happy bride, which meant less hissy fits. Her lateness could be smoothed over with a bribe, in the form of a specially designed, one of kind, crystal cake topper.

Humming softy she watched the large sliding doors of the elevator open. Stepping in, she hit the button for the lobby and leaned against the back railing as she waited for the cab to reach its destination. It didn't take long until she was at the lobby and out of the building. A cool breeze brushed her face and her heels clicked on the sidewalk as she made her way to the parking lot.

"Beware, the end is near, Pluto will rise again."

Iriana passed by an old woman dressed in rags, holding up a sign that declared the rise of Pluto was imminent. She just shook her head, "Hate to tell you but Pluto isn't even considered a major planet anymore."

The woman rushed after her, grabbing her sleeve. "Beware, Pluto will rise again."

Iriana paused, "Sorry but I don't think so. Here, take this."

She dug into her purse, pulled out her wallet and slipped out a twenty dollar bill. "I'm sorry it's all I have on me right now."

"I don't want your money," the woman hissed, shoving Iriana's hand back. "I'm here to warn you, Pluto will rise again, they all will."

"Uh, okay," She slipped the money back into her wallet and shoved it into her purse. "Look, is there family I could call, friends, maybe a doctor. There's a homeless shelter just round the corner, it's got rooms and a job center and helps people get back on their feet. I can take you there if you want."

The woman pulled back, looking as if she'd been slapped. Drawing herself up to her full height which was much more that Iriana's five foot three stature, the woman loomed over her. "I, madam, am a seer, gifted by the divine. Mark my words, Pluto will rise and you will meet him."

She blinked, "Pluto as in the Roman god of the Dead? Uh, okay. Look, I gotta go, it was nice meeting you and please do see someone or use the homeless shelter I was telling you about. It's called the Sheltered Pines, run by a really nice woman named Ricki."

Iriana pulled her arm away and turned on her heel, walking away. When she got to the entrance of the car park, she glanced over to where the old woman was but found her gone. Shrugging, Iriana headed for her car. That was the only part of her day that went right. The crystal cake topper hadn't arrived yet and she had to wait three hours for it. The bride threatened to sue her but Corrina managed to smooth things over. She got hit on by no less than three drunken groomsmen and accidentally sat on cake that someone had left on their seat. By the time the wedding was over, she was tired, hungry and had a pounding headache.

Leaving her favorite coffee shop with a nice ham and cheese sandwich, she made her way to her car to find a parking ticket stuck between the windshield and the wipers. Growling she looked over at the parking meter that had taken her coins. "I fed you, gave you money and this is how you treat me? What the hell?"

Thankfully the fine wasn't too high so she wasn't too mad. After sliding behind the wheel of her car, she put the key in the ignition and turned, nothing, not even a little sputter to tell her that the engine had some life in it. When she tried to call for a cab and the towing company she found her cell phone batteries were dead. Hanging her head she headed back to the coffee shop to find the phones were out of order. Rushing from store to store the same she found the same thing until she reached a tiny little TV repair shop.

The owner, a tall man, with messy curly brown hair, blue eyes and sweet boyish look about him, let her use his phone. As she exited the shop a downpour started, lightning crackling in the sky and thunder rumbling after it. Shrieking, she rushed back into the small store. "You have got to be kidding me. Does God hate me today?"

"Something wrong?" The shop owner asked coming out of the back room.

"Sorry, can I wait here? As you can see the weather has gone crazy." She gestured toward the front window and looked back at the man.

"Uh sure, stay as long as you need to. Would you like some coffee?" He smiled and gestured to the best thing she'd seen all day, a Java Express 4.5, the best coffee, cappuccino, espresso, latte maker in the world.

Her shoulders sagged in relief. "Yes, yes, yes, I would love a cup. Can that thing do a mocha cappuccino?"

He grinned, eyes crinkling at the sides making him even cuter than before, "Of course. I'm sort of a coffee snob. If it can't make all my favorite coffee drinks the way I want them, then it's not worth the metal that's used for its casing."

She laughed. *He's weird but cute.* "Do you have a bathroom? I'd like to try and dry off, if I can."

He pointed to a darkened hallway. "At the end, the last door on the left."

"Thank you." Iriana followed his directions and found herself in a small bathroom with just a toilet, sink and small mirror. The naked bulb overhead gave just enough light that she could see what a mess she was. Her makeup was smeared, hair soaked and her suit was wrinkled. Looking around she didn't spot a hand dryer so she settled for paper towels. Undressing, she dried herself off first before squeezing out the jacket and skirt as best she could, then blotting the material with the towels.

When there was nothing else that could be done she got dressed again and made her way out to the front counter only to find the shop keeper gone. Figuring he had something that needed repairing she waited for the coffee to finish. When the timer went off and he didn't show up, Iriana shrugged, made her way around the counter and picked up the cup of coffee that smelled like rich decadent chocolate and coffee. Inhaling the scent deeply, she blew away some steam and took a tentative first sip. Her taste buds sang at the bitter sweetness that rushed over her tongue.

She drank slowly. When her stomach growled she was reminded of the ham and cheese sandwich from the coffee shop that she had stuffed into her purse. She took the sandwich out of the bag in her purse, unwrapped it, and then proceeded to devour it taking large bites. When that was done, she found herself feeling sleepy. Yawning, she looked around. The shop keeper had yet to appear. She walked around the counter and sat down on a small wooden chair. Tilting her head back she yawned again. Her eyelids became heavy and her vision blurred. Arms hanging at her sides, shoulders sagging, then darkness rippled at the edge of her vision.

In the distance she heard heavy footfalls. "Looks like the sedative finally took. I felt like I've been waiting forever. What do you think?"

"She's perfect. Pick her up and bring her to the back."

Iriana tried to open her mouth but found it too hard to do. Her eyelids fluttered and then closed as sleep overtook her. She didn't even feel her body being lifted and moved.

The shop keeper dropped Iriana on a couch with a soft oomph and stood up. "I don't feel right about this."

"It's for the best. We need a guinea pig." The old woman said as she removed her rags to reveal jeans and an oversized sweater.

"Why her?" He asked, looking at the sleeping woman.

"Because she's here and the damn thing seems to be working."

"But mother -" He was interrupted by the older woman.

"I know, I know, but we must know if it works. Those damn cult leaders thrust us back in time as punishment. We need to get back and she's our ticket to the other side. If the wormhole holds when we push her through, we can go back. If things remain stable we can send her back to this time and all will be well. Don't worry; no harm will come to her. Besides she's a kind woman. I met her outside of her apartment complex, she tried to be helpful."

"So, first she goes then I go?" He began to push buttons and pull levers. A large machine whirled to life, a black and white vortex opened up in the middle of the room, papers blew all around the room and objects began to move.

"Right. Now get her to the machine and we'll push her in," the older woman yelled. The shop keeper walked away from the panel of controls and scooped up Iriana in his arms.

"Sorry about this," he said to her sleeping figure. He walked over to the vortex and held her before the swirling vortex. Squeezing his eyes shut he pushed her through and rushed after her. Icy air rushed over his body, it was like he had walked through a waterfall of freezing water. His body felt as if it was being pulled in multiple directions. He grabbed his thighs, digging his fingers into the fabric covered flesh. Gritting his teeth he prayed the ride would end soon. His heart was pounding against his chest, his head was threatening to explode and then it was all over. Breathing harshly he stumbled forward and tripped over something. Crashing into a wall he slid down, his head spinning, vision blurry.

When he finally recovered he looked down and found that he had tripped over Iriana's crumpled body. Scrambling forward he checked to see if she was still alive. Thankfully her pulse was strong, her breath was slow and even, the only downfall was that she was icy cold. Looking up at the vortex he was relieved to see it hadn't dissipated. A few seconds went by before his mother joined him. Breathing harshly, she bent over, "Give me a second before we send her back."

Joy over their success at returning home soon turned to fear. The vortex was breaking up. Bits and pieces were floating away from the swirling tunnel. It was as if the phenomenon was cracking like a mirror, first one crack appeared, and then another and another and another until the whole thing looked like a tie dyed spider web. The shop keeper watched in horror as pieces of it fell from the whole and disappeared until there was nothing but a tiny cloud left. His mouth fell open. All he could do was stare.

"What? What's the matter Josiah?" The older woman turned and looked behind her. "What happened, where is it?"

"It just seemed to shatter then disappear."

Footsteps prevented them from discussing things further, "Quickly we must hide her. Help me get her somewhere safe."

Josiah nodded, picked up Iriana and dashed after his mother. Much to their relief they were in their old compound. Weaving the familiar halls they found their way to their old set of rooms. There they placed Iriana in a guest room afterward they went to their respective rooms bathed and changed before joining the rest of the community.

"We must discover what has happened in our absence and plan accordingly. Once we have the lay of the land so to speak, we will figure out a way to return her back to her own time. Come let us mingle among our people." With that they left their quarters.

Iriana awoke in the dark. Head pounding, body freezing. Grumbling she pushed the covers off of her, swung her legs over the side and stumbled out of bed. Blindly she made her way across the room and out the door. Squinting against the sudden harsh light, she traversed a landscape filled with blurry outlines of shapes large and small. A door swished open and she tripped over something raised on the floor. She fell into a hallway, too slow to react, she landed flat on her face, air rushing out of her lungs on impact. "Omph."

Murmurs sounded around her, blinking rapidly, she found her vision clearing. When she could finally see her eyes widened, all around her were people dressed in black togas, long and short. Scrambling up to a standing position, her head turned this way and that. She quickly backed up, heart hammering as confusion set in. "Where the hell am I?"

The murmurs grew louder. She watched their eyes roam over her figure. Looking down she tried to understand what the fuss was about. Her suit was wrinkled but thankfully none of the buttons were undone on her jacket and her skirt hadn't ridden up. She was missing her shoes, but she didn't pay much attention to that.

"Witch!" Someone shouted. Another person echoed that word and soon the crowd began to chant it. "Witch! Witch! Witch!"

"Who? Me?" She asked. *Okay, Iriana, this is dream, pinch yourself and wake up.* She did exactly that, only it hurt. She did the next best thing, she slapped herself. That only hurt more. The crowd swarmed her, making her panic. Closing her eyes, she forgot all of her self defense training and started swinging her arms around her like a mad woman. It didn't help, someone managed to grab one wrist and another person grabbed the other. Arms circled her waist and she was hauled against a hard body. A harsh voice in her ear hissed, "Stop resisting witch. We know what to do with people like you."

"Look, I don't know what you're talking about. I'm not a witch, I swear. I can barely make a cup of tea. I kill plants. I know nothing about magic. Okay, I did want to curse my ex-boyfriend but come on, is it my fault the guy got into a car accident? He's a horrible driver. It's not my fault he crashed into a cop car, it was pretty funny." The man holding her against him growled and she felt sick, "Okay, it's not funny. I swear, I wasn't laughing. Look, I'm not a witch. I can't even do that nose wiggle thing that Samantha can do and aren't you supposed to have a cat or something as a familiar? My building wouldn't allow it. Please, put me down, I'm not a witch, I swear it."

"Quiet witch, your fate will be decided soon enough."

Iriana wanted to hurl and cry but didn't dare do either for fear of what would happen. Instead she stayed silent and concentrated on her surroundings. The walls were all metal. Large panels were set every few feet, some blinked while others were lit up. Bright light streamed overhead. A glance up revealed skylights that showed dark and threatening clouds, thunder rumbled in the distance signaling a storm was near.

She turned her attention back to her surroundings, strange symbols were carved into a wall and then they passed a painting of a tall, faceless man holding a helmet under his arm standing on what looked like dark earth, black water seemed to lap at the shore, curling ink black hair fell around his shoulders to his waist. Just looking at the portrait made her break out in goose bumps. The hair on the back of her neck stood up. Iriana turned her head away from the painting and focused her attention ahead of her. They were approaching a large metal doorway. The doors slid back with a soft woosh of air and she was confronted by a cavernous hall filled with people, the walls and ceiling, were painted a shiny black. A large cast iron chandelier came down from the ceiling, blue flames danced on the wicks of black candles in an unfelt breeze.

In the distance came the sound of rushing water, the air smelled of rain and wet earth.

"What is the meaning of this?" A large voice boomed. Iriana struggled even more. The arms around her increased their hold making it hard to breathe. She stopped struggling hoping he would loosen his grip, he didn't. *Bastard*. Iriana's hand felt numb and cold, her head ached and she felt another wave of nausea. She managed to tamp that down quickly. But the words of the man holding her made her want to vomit. "We found a witch among us. We don't know from where she came or how she infiltrated our compound. I say we offer her as sacrifice."

"Bring her here." The loud voice boomed. The crowd in the hall murmured and Iriana began to struggle again. She felt eyes looking her over, their voices getting louder. Despite feeling light headed she demanded, "Put me down, put me down you bastard."

She didn't care if she was using up most of her oxygen as he increased his hold around her waist. Iriana just wanted to be free of him. Unfortunately when he did release her, she fell to the floor, her knees and hands hitting the ground hard. On all fours she tried to regain her breath.

"She is lovely for a witch. Flawless mocha skin, large brown eyes, full lips and high cheek bones. Her breasts and hips need to be larger but we can't help that. We need a sacrifice now. She will do. Take her to the boat and tie her down."

Iriana had no time to be angry, she was hauled to her feet and duck marched to a small boat. They set her down on a seat in the middle of the craft, picking up shackles that were attached to the boat; they grabbed both of her wrists and closed the cuffs, the lock snicked into place. She tried to tug on her restraints but they were bolted into place. Her stomach dropped as the sound of rushing water grew louder. The boat suddenly rose up in the air and moved toward the din. Her heart threatened to burst through her ribcage. Looking around, frantically she tried to understand what was happening. To her right was the hall. To her left were black rapids crashing against tall stalagmites that rose out of the water like jagged teeth of some ancient monster. Understanding dawned on her.

"No, no, no, no, please, I'm not a witch. I can explain or at least I think I can explain. This is all some sick dream or a prank really gone wrong. For the love of God, please don't do this." She pleaded. Her words were drowned out by the water. The boat dropped and she screamed. The small craft hit the water, icy liquid splashed up around her and sloshed into the boat, bathing her feet in freezing water. Cold air and moisture hit her face as the boat took off, pushing forward at a frantic pace, riding the currents. She opened her mouth to scream only to get a mouthful of freezing cold water. Though cold, she found the water refreshing, rejuvenating even. Swallowing it, her body began to surprisingly heat up.

Using her new found energy she tugged frantically on her bindings but they still wouldn't budge. She sent up several silent prayers that the boat wouldn't hit a rock or tip over. The dark world rushed past her in a blur of gray. By the time the pace slowed she was dizzy, nauseous and hot, sweat mingled with the cold water that splashed her face. When the boat drifted to a stop, the manacles fell off and she scrambled over the side to throw up. She retched until her stomach was empty and she was just dry heaving. Wiping her mouth with the back of her hand, she flopped down to the bottom of the boat, breath coming out in pants. "I never want to do that again."

Heavy footfalls signaled someone's approach and, based on how loud the footsteps were, they seemed to be a big someone. Fear raced up her spine. She rolled into a little ball and began to plead with the universe, "Please, don't eat me. Please don't let it eat me. I don't taste good, not even with ketchup. Please, whatever it is, don't let it eat me."

"Who are you talking too?" A smooth deep voice edged in roughness asked.

Her stomach tightened, heat washed over her body as her nipples tightened painfully, her sex became heavy and knees felt like jelly. Slowly she moved to one side of the boat and peeked over the side. Her eyes met knee high black boots with what looked like black metal shin guards. Her gaze traveled up over tight black breeches, a long black silk shirt and then to the pale face of a man with stormy gray eyes and long, curling ink black hair that fell around his shoulders to his waist. He reached up and brushed some hair out of his face and she just stared mouth open. *Normally I don't go for the pale type but dayum.*

His face looked like it had been carved out of marble. He had high cheek bones, a square jaw, high forehead and long straight nose. His eyes were hooded with a thin slash of black eyebrows and framed by thick, long, black lashes. His lips neither full nor thin, although the bottom lip was a bit plumper than the top. She just sat at the bottom of the boat staring up at him. He, in turn, looked down at her, hardly blinking.

"Could you blink or something, you're creeping me out." She declared finally breaking the silence. He did as she asked, lashes moving slowly down then up.

"Is that all right?" She shivered at the sound of his voice, like whiskey, smooth and yet rough around the edges, warming you from within. Swallowing she just nodded, not trusting her voice to be even.

"Good, I suppose you are their latest sacrifice to me. Please come along then." He turned and she got a wonderful view of the back. His tight breeches, showed off his high, ass perfectly. The cheeks looked so hard you could bounce a quarter off of them and get change back.

"What lovely peaches," she murmured.

He looked over his shoulder, an eyebrow raised in question, "What?"

"Nothing, nothing. Um, excuse me, but who are you?" She scrambled up quickly and leapt to shore as the boat rocked back and forth.

"I am Pluto, Roman God of the Dead."

Chapter Two

Pluto tried to ignore the way his body was reacting to his latest sacrifice or captive as he preferred to call them. His heart was hammering against his chest, he felt light headed, his balls ached and his cock was pressing against his breeches demanding its freedom. He absently adjusted himself as he walked toward his palace. He almost stumbled twice when his thoughts drifted back to the sacrifice.

She is lovely, her lips are quite tempting and despite her soaked appearance she is attractive. I just wish I could get her out of her clothes. He came to a sudden stop and cursed at himself. *I am not going to sleep with her. She is obviously not of this time. I will send her back and wait for them to send me someone else. Someone who actually wants to be here.* He continued walking. Keeping his senses open just in case she needed help walking over the rocky shore. A soft squeak caused him to turn around and find her on her butt, knees together, shins apart. Starting back to help her, he stopped when she pushed herself up and got to her feet, reaching behind to dust her bottom off.

She made her way carefully over the stones until she reached him. "So let me get this straight, you are Pluto, Roman God of the Dead?"

"That is what I said."

She blinked. "And this is all real?"

"Yes."

"Uh huh, do you have another name? You know maybe Hades?"

"That is my cousin."

"Okay, so no other name. Can I call you P? Pluto reminds me of the dog, you know from . . ."

He held up a hand, "I understand, yes, you can call me P as you put it."

Trying to hold back a chuckle, he turned and began walking. He could feel her behind him, carefully picking her way over the rocky terrain. Stopping again he turned, "Do you want me to help you?"

"Nope, nope, I got it P. I don't mean to be rude but did your parents hate you?"

"Excuse me?"

"Did they hate you? I mean come on; you've got a planet named after you that was demoted and a dog from a cartoon. I can't take you seriously with a name like Pluto." She looked up at him and he couldn't hold back the laugh. He laughed long and loud. The sound echoed off the walls and ceiling of the cavern back to him. When he finally stopped, he was wiping away tears. When his vision cleared he found her standing before him, her lips twitching as if she was trying to resist smiling.

"My parents did not hate me, perhaps they are disappointed with me but they don't hate me. Come, I'm sure you're hungry and need a change of clothes." He nodded his head toward the palace and began to move.

"You really need to look into paving, walking this shore or whatever the hell it is, is a bitch."

He chuckled in response. Pluto was quite thankful that she wasn't peering closer at the stones; she would have found she was walking on skulls and bones mixed in with rock. When they finally reached the steps of the palace she looked tired. He felt bad for her so without asking, he stooped down and scooped her up in his arms. "Hey, put me down, I can walk thank you very much."

"Yes, but you shouldn't have to. You made it this far, let me carry you. You must be tired."

She didn't look at him when she muttered, "I have legs and I know how to use them."

"Yes, but you're tired. Let me carry you. Please, it's the least I can do."

Iriana finally turned her head to look at him, weariness in her eyes, "You're going to eat me aren't you?"

His cock twitched in response. "Not unless you want me to."

He swallowed and cursed silently, he hadn't meant to say that out loud.

Much to his relief she didn't respond to his comment instead saying, "Well, there is a rock in my shoe. Fine, you can carry me. But just so you know I'm not letting my guard down."

"Of course. I'll put you in the best guest bedroom where a nice bath will be drawn for you, some warm clothes put out and a meal sent up, does that sound okay?"

"Yes. Question, how come you speak so well? I mean, that didn't come out right."

He understood what she meant perfectly so he interrupted her, "I watch TV."

Her jaw dropped and he chuckled. He began to walk, holding her close to him. Her body weight in his arms felt right. When it was time to put her down, he was reluctant to let her go. He did what he needed to do, gently putting her on her feet and taking a step back to prevent himself from taking her in his arms again. "You'll find your room right beyond those doors. I'm sure you have a lot of questions, I'll answer them later. Please, for now just relax. You've been through so much."

Before she could say anything he turned and walked away, regretting each step he took. He had a feeling that unlike the other sacrifices she would be the hardest to let go of. He put as much distance between them as he could, retreating to his study in order to gather his wits about him, unfortunately his mind had other plans, X-Rated plans that had him picturing her in a bubble bath, the bubbles barely covering her slick mocha skin.

Groaning he gritted his teeth. "I should not be thinking of her like this. I'm only going to let her go."

Taking deep breaths and blowing them out, he tried to concentrate on something else, anything else. As his body calmed down he entered his study and took in his solace, the one place in the palace that didn't remind him of his job. Breathing in the scent of old parchment, he let out a relieved sigh. Here death didn't touch him and the weight of fate didn't hang heavy over his head.

Closing the door behind him, he wandered toward his favorite wingback chair, covered in black leather. Picking up the book he had been reading before he had been alerted to the cult sending him a new "sacrifice," he sat down and began to read, determined to ignore his current houseguest. But it was hard, his thoughts kept wandering back to her. There he had been standing on the shore watching the boat coming closer and then he heard her pleading with the universe that whatever was approaching her location, would not eat her. It had been both amusing and confusing. The cult told the sacrifice many things depending on the person, their crime and the reason why they had been selected as an offering.

The leaders of the cult itself knew nothing about what went on once an offering reached his end of the cavern. They were just following tradition just as the leaders before had. It had been an odd occurrence to him and his fellow deities to suddenly be recognized and worshipped again. Almost like coming out of deep sleep to find the world suddenly remembered you were there. At first the offerings of food and flowers had been nice and then someone thought it would be wonderful to send living people down the river to him. He had been confused at first, finding a person bound and gagged at the bottom of the boat. After some explanation he understood.

The traditional big three faiths had broken down and war was declared. With the destruction of the big three imminent, people turned to old times when polytheism was popular. Now, he was back in vogue and he wasn't sure what to do with this sudden recognition. He had a cult like the other gods but he didn't desire the notoriety. He preferred his solitude. To go to shore every month and calm some poor person down and then send them on their way was irritating. Now he was attracted to one of the offerings. Sighing he put down the book and hung his head. He could ring up one of his brothers for help but they would only laugh in amusement.

He allowed his mind to wander toward his attractive guest. "If I indulge in the attraction, it may be easier to let her go."

Getting up he made his way to his suite of rooms. Once there, he undressed and climbed into bed. With his mind he pulled open the drawer of his nightstand

and took out the lube. Flipping up the top he squeezed a small amount into his palm and returned the tube. Reclining against a pile of pillows, he closed his eyes and pictured his guest. Her visage came easily to him. He could see her flawless mocha skin, large almond shaped brown eyes framed by long black lashes, her cute button nose and tempting full lips. He could see her naked in the tub easily, skin glistening from the water, bubbles sliding gently over her flesh.

Her back arched, her breasts rising above the white frothy wonderland. Her dark chocolate nipples, tightened from being exposed to the cool air. He longed to lick the turgid peaks, sucking one into his mouth as his body slipped into the water, covering hers. He could feel the slick glide of her flesh against his. Groaning, he wrapped his hand around his cock, slowly pumping the hot, hard flesh. With his other hand, he cupped his balls in his hand, rolling and tugging the delicate eggs. Sparks of pleasure rushed through his body as fire washed over him.

He could taste the salty sweetness of her flesh; hear her sigh softly as she buried her fingers in his hair. Her back arched as she urged him closer. Their bodies brushed against each other in the water, his fingertips traced her side, over her ribcage, following the curve downward to her hip. Her body shifted underneath him and like a dance they moved against each other, each bump, each glide, each caress only heightened the fire that danced between them. Each touch teased, offering just a taste of what it would be like to feel her body fully against his.

Taking hold of her hip before she could float away, he pulled her against him, groaning at the feel of her hot silken flesh against his. He released her nipple with a pop, looking at her. Their eyes met and sparks arched between them, the fire burning in her eyes could scorch him alive and he would gladly burn. Never had he felt so alive, so connected to another person.

"I don't even know your name," He murmured, "And yet you've captured me."

Her lips curved into a smile, "My name is Iriana."

"Iriana," He repeated, the name rolled off of his tongue easily. So exotic and beautiful, befitting the enchantress before him. "I love it."

"Pluto, make love to me." The husky timber of her voice trailed up his spine like fingers of fire. He moaned, cock twitching in his hand as he stroked his shaft faster.

"Gladly my sweet, gladly." Taking hold of her other hip, he pulled her closer to him. She wrapped her legs around him. He kissed across her collarbone, up her neck, tracing her jaw with the tip of his tongue before pressing his lips to hers. She opened her mouth and the tip of his tongue tentatively traced first his bottom lip then the top before running along the seam of his lips. Thrusting his hips forward, he mimicked the act of love he wanted to perform with her. She rocked her hips against his as his cock slid along her stomach.

Their bodies slid against each other, hips grinding as he deepened the kiss. Burying his fingers in her hair, he tugged her head back. He shoved his tongue in her mouth, withdrawing, matching the pace of his thrusts. Moaning, her hands ran over his back, her fingernails racked the skin. The pain added to the pleasure, growling he pulled his head back and released one of her hips. He floated above her, reaching between them he positioned his cock at her entrance, with one thrust he was inside of her slick wet heat. They both cried out. Her inner walls contracted around just his cockhead. Withdrawing he shoved his hips forward sinking deeper into her tight channel.

They moved together, thrusting forward, pulling back, fucking slowly; stoking the fire that threatened to turn into an inferno. His hand moved in time with his fantasy self's hips. He could practically feel her vaginal walls squeezing his cock, the slick heat surround him. Groaning he thrust his hips, his dream self matching his pace, faster and faster they moved, fucking her harder and harder. The fire built, higher and higher it climbed. His balls drew closer to his body, aching with the need to be emptied, the base of his spine tingled and trails of heat rushed up and down the column. His cock twitched and expanded, he cried out as he came. Hot, streams of cum hit his chest, stomach, coating his hand, hips and balls. He didn't stop pumping until every last drop of seed dribbled down his hand.

Breathing hard, body covered in sweat, his heart was threatening to burst from his chest. He was surprised to find he felt dizzy. Never had he come so hard with a partner or alone. He could only imagine what it would be like with her. He let out a growl of frustration. Now he wanted to be with her in reality. Masturbating had done nothing to squash his desire for her. He let go of his now limp cock and crawled off the bed. He made a beeline for the bathroom, showered and changed into jeans and a button down T-Shirt.

He made his way to the room she had been given and knocked, praying she was still in the bath.

"Come in."

His cock twitched at the sound of her voice muffled from behind the door. Sighing, he ordered his body to calm down and opened the door. His breath caught in his throat when he saw her. She was wrapped in a large fluffy towel; her hair was also wrapped in a towel.

"Hey, P. I just got out of the bath. Thank you for your kindness."

"No, problem."

"So, questions, I have several." She gestured toward an empty chair but he couldn't move, couldn't think, all he could do was stare. Her face was free and slick with moisture. She looked so beautiful, he was in awe. Swallowing he ordered himself to move but his feet wouldn't cooperate.

"Okay, so stand there why don't you. I'll just sit down. She padded across the thick carpet in her bare feet and sat down in the chair she had offered him.

"I'm Iriana by the way."

He kept his mouth shut. He had unconsciously delved into her mind during his fantasy. Cursing himself he prayed she hadn't noticed the intrusion.

"So what am I dealing with here? I went back in time? Judging by your dress I think not. What's the year?"

"The year is 2025." He launched into a brief explanation of what was going on now currently. "Basically the major three religions launched an all out war on each other. People got tired of the fighting and turned to other means of spirituality including polytheism."

"So you're telling me that all those gods I studied in school, you guys are real?"

"Yes."

"Cool."

"Cool? You're not scared, freaked out?"

"Well, I was thrust through time, branded a witch, offered up as a sacrifice and now I find out the gods are real. I've freaked out, hurled, freaked some more and now I'm good. I'm drained. Maybe I'll wake up in the middle of the night screaming but for now I'm good. Sooo, Mr. High and Mighty God of the Dead, what do we do now? Do I stay here? Or are you going to kick me out into the great wide, unknown future so I can fend for myself? What's the plan here?"

She turned away from him, her eyes roamed over the table loaded down with enough food to feed a small army. He took that small reprieve to think. He knew he had to tread carefully.

"You have many options," He started off, "You could stay here or return to your time."

She stopped looking over the table and turned toward him. "What?"

Her eyes were wide and glistening, he could see hope. Reaching up he rubbed the back of his neck and looked away from her. "You can stay here or I can return you back to your own time. It's not difficult but it will take some waiting. I can only open a portal in time on a full moon. That is when the connection between worlds is the greatest. Don't ask me why I'm not sure." The thought of her returning did cause an ache in his heart. He wasn't sure why, he felt anything at all. There was the spark of attraction but there shouldn't be anything else. She wouldn't be staying and yet he wanted her to.

Her attitude toward her current situation astounded him. She was so calm and collected. He marveled at how contained she was. He admired her for that. He didn't want to but he did.

"So the full moon is what a month away. Well, that's a vacation I wasn't counting on and I do need a break. Sooo, do I get to stay here or am I going to have to go out there?"

"Out where?" He asked, not liking the idea of her wandering around out in what she would consider her future world or a possibility of the future.

"Out there in that world. I'm curious about it. Have you ever seen it?"

"Well . . ." He didn't finish. He felt a sudden sense of idiocy. He had never really ventured beyond the safety of the underworld. *What would happen if I left for just a month? Hades wouldn't mind, he always said I needed to get out more.* Looking her over he had a sudden urge to see the outside world with her. Discover the wonder with her. *What's a month?*

"No, I've never seen it up close. But if you'd like we could go together. You don't have to say-"

"Wonderful, so we can search this world together. I'm so curious to see this future. I mean I know things may not happen to make this my future but it's so cool. When can we start?"

Eagerness shown on her face and his heart swelled. "Are you scared of anything?"

"Spiders, falling out of a perfectly good airplane, sharks, aliens, really horrible B movies and Botox. What are you afraid of?"

"Being alone." The words came out before he could stop them. They hung in the air like vapor. He felt scared at her reaction, relieved that he had said the words out loud and angry that he had let his control slip like that. He watched warily as she processed the words.

"That too. It can be both exhilarating and scary to be alone. Do you have anyone? I know Hades has Persephone but do you . . ."

"No, there is no one." The words didn't make him feel as lonely as they had in the past. The emotion he had, when making his confession was indescribable, part happy he had no one and part afraid she would say she did have someone. The thought of her having left behind someone she cared about caused him to ask, "Do you have someone?"

"Nope, no one, thank goodness. Although I'm sure my friend Corrina is freaking out right about now but nope no man in my life." She said it with a smile. "Not that I don't want one. I would love to have someone but my life is sooo busy right now. I plan weddings and try not to kill the bride and/or members of the wedding party. So far so good, no having to get bailed out and no one suing me for assault." She grinned and he laughed. She was enchanting.

"So what's up with the clothes? They wear jeans in the future?" Her eyebrow rose as she took him in causing warmth to spread in the wake of her gaze. Licking his lips he tried to find the words but arousal was clouding his mind.

His cock pressed against the fly of his jeans and his balls ached. He wanted to turn around and walk away but couldn't. Never in his life had he felt so nervous, scared and unsure about someone.

"They have yet to invent those space age clothes you see in the cartoons and movies. Instead style of dress depends on your comfort, what cult you belong to, so on and so forth. So jeans are still around."

"Why then the garb you wore riverside? Not that I'm complaining, you looked good in them but couldn't you just have shown up in what you're wearing now?"

"Would you have believed me if I had shown up in jeans and a T-Shirt?"

She tilted her head to the side and a smile spread across her lips, his heart warmed in response, "You never know. Maybe, I was having one hell of a day."

Pluto laughed and she joined him. Her laugh was filled with joy and happiness, it was like sunshine and something sweet all mixed into one. He loved it. Silence fell between them and it wasn't uncomfortable. It was easy, friendly, content. The small moment was interrupted by the sound of her stomach rumbling. She chuckled. "I guess that's a signal that I better eat. Join me? I want to know more if you don't mind me picking your brain."

"Not at all." He finally moved forward and sat down across the table from her. "Please do ask any questions you may have and I'll try and answer them." For the next hour she asked everything and anything that came to mind. She didn't hold back and he found that refreshing. He answered every one of her questions about television, the state of movies and science. Her range of interest was delightful. She seemed to be curious about everything. Their evening came to a close before a fire, while they sipped hot chocolate. She tried to smother a yawn with the back of her hand but couldn't hide it.

"You are tired. It's time I left you. Sweet dreams Iriana."

She gave him a sleepy smile before placing her cup on the table and heading for the bed. He watched her progress hungrily. When she stopped and turned around to look at him, he wasn't sure what she was about to do. With a cheeky smile. "Sweet dreams, P."

With that she undid the tie on her robe and shrugged out of it exposing her naked body. Her breasts were just as he imagined. Her stomach was slightly rounded, hips flared out sloping down to show off her shapely legs. Her mound was bare except for a single thin line of pubic hair that disappeared between her legs. He groaned, wanting to see the treasure between her thighs. Movement caught his eye causing him to look up. Reaching up she pulled the towel off of her head, her long dark hair fell around her shoulders in waves of varying shades of brown.

"You're beautiful," Pluto murmured.

"Thank you, now I've given us both a thrill and I know you're attracted to me so it's time for you to go."

"What?" He groaned. Arousal flared white hot, rushing through his body riding him hard. He wanted to undress and worship every inch of her body.

"You have to leave now." She pulled back the covers and climbed into bed. Pulling the covers up to her chin she gave him a look of innocence but her eyes sparkled with devilish glee.

"Tease, you'll pay for this. Out of politeness, I'll leave but next time I won't be so accommodating." He stood up and headed toward the door.

"You promise."

He looked back at her and gave her a wicked smile, "You have my word."

"Good," she yawned and snuggled down, her eyelids drifting down. He didn't leave the room, instead watching as sleep slipped over her. He couldn't resist, walking silently across the carpet he walked toward the bed and stood over her taking in her relaxed features. Without hesitation, he bent down and brushed a kiss across her forehead. "Good night, Iriana."

Chapter Three

Iriana awoke surprised by the sound of birds chirping. Getting out of bed, she walked, nude, toward a large wall of curtains. Taking a deep breath, preparing herself for anything, she pushed back the panels and was awed by what she saw. Light flooded the stony shore, whites and grays of varying shades decorated the ground, the boat rocked gently in the black water. Ravens and little black birds she had never seen before hopped over the ground, flowers in varying shades of red and white hung low, wet with dew. There was no grass that she could see but even without it, all was beautiful and then he came into view.

He rose up out of the water like the god that he was, his pale torso decorated with slivers of dark water trailing down his body then disappearing into the black trunks that hung loose around his waist. She swallowed, his shoulders were broad, his chest looked hard and his abs were more like an eight pack than a six. He had a swimmers build but his arms were heavily muscled, not in a body builder sort of way, but a man used to hard labor with his hands. She shivered, nipples tightening, body slowly heating up. Her stomach clenched as her core clamped down on nothing, her sex was heavy with desire.

Licking her lips she continued to watch in awe as he walked up the rocky shore without wincing, toward a small flat white space. He stopped, ran a hand over his face and then through his long, curly hair, that fell all the way to his waist. Her mouth went dry when he hooked his thumbs into the waist band of his trunks and pushed down, exposing, thick muscular thighs. His cock hung flaccid between his legs. She was surprised to find he was circumcised. She wondered what he would look like aroused. She squeezed her thighs together trying to ignore the ache that had begun.

He looked up and she stilled, hoping he hadn't seen her. His eyes remained on her, lifting his hand he brushed his finger tips down the middle of his chest and over the ridges of his abdomen, through the thick dark patch of hair to take hold of his not so flaccid cock. She swallowed as she watched him stroke himself. Looking back into his eyes, she shivered at the blatant desire that burned in his stormy gray depths. *Payback*. She knew that he had to be doing this to repay her for last night. Her eyes drifted back to his hand. Raising a hand, she let it drift between the valley of her breasts, over her stomach and slip between her thighs. She ran a single finger up one plump pussy lip and down the other, pausing to circle the wet entrance of her core.

Her finger traced a path up, delving between her nether lips, she found her clit, circling the hardened nub before brushing the head with just a light touch. A shiver ran through her at the light touch. Running her finger again over her clit with more pressure she watched as his hand began to move faster. Bringing her other hand up, she cupped one of her breasts, kneading the mound. Moaning she found her nipple, pinching the tightened peak. Electricity shot straight to her core, her cunt contracted as juices slipped down her thigh. "Fuck."

Squeezing her thighs tightly she worked her clit, increasing the pressure. Her hand moved in time with his. Iriana pinched, rolled and tugged her nipple, while watching him stroking his cock. A glance at his face made her knees weak. His eyes were practically glowing with gray fire. *I want you.*

His voice slipped into her mind making her knees buckle. *I want to fuck you so badly right now.* She sank to the floor slowly, her hand still moving between her thighs. She rubbed her clit harder, her orgasm building, curling within her. She felt as if she was being burned alive, by desire and his gaze. "Please."

Her plea was a husky whisper that hung in the air. In the time it took to blink he vanished from her line of sight. He took hold of her waist and helped her up to her feet. Heat surrounded her, blazing from in back of her. She felt the hot press of his flesh against her back. She felt the hardness of his cock against the cleft of her ass.

"Tease. You shouldn't tease me like that." His hips rolled against her ass letting her feel the hard heat of his shaft.

"I will fuck you. But not yet, not now." His lips brushed the side of her neck, causing her to groan softly. Her hand moved faster between her thighs, rubbing harder, her juices slipped down her thigh as she pinched and tugged her nipple harder. "Pluto."

He nipped her ear lobe taking the delicate flesh between his teeth and tugging softly. "I want you but not yet."

His moist breath caressed her ear a shiver rushed up her spine. He stepped back taking his heat with him. "Show me that you want me."

She turned around slowly, hands dropping from her body. Iriana watched as he crawled onto the bed she had just abandoned. Plumping up the pillows behind him, he spread his legs and took hold of his now fully hardened cock. He was thicker than her past lovers but not longer. "Show me."

He gestured to a chaise lounge that had not been there before. Without thinking she sat down on the chair and sat back, spreading her legs exposing her slick nether lips.

"Perfect," he murmured. He began to pump his shaft slowly. "Touch yourself. I want to watch you come."

She spread her pussy lips and touched her clit, tentatively at first. She had never masturbated for a lover before much less a soon to be lover. Even though they had only known each other a night she felt more comfortable and safe with him than anyone else. Giving herself over to the heady feeling of him watching her as she pleasured herself, she began to circle her clit, faster and faster, her climax building higher and higher. She pinched and rolled her nipple with her free hand, tilting her head back, relaxing under his gaze.

"Look at me, watch me, watching you."

Raising her head, she watched his hand moving up and down his cock, matching her rhythm perfectly. Just watching him increased her arousal. Closer and closer she moved to breaking apart. A wave of fire washed over her, her core clenched on nothing as her limbs shook. Her eyelids slowly lowered, she was falling, breaking apart on her descent. A moan in the distance caught her attention. Her eyes flew open and she watched as he came, ribbons of cum shot into the air, landing on his chest, stomach, thighs, coating his hand. She watched his chest move up and down rapidly as he caught his breath.

Arousal still burned deep inside of her. What she had just witnessed made her want to lap up his seed, tasting the saltiness of him. Sliding off of the chaise lounge, on wobbly legs she made her way to the bed. Climbing up, she crawled toward him, taking in his legs lightly dusted with black hair. She could smell his musk, her pussy tingled with awareness. When she reached his groin, she took his hand, lifting it off of his flaccid penis. Gently she opened his fist and spread his fingers. Bringing it to her lips she lapped up his semen, her tongue moving up and down slowly over each digit. Growling he jerked his hand away and wrapped it around her wrist, yanking her forward until she fell on top of him. His skin was hot, slick and sticky.

She planted a hand on the mattress and pushed up, scrambling up until her face was over his. "That was sexy."

She kissed him softly. Pulling her head back she smiled, feeling warm and cozy. She had never had an afterglow after sex or masturbation. She felt so relaxed. Laying her body down, she placed her head on his shoulder.

"We could do it again. It was satisfying. Although I would prefer to come inside of you next time."

She shivered, her pussy fluttered at the thought. "Next time. For now, we'll just relax, shower and head out. I want to see this new world."

She pinched his nipple causing him to moan. "Oooh, I'll have to try that later."

He laughed, and smacked her on the ass. "Oh!"

Warmth spread after the sting causing her to wiggle a bit.

"Stop that or I will take you."

She gave him another kiss before scrambling up and getting off the bed. "Shower, get dressed and then we leave."

"Is that an order?" He rolled over onto his side.

"Yes, that's an order. God or no, you're showing me this world. I only have a month here. I haven't had a vacation in so long I forgot what relaxing is. So get moving." She dashed out of the bedroom and into the bathroom, locking the door after her. In the shower she couldn't stop herself from giggling. She had just masturbated in front of a man who was nearly a stranger and enjoyed it. Iriana felt so free, there was no pressure from her other life to look perfect.

She was one of the top wedding planners in the city. She had several high profile clients. She had an appearance to maintain. For the first time in years she could drop that façade and have fun, leave work behind. She was actually excited which surprised her.

"I actually can't wait to see this. I'm in the future, spending time with a Roman God and I'm having fun. Oh if Corrina could see me now. Whee!" She washed up not bothering to wash her hair and got out of the shower humming. After drying off, she headed into the bedroom to find clothes laid out on her bed including underwear much to her relief. Getting dressed she put her damp hair up in a messy bun and left the room. Her bare feet slapping against the hard wood. She was amazed at all the artwork on the walls. It was beautiful; some paintings were of lush landscapes, other of Gothic scenes depicting what she interpreted to be Pluto among the dead. There were statues, vases, urns, plants everywhere. Despite the dark brick walls, dark wood and black marble the place did not seem dreary. There was a peacefulness and warmth about the place. She continued to wander down the corridors until she came to the entry hall.

"May I help you madam?" A deep voice asked. Turning around she was startled by a man with pale white skin and black stripes, golden eyes looked down at her, his long black hair fell in curls around his shoulders. He was dressed all in black, right down his knee high boots. Looking back up at him she blinked.

"Um, hello, good morning, I think, have you seen Pluto?" She wasn't sure how to approach this man. He made her uneasy. He blinked slowly, "He approaches now. Would you like shoes?"

She looked down, becoming aware of her bare feet. "Oh, I forgot, um yes, do you have a size six and half?"

"I can find some, excuse me." He turned and walked away.

"Thank you," she called after him, he made no response.

"Who are you talking to?" Pluto asked from behind her.

She whirled around and ate up the visual. Today he wore worn jeans and a black, button up shirt, the top three buttons were undone showing off just a hint of pale flesh. Heat rushed through her body like a tidal wave. Her panties became damp. Her skin felt too tight, her stomach clenched, her pussy clamped down on nothing. She groaned softly. The events of that morning rushed through her mind and she wanted to replay them with him, only he was inside of her when he came.

"Not now, Iriana, later." His voice was so rough, the sound slid up her spine making her shake. "Who were you talking to?"

She composed herself by taking a deep breath and blowing it out slowly. He may be god of the dead but he's making me feel like I'm in the presence of Eros. Clearing her throat she tried to remember the golden eyed man. "He had stripes, was really pale, like porcelain but had black stripes on his face and neck and dressed all in black . . . oh with black curly hair."

"Ah, you met Rory. That's nice. He doesn't come out much. Never really interacts with the offerings." Pluto tilted his head to the side looking thoughtful. He shook his head, "What did you need?"

"Shoes, you forgot to give me shoes. How did you know I needed something?"

"He is my servant. If you need something he can assist you. What size are you?"

"Six and half."

She felt the room get warmer, his body began to glow. He held out his hands, palms up and in them was formed, much to her surprise a pair of black platform flats.

"Those are so cute, can you make me some Jimmy Choos too? I want stilettos, black ones and the straps have to go up my calves. Oh and some Manolos too, red only strappy but not with leather silk ribbon and. . ."

He held up a hand stop her. "I can create things. But those I'm sorry to say no."

Iriana pouted and pointed, "But you made those cute ones."

"But I am only Pluto, not any of those designers."

"So I take it those shoes are still popular?" She asked taking the flats and putting them on.

"Yes, many of the old TV shows are still popular. Some are even being remade today. A lot of the old fashions are making a comeback. Although, those brands of shoes are still highly prized."

"Interesting. So are you ready?"

"Don't you want to eat first?"

She reached out and grabbed his hand, "Nope, besides I know the myth, eat the food of the dead and you stay here. You aren't tricking me mister now let's get to it."

She tried to pull him toward the door but he wouldn't budge. "You do realize you ate some of that food last night don't you."

She stopped tugging and her body went cold. She dropped his hand and just stood there. Her brain just froze, it became hard to breathe. "I have to stay here forever?"

Her voice came out in a strangled whisper at the thought of never seeing her friends again, her family, not doing her job again. She may hate some of the people she had to work for and some days were more of a pain in the ass than others but still, she loved her job. Reality slammed into her. Sadness descended on her so fast she couldn't hold it back. *I could be trapped here forever.* Her legs began to shake and she sank to the ground. She felt like crying.

"Iriana, what's wrong?" Pluto dropped down in front of her. He reached out and took her face in his hands, thumb stroking her bottom lip.

"I could be stuck here just like Persephone. I might never get to see home again." She let out a sob, tears began to fall unchecked.

"Oh, Iriana, nooo, that's not what it means. You don't have to stay here forever. But it does mean you and I are connected. You are now a part of this world, alive but not of this world and time. You have ties here but they do not bind you here, not like Persephone."

"But I'm just like her. I ate the food of the dead." She sniffled and looked at him.

"My rules for this part of the Underworld are different. You are different. You are not of this time, the rules are different. But we will have a connection you and I, can you handle that?"

She sniffled one last time and wiped away the last traces of tears. Looking at his face, she had to be honest with herself, she wanted to know more about him. There were hidden depths and a sadness that hung around him and yet there was fire and passion burning inside of him. She wanted to explore every bit of him, not just his body but mind and heart. He called to her. She felt safe with him and desired. He was the first person to interest her in a very long time.

Nodding slowly, she smiled up at him, "Yes, I can handle that."

"That means if I wish it I can appear before you at any time and I can bring you to me as well. If you call for me I will answer you."

"So, what, just say your name and poof?" She couldn't help but giggle.

"I'll explain it before you go. So are we going to eat breakfast or just crouch here in the foyer?" He smiled, and her heart melted. Iriana's stomach grumbled answering for her.

"Okay, let's go eat but we must be quick about it, we're burning sunlight or Underworld light or whatever the hell is lighting up the Underworld." They laughed and he helped her up. He led her to a small nook where breakfast food was already laid out. Her mouth watered at the sight of pancakes drenched in maple syrup, waffles, bacon, scrambled eggs, toast, and crepe suzette with what looked like strawberries on top. "Maybe we shouldn't be so quick about eating, you taking it slow and all that."

She went up to the table, slid into a seat and began to load down the empty plate before her. When Pluto hadn't moved she looked back at him, "Well, aren't you going to eat something?"

"I've never really eaten breakfast with someone else before, not since I was young. It's both odd and nice."

"Then get over here, sit down and eat." She gestured to the chair next to her. For half an hour they ate and talked sharing small tidbits and details of their life with each other. By the time they left for the outside world Iriana wanted to know more about him, she wanted to spend more time with him. As they took a small boat to the mainland, she admired her surroundings. The trip to the Underworld had been scary, dangerous and fast paced. Now she could see how high the cave's walls went, the plants that grew in small places, and the fish that swam in the water. It was all so peaceful, so relaxing, she actually found herself nearly falling asleep on the ride over.

"Iriana take a look behind you." He called out as he continued to row. She turned her head and was awed by the splash of color on the shore. Surrounding the dock and on the shore, flowers of every variety were growing, as they floated slowly toward the wooden berth. Once there Pluto dropped the anchor and leapt up. He tied the boat to a small post and helped her out of the craft.

"Thank you." She couldn't help but smile up at him. Taking her hand in his, he led her toward the explosion of color. Bending down he broke off a red and orange tiger lily. "For you."

He gently tucked some strands of hair behind her ear and slipped the flower in her hair. Heat washed her face and she had to look away, suddenly feeling shy and unsure of how to react. "Thank you."

He tugged her hand and she stumbled, falling against him. "It's nothing to thank me over."

Iriana righted herself and looked up.

"Ready?"

"Ready." He led the way down a dim passage into daylight. What waited for them on the other side astounded her. A bazaar was in progress. There were so many people in all manner of dress and so much going on she wasn't sure where to look first. There were belly dancers, snake charmers, magicians, and people climbing up ropes that weren't attached to anything. There were so many stalls of food both cooking and not, stalls with spices, jewelry, oil, art.

Seeing it all made Iriana, go into work mode. Her imagination went wild with all the scenarios she could create. Squealing she rushed forward dragging him behind her as she went from vendor to vendor asking all sorts of questions. She even tasted some of the cooked food. Pluto went with her willingly, not protesting one bit at all the walking they did or the sights she dragged him to see. As night fell, they found themselves outside of the city, sitting on a crumbling wall.

"Did you have fun?" He asked, passing her a piece of candy.

"I was in heaven. For the first time in a long time I loved the creative process. I'm sorry we didn't get to see anything you wanted to see. You should have stopped me."

He shook his head. "No, no, I was just glad to be there with you. I had nothing in mind to look at. I just wanted to spend time with you."

Laying her head on his shoulder she looked at the midnight blue sky. "The future isn't so bad."

"But this is merely one of many places we could see. I could show you a place where people live in the skies, would you like that?"

She bumped him with her shoulder, "I thought you said that you never seen the outside world."

"When the dead come to me I do ask questions. There is also what the sacrifices tell me, such wondrous tales. There's even a world of people who live in bubbles, just bubbles in the ocean and the sky."

"We can visit all of these places?" She reached over and broke off another piece of the large candy flower Pluto had gotten them.

"Yes, we can, but we must return to the Underworld now. It's getting late." He slid off the wall and held his hand out to her. She took it and jumped down to the ground taking one last look at the soft glow of the city below them. Excitement boiled within her. Only thirty days left to see what the future could bring. By the time they got back to the palace she was tired, her feet and legs ached from all the walking they had done. When she got back to her bedroom all she could do was flop down the mattress and stare up at the canopy.

"I'll go run you bath." Pluto called out.

"Okay."

Closing her eyes, she smiled. For the first time in a long time she was genuinely happy and excited about something.

"It's ready, get undressed and I'll bathe you."

~168~

A shiver of excitement raced up her spine at the thought of his hands on her. It surprised her how much she not only enjoyed his company but wanted him. No other man had made her act like this and yet all he had to do was speak and she was putty. Smiling she sat up, slid off the bed and undressed, walking slowing toward the bathroom. Anticipation sung through her veins, she hoped he was naked. Taking a deep breath and closing her eyes, she walked through the doorway. The scent of lavender and lemon wafted in the air, a warm humid breeze brushed along her skin causing goose bumps to rise. Her heart hammered against her chest.

Opening her eyes slowly, the image that met her gaze made her breath stall. He stood next to the tub in nothing but a towel. His alabaster skin, covered in a light sheen of sweat. He reached up and ran a hand through his hair. She watched as his hair swung back into place as if in slow motion, inky black strands slipped over his skin, shining in the light. He snapped a finger and the room became dim. Blinking, she tried to comprehend what just happened.

"Ready?" He held out a hand. She took it without hesitation, ready for what they were about to do. Her skin felt tight, the room was too hot. Her sex felt heavy, clit pulsing with need. The feel of her hand running over his callused palm only made her want to feel the roughened skin against the rest of her body. He pulled her toward the tub which seemed to have lengthened since the last time she was in it.

"This place is very interesting, one minute that's a normal sized tub the next it could fit at least four people in it."

He chuckled, "Yes, very interesting. Come let's bathe together."

She stepped in the tub first and settled in, turning her attention to him. She watched as the towel dropped, exposing his completely nude body to her gaze. She smiled, seeing that he was already aroused. "So the towel was what, a deterrent for not taking me right then and there?"

Pluto chuckled as he climbed into the tub, "Yes. I find you quite irresistible. Besides I don't want our whole time together to be just sex. I want to finally experience life with you."

He sat down next to her, placing his arm around her. She laid her head down on his shoulder. "So we're taking it slow?"

"If you don't mind. I've never done this before. I normally keep to myself. I'm quite comfortable staying in my palace, being alone. You have come into my world and given me a dash of color. I want to enjoy every second I have with you in and out of bed."

"I have yet to see your bed." She pointed out with a giggle.

"If you behave tonight maybe you will." He teased.

Raising her head, Iriana looked up at him, "I want to see your bed tonight. I want to see more than your bed tonight."

"What do you want to see?"

"It's not what I want to see, it's more like what I want to do," she corrected.

"What is it that you want to do?"

"This." She sat up and turned, threw one leg over his legs and sat down straddling him water sloshed the sides of the tub but did not spill over. Placing her hands on his chest, she leaned forward her breasts pressing against the hard wall of muscle. She traced her tongue slowly along his bottom lip, then the seam of his mouth before pressing the softest of kisses on his lips. That gentle touch fired her up, she wanted more, needed more. Reaching up, wrapping her arm around his neck, she buried one hand in the silken strands of his hair.

She took control of the kiss, pouring passion into it. She took a hand full of hair and pulled back, rising up on her knees, her nipples brushing his chest as she rose. She nipped his plump bottom lip, tugging it with her teeth before sucking it into her mouth. He groaned, his hand sliding up and down her back, hardening cock, gliding up her stomach. He slipped his hand over a cheek of her ass, he squeezed the rounded mound causing her to moan, releasing his bottom lip. He chose that moment to bury a hand in her hair and grab a handful, tugging her head back, her neck arched.

He lowered his head, blazing a slowly trail of fire up her neck and along her jaw with soft nips and kisses. She moaned, "Pluto."

He let go of her hair and she looked at him. Their eyes met and a silent conversation began. Their gazes spoke of their desire for each other, their yearning for more.

"I want . . ." She started.

"We have a month, after that, we shall see." He replied, reaching up to brush back a strand of hair that had fallen in her face. They didn't speak again. She leaned down and kissed him. Taking his face in both of her hands, she poured into that one simple action, all her need and desire. The kiss spiraled into one of possession, need and dominance. She was declaring him hers. Releasing his lips, she dusted kisses down his neck, nipping his shoulder before moving down. Iriana circled his nipple with the tip of her tongue before scraping the hardened peak with her teeth.

She continued to trail kisses down until she reached the water's edge. Looking up at him, "What do you want Pluto? Do you want to be with me tonight?"

"Yesss." He hissed. Iriana kissed her way back up his torso. "Let's go to your bed Pluto."

She stood up, water slipping over her skin. Turning, she stepped out of the tub and grabbed a towel. She heard the splash of water behind her but didn't look back. Instead, she dried off and left the bathroom. Sinking into a padded chair she waited for him to join her. When he appeared in the doorway, her breath caught. Closing her eyes, she composed herself before standing up. "Let's get to your room."

He walked over and took her hand. They left the room and went down the hall. He pushed open a set of double doors. Stepping over the threshold, Iriana gasped. The room was huge, the walls were covered in fabric in varying shades of red and black. Candles blazed away in a large bronze chandelier. The only piece of furniture in the room was a massive bed, covered in furs and silks.

"Go lie on the bed Iriana," Pluto ordered. She didn't have to be told twice, she left his side and climbed up on the huge bed, crawling on the wide expanse of furs and silk. When she reached the mountain of pillows she lay down and waited for him. She didn't have to wait long. He joined her in a matter of seconds. He didn't hesitate to cover her body. His head came down and he took her lips in a soft kiss. "Forgive me Iriana, but I can't wait. I need to be inside of you now."

She responded by spreading her legs wide for him and tilting her hips upward.

"Take me," she whispered. Reaching between them, he took hold of his shaft and positioned himself at her entrance. With one thrust he was inside of her, stretching. She cried out at the unexpected pain. Pluto paused and she shook her head, "No, don't stop, please, I want all of you inside of me."

She wrapped her arms around him, sliding her hands down his back and over his buttocks. She urged him forward. He pushed his hips forward, sliding more of his hard length inside of her. Moaning, she wrapped her legs around his hips, squeezing her vaginal walls. He withdrew only to slam into her hitting her cervix. She cried out, arching her back. He lowered his head, flicking her nipple before sucking the tight peak into his mouth. His pace was slow, building the fire between them. She met his thrusts with ones of her own, squeezing her muscles around him every time he withdrew.

Like a dance they moved together matching each other move by move. The fire was stoked higher and higher. Her orgasm built, twisting and curling tighter and tighter until the fire exploded within her, washing over her causing her to cry out as she came. He followed her, cock twitching before she felt the hot gush of his seed inside of her channel. He continued to fuck her until he was flaccid inside of her. She felt their combined juices slide down, coating her thighs and anus.

Panting, he buried his head in the crook of her shoulder. "Let us rest before the next round."

She ran her hands through his damp hair. "Okay."

Closing her eyes she let out a sigh. A sense of heaviness descended on her heart. *One day down, thirty to go*, she thought sadly.

* * *

The days went by quickly. She got to see as much of the future as possible. She even met a few gods and goddesses. However the thrill soon wore off as the day for her departure drew near. As the time drew near, Pluto became distant asking questions about her life, what she would do once she got back to her own present. As much as she missed her friends, family and her job she didn't want to leave him, not yet. She wanted to bring him with her or at least find a way to see him when she did return.

Sitting in a window seat in one of the palaces many little nooks, she gazed out on the black water. It was a gloomy day. Light came through in patches.

"Is there something wrong?" Rory asked. Glancing up, she saw he was wearing his usual all black.

"I'm going to miss this place."

"You will be missed."

"Is there any way . . ." she started only to stop. Rory couldn't help her with her problem. "Never mind."

"You wanted to know if there was a way to see him again once you've returned."

She didn't respond, instead turning back to the river.

"You have eaten the food of the dead he can find you in any time you are, wherever you are. It must be him who seeks you out, not the other way around. You have given him life. Let us see if he chooses to live it."

"What if he doesn't?"

"Then there is nothing we can do. Do not worry. I do not think he will let you pass him by."

She looked up at the man with the stripes and eerie golden eyes. "How do you know?"

He gave her a Gallic shrug before turning on his heel and leaving her. Iriana let out a sigh, "I hope he does find me again."

For the rest of the day she wandered the halls, going into her favorite rooms. Reliving the memories she and Pluto had made. They had made love in every one of his favorite rooms. Night fell and the clock struck eight, dinner time. She made her way down to the dining room to find Pluto all dressed up.

"Let us have dinner one last time and then make love. I need to be with you again before you go." He said softly.

Smiling sadly, she nodded. "Okay, P."

They ate in silence both of them buried in their own thoughts. When the meal was over, he led her upstairs to his room, where she had slept every night since they had first made love. They undressed slowly, each one savoring the look of the other, memorizing every dip and hollow of their lover's body. Once on the bed their lovemaking started off soft and tender. When she came tears slipped from her eyes. Burying a hand in his hair and urging his head down, she took a kiss from his lips. The action was meant to keep her from saying the words she really wanted to say, *I love you.*

In one month she had fallen in love with the God of the Dead, knowing their relationship could never truly be. When he came, he pulled his mouth away from hers, crying out her name as he pumped every drop of his seed inside of her. She fell asleep in his arms and awoke the next morning alone in her own bed. Curling up in a ball, she cried, mourning the loss of her lover. When she finally did stop crying, she took a shower and ate something but refused to leave her apartment. When she did leave, she found out that she had only been gone for a few hours not days. Although relieved that no one had missed her, she still ached to see Pluto again. By the next morning, she was back at work feeling terrible but wanting to bury her emotions in a large workload of planning other people's happiness.

"Okay what's wrong with you? You've been moping around here like you lost your best friend and I hate to break it to you but you haven't lost me so what's up?" Corrina sat on the edge of Iriana's desk.

"I met a guy a few weeks ago."

Corrina hopped up, "What? And you didn't tell me? What the hell? That's it, this friendship is over. I'd like my handmade, craptastic friendship bracelet back."

Iriana let out a sigh.

"Okay, you can give me the bracelet back later. Tell me about this guy. What's going on?" Corrina sat down again and Iriana looked up at her.

"He's fantastic, intelligent, a bit quiet but that's okay, caring, sweet and a good person but unfortunately we can't be together. He lives really far away and it's just hard. Work is getting us both down so we don't have time to be together. I haven't known him that long but I really like him."

"Okay, so take some time off and go see him. I know my way around and I promise not to beat the crap out of any bridezillas."

Iriana didn't tell Corrina that seeing him was impossible, the only way to do that was to either die or go into the future and she couldn't do either. Opening her mouth to tell Corrina to forget it, she was interrupted by the bell over the door ringing. Looking at the front of the store her mouth dropped open.

"P?" She stood up so fast her chair toppled over.

"His name is P?"

Iriana rushed around her desk, hating that she chose to wear a tight pencil skirt and stilettos that day. She ran as best she could and jumped up into Pluto's extended arms. "Iriana, I missed you so much. I couldn't go on not seeing you again."

He wrapped his arms around her, hugging her to him. She closed her eyes and savored being surrounded by strength and feeling his hardness against her. Pulling back she titled her head up, "Kiss me."

He did as she ordered giving her a passionate, dominating kiss that made her melt. He pulled back his head, "Let's go to your place. I need to be with you."

She giggled. "Okay, Corrina can you lock up?"

Pluto carried her out of the shop. In the distance she heard, "Oh sure, don't introduce me to your new boyfriend, just ignore me for that hot piece of marble. I hope you do the same for me when I find my own hunk."

Iriana just laughed and wrapped her legs around Pluto's waist. How they got to and in her apartment was a blur. All she knew was that he was here and wanted to be with her. As soon as the door was closed the clothes came off. He took her against the wall, fucking her with an intensity that overwhelmed her. With each thrust he claimed her as his.

"You are mine, forever, you and I will never be apart. I don't know how we'll work it out but you and I will be together."

"All yours, forever," she whispered before taking his lips in a passionate kiss. When she came she screamed, not caring who heard her. That only made him thrust harder and faster. He pumped his hips once, twice three times before meeting his own climax. They sank to the floor, their arms still around each other. Laying her head on his shoulder she let out a sigh.

"So, have they continued to send you sacrifices since I left."

He laughed. "I asked them to stop sending me people. Now they are sending me animals. The palace has become a veritable zoo. I need to find a temporary place while Rory finds homes for them."

"You can stay here, that's if it doesn't affect death and all that."

"The other Gods of Death have that covered, don't worry."

"Good, so I have you all to myself."

"Yup, all to yourself. Perhaps now that I'm in your world, you could show me around?"

"I'd be glad to, just let me recover and I'll take you to the best sushi bar in the city."

"I'd rather eat in."

"But how will you . . ." She gasped when he thrust his hips, he was now hard and ready for another round.

"Yeah, eating in sounds really good right now."

SEDUCTION IN MOONLIGHT

Diana DeRicci

Chapter One

Moonlight bathed the fields. That was her gift every night to the mortal realm, be it on a star struck, crystal clear night like tonight, or buried behind the tempest of her brother's will, she shined brightly across seas and continents. It was her honor, and her privilege. Most nights she struck her duty as she had for millennia.

Tonight she knew something was different. There was a scent, a wafting lure that danced between earth and sky on the nighttime breeze. Selene's travels through the night sky hadn't changed course in all her time, and she knew it never would. Her place was in the sky, the passions that cocooned her brilliance reflected in her joyous giving to those beneath her.

Yet tonight, she craved. She craved the beauty of affection, the liberation of adoration. A witness to the same emotional bonds of her fellow brothers and sisters high in the sky atop Olympus, a connection she had yet to experience. An ambrosia she had yet to savor. Tonight she would seek her pleasure. Tonight the knowledge that she would find the freedom she sought consumed her. And she gloried in that epiphany. Fresh. Free. Beckoning.

Traveling easily on the comforting silvered sliver of a moonbeam, she alighted to the cool darkness of the mortal plane.

Edmon looked up, searching the night sky as he did every night. The beauty in the natural glow of the stars that sparkled from above always brought him peace. The heat of the day washed from his skin beneath their watchful glint. He drew air deep into his body, enjoying the brisk spring air. The seductive wave of the lake beside him reflected the full bodied glow of the moon, nearly at her peak, the reflection pearl white on the water's surface with the pure silver of her face. He had always envisioned a woman when he caught sight of this opalescent purity. Bold yet genteel. Fierce yet loving. A woman of pure light.

He spread his arms wide and basked in her glow, feeling her heat even though Edmon knew no such thing existed on the frigid face of the moon. He still felt warmed by her. He always had and tonight, somehow, she felt closer. His skin tingled as though a woman's touch caressed his skin.

It was a private desire, one he had never shared. A woman who had no face, no name, no body, but he had always imagined her as his. During the day, he was a warrior, a legion commander, but on the rare nights he could spend beneath this beauty, he regained his humanity. And every night he thanked the lovely lady of the moon for the beauty that she bestowed upon him to reinvigorate his waning sense of humanity. When blood and battle tirelessly called on his strength and his duty, he always found a way to return to the mistress of the night, and groveled if only in his heart for the love and attention he would never find in the capacity that he desired--hungered for.

Trees waved in the calm breeze that blew across the

flat lands, bringing the scents of spring to him.
And one other that had nothing to do with the land surrounding him.
He turned.
"How..." he stammered. "My lady, why are you traveling alone on these dark roads?" Not a sound had alerted him to her arrival, neither chariot nor horse, yet there she stood in calm contemplation, regarding him. She was ethereal in her beauty. Rich brown hair, as dark as his charger's mane sat piled atop her head in thick roping braids, woven through with pearls and pure stones. She stood as tall as he, but had a swaying reed like beauty in her body as she moved, walking closer to him.
He searched in both directions. They were alone. Out of reflex and a caution that was as ingrained as his own voice, he wrapped a hand around his sword. She never flinched.
The tunic she wore draped to the ground, silver and white with threads that glittered in the moon's white light. Never before had he seen a fabric of its like. It seemed to create an aura of silver light around her frame, the tie at her shoulder flowed behind her, drifting on the wind like a silken sail. A single silver arm cuff graced her sleek build about half the way above her elbow, reflecting yet more of the moonbeams from overhead. She was a woman of uncommon beauty, and he swallowed to remind himself to breathe.
"You called to me," the vision replied, when she drew close enough to speak.
A shiver of sheer want struck his spine at the melodic sound. *Gods,* he thought. "What kind of magic do you have to hold sway over me?" he asked, stunned, nearly frozen to the ground by her beauty. Fair skin, lovely

bright brown eyes and a mouth that knew how to smile, and did so frequently. She was delicate yet Edmon sensed what he saw was not the truth of the feminine beauty before him.

Her lips lifted in one of those soft smiles, the kind he instantly knew she was naturally capable of. Nearly ruby red lips, which he already craved with nothing more than a few words spoken between them. Soft and full, they drew his attention like the nectar of the sweetest flower to the bee.

"I hold no magic, my dear warrior. It is you who summoned me from my palace on high." She lifted her gaze and looked proudly at the moon.

"Goddess," he managed. Edmon knew he was staring. How could he not?

"Indeed," she answered, her smile broadening. "Walk with me." She gave him an enticing look, turning to stroll along the lake's edge.

Selene cast a look at her companion. He was unbelievably handsome for a human mortal. Strong and tall, wide and deep, like the valleys and canyons of the Earth herself. Timeless in his construction. His stride was confident, his expression bordering on arrogant, but she knew it was not the man behind the chest plate that she saw. The man who appealed to her was the one who could walk this same pace, with nothing on at all and she knew he would be aware of that fact. He exuded a confidence that called to her. A man in possession of his own destiny. Did he know how very rare and precious that privilege was, to be in control of your own life in this way?

His hair flowed in a midnight swath down to his

shoulders, as dark as the night sky. Selene pulled her lips together, aware that a man, who took after her Olympian brother Helios, bright and fair, would not have appealed to her at all. Her brilliance had bathed mother Gaia for far longer than these mortal beings had been around to enjoy her wonder. This man knew the gift she gave them nightly and reveled in it.

That alone was enough to have caught her attention. Anything less would not have even caught her attention for a fleeting moment. Seeing him now, Selene understood why she had felt so drawn to the mortal realms, had craved when eons had passed without so much as a flicker of starlight to break her nightly progress. This mortal warrior could fulfill something within her, could appease a hunger that until she had seen him, heard his voice, she had been unaware of it. Maybe it was because they walked side by side rather than her watching from overhead as she had done since the beginning of time. Maybe it was because he saw her as a woman and perhaps knew what he saw appealed to him, just as he appealed to her.

She only knew she planned to find the answers to these quandaries before the end of the full moon.

Chapter Two

Selene drank in the beauty of the night, her realm with each breath, hearing the quiet heartbeat of life surrounding them.
"My lady, it is not safe on these roads to be traveling unescorted." Stern words from such a calm male.
"But I am not alone," she explained. "I am in no danger, and neither are you."
He only raised a dark brow. He did not reply.
"You have looked upon me often warrior. Do you not recognize me?" There was no condemnation in her tone, just a quiet curiosity.
"No, my lady. Had I visited upon your beauty before, I know I would remember."
Selene looked up into the carved face of her new found escort. She lifted a hand, touching his forearm lightly. He stopped, as still as a statue. The skin beneath her fingers burned with the sun's own fire, with a heat she was drawn too. Muscle and sinew moved and clenched beneath her touch.
"Ah, but you have. You have sought me out on many nights and tonight I am here." She trailed her fingers up his arm, a timeless, natural motion until she had caressed his upper arm and his shoulder beneath her palm. Satin and steel. Warm and undeniably solid. Just the feel of him made her heart beat with a vigor that shook her. "But only for three nights' time."
"I summoned you?" he asked, his tone ripe with disbelief. "I have no such powers."

Weaving her fingers through the heavy fall of his hair, she stepped closer. His eyes focused directly on her, his gaze penetrating and unmoving. The beat of his heart pounded against his neck, pulsing within the vein below his skin. His shoulders rose and fell with deep draughts of air. With a touch to the buckles of his chest plate, it slid away from his body, baring his undershirt and short battle skirt. She knew what would be beneath it.

Nothing save the man himself.

"Powers are irrelevant," she informed him, as he watched the plate armor fall to his feet. "Right now, you have a power over me."

"Impossible."

"Kiss me and try to say so again."

The strength in his sudden kiss was a plundering passion, a fierce deliciousness that stole her breath. How long had he been holding his control? She couldn't know, but the depth of his kiss seared her. He dragged her closer to his body, her form fitting to his like the softest of fabrics against her skin. The hard planes of his chest pressed her breasts high and sent lightning to her nerves. She could even feel the hard ridge of his shaft just above her hip. She shivered in wanton delight. His hands were firm but did not hurt, decisive yet not strangling on her sensitized flesh beneath their heat. She whimpered at their movement, craving more, craving anything he had to show her.

He plunged his tongue between her lips and truly tasted the ambrosia of the heavens. She met him, dueling with a passion that made him growl with hunger. She was so soft, so lithe yet there was a hidden strength in the woman in his arms. The scent on her skin was unlike any bath he knew; delicate like the spring breezes yet so much a part of the woman in his embrace he would know her anywhere, instantly. The sloping curve of her firm breast rubbed against him with hardly more than a few layers of cloth between them. The hard nubs of her nipples rubbed against him with every breath.

He released her mouth, but only that part of her, both breathing as though they had been under water for far too long.

"Who are you?" he rasped, searching her face. He would have never forgotten a woman such as this one.

"I am the moonbeam, the pale calm that you seek, warrior. I am heaven and Earth everlasting." As she spoke the aura around her body glowed brighter.

Goddess, he thought again. And then knew he was the chosen blessed. "Goddess," he whispered, in reverent awe, bringing her flush against his body. Her hands were both twined into his hair and the slow pull against his scalp, the scratch of fingernails sent a thousand fingers down his spine in reaction. "Why?" His lips rested at her temple, panting even as he craved. He inhaled the sweet scent of flowers and spring on her skin, as though she was surrounded in the lusciousness of the season. He had never felt so heavy, so full and filled. The desire raging through him would not be slaked on just any woman.

His cock twitched just thinking of what he wished to do with the woman in his arms.

"Because your desire is mine," she breathed against his throat. He shuddered when the liquid warmth of her tongue caressed him. He arched in answer to her seduction. "Because I have chosen you."

"I will owe no payment?" Trickery was not unheard of when it came to the denizens of Olympus.

"No, my good warrior. All I ask is your passion for the

next three nights, until the beginning wan of the full moon. Then I must retreat to my palace once more."

"I am truly blessed," he said. "I will fulfill your wildest dreams, Goddess." He sought to find her succulent lips once more and swallowed her whimper of heated delight when he did. Her fingers delved deeply into the hair at his nape, twining and tugging, sending little shocks down his body, tightening his groin even more than when he had first seen her. It was hard to keep his desire in check, to not envelop her and love her but he was not an animal. She deserved to be loved. The seducing pressure of her body against him curled over his nerves until he felt her skin up and down his length. And craved them body to body.

"Sister, what trouble is this that you seek?"

Selene looked around the broad shoulder of her warrior. *Apollo.* She frowned. "What brings you to my meet?" The warrior had stopped moving, his kisses silenced. Although he breathed, there was no other sign of his awareness to Apollo's approach.

The tall, blond male glowered at her across the green slope of the lake's edge in the dark. He was swathed in a single wrapped tunic around his hips, rising over one shoulder clipped with a golden winged clasp and sandals that curved like winsome snakes up muscular calves. He was male perfection, in the way that she was feminine beauty. But he held no interest for her.

"I owe you no explanation," she stated, refusing to relinquish her hold on the mortal's body. Her fingers tightened in reflex. Apollo's many loves were no secret. Selene only asked for one.

"He is mortal, dear sister. He will betray you."

"No sooner than my own blood," she retorted. Gods could be as petty as any child when they so chose.

Apollo shrugged. "Come away for one night and think

on your deed before it is done and cannot be undone." What could not be undone? She searched the warrior's face, suddenly fearful she had done something that could hurt him. "I will bring him to the palace." It was a sudden desire, and forbidden.

Apollo's expression darkened. "A mortal? On Olympus? Impossible."

Selene would not beg. She was a goddess, the ethereality of the moon, of the night sky. She stood away, coaxing the warrior's hands to his sides. She still burned, her skin sensitive to the caress of this man's fingers, of his lips. Sadly there was nothing she could do tonight to discover what these new sensations and feelings meant.

"If you need, there are many better suited," he told her, trying to soften the pain of her departure.

"No," she replied, stepping back from the warrior who had called to her, in a way that Apollo would never understand. She leaned toward him, brushing a last kiss to the mouth that had just made her tingle in the most unexplainable ways, made her body ache in sinful delight. "I will return, my brave warrior," she whispered against his warm skin, delivering the promise. "Wait for me, wish upon the glory of the moon and I will return."

She stepped back and in an instant, she vanished along with her overbearing, overprotective brother of Olympus.

Chapter Three

Edmon returned to the calm lake the following night. He had awakened from the most glorious dream that morning beside the lake where it looked as though he had fallen asleep. He had rested well, which was unusual. It had been a dream of a beautiful woman, a goddess that had bedazzled him. He had not drunk himself into a stupor that night, but could not think of one reason he would be dreaming of such a woman when his head should have been filled with battle strategies, wars lost and won. The occasional relief he found with a faceless, nameless woman seemed distant in his memory. This dream had felt so *real,* far too detailed. The color of her hair, the jewels that had been wound throughout, the scent of her skin. One that could make him ache with just the memory. He lifted a hand and stroked a finger across his lips, as though he had just shared her kiss. He swore he still tasted the sweet touch of her lips on his own.

He walked the edge of the lake far from the road, studying it in the darkness, taut with an ache that he could not release. Not even by his own hand, and he had considered it. Training in the fields until he was ready to collapse, had taken the worst of the boiling desire from his thoughts, but not now. Not in the place he had envisioned the woman of silvery light and beauty unlike any woman he had ever known.

He tipped back and looked at the luminous globe in the sky, hanging like a silver dusky disk still low in the horizon, her rise just beginning. A glowing jeweled nimbus created by the wisp of traveling clouds between the earth and the moon gave the sight a mythical and magical touch. Then he cursed at the cold beauty of it, craving what he should not.

His hands curled into fists, frustrated at his unknown tormentor. "Goddess, do you taunt me? Do you sense my touch still as I yours?" He ground out the words, his eyes drifting closed as he let the sensations course through his body, the memory of every caress, of each kiss swarming him now that he allowed the memory its freedom. The heady rush of desire almost blindsided him. It engulfed him, enflamed him. He ached painfully.

"I do."

He whirled, sucking in a sudden growl at being taken unawares by the whispered sound of those two words. There she stood, as beautiful as he remembered and more, bathed in a brilliant moonbeam.

"You taunt me?" he demanded, a flare of anger rising at her unknown games.

"Never, my brave warrior," she soothed. She approached him and reached to touch his arm. "I feel you." Words on the quietest song of the breeze. They sent his heart pounding, racing not unlike the thunder of the horses' hooves in front of his chariot during the day. Suddenly his anger evaporated, staring into her pure earth brown eyes. "I promised should you return, so would I."

Her fingers were cool but still burned his taut muscles as they stroked up his arm. He wore no chest plate tonight, his body and hair bathed and washed from his training exertions. Exercises where he had demanded the most of his body to push away the yearning in his blood. He realized it was an effort in futility. He had never felt this deep a hunger in his lifetime.

Something settled for the night in the trees far beyond the reach of the lake, but the rustle of life quieting seemed loud between the two whose stares were locked, neither willing to break the energy between them.

His fingers curled around the smooth skin of her arms, pulling her tightly against his frame. She did not resist, or appear to hate the move. This creature was no dream, her skin supple, warm and delicate beneath his firm hands. Her breasts were nearly visible in outline beneath the silken wrap she wore with grace. Once again the tautness of her nipples drew his gaze, and he could not resist their temptation. Palming one luscious globe in his hand, he lowered to her lips and supped on their sweet fullness like the finest wine. She whimpered and he answered her, licking with decadent slowness across her lip, tickling the corner until she opened for him. He groaned when she welcomed his kiss, taking him, her passion swiftly rising as her kiss deepened with his. Her breast swelled into the curve of his hand. A shiver rocked her shoulders as he tugged lightly at the peaked bud between his fingers, rolling her flesh, the slippery feeling of her robe between him and his treasure increasing the pleasure of the moment.

He pressed against her, his shaft throbbing with the new assault of desire and burning longing that engulfed his body. Edmon had rarely felt thoroughly engrossed in his feminine conquests, rather only seeking the immediate relief of the body.

This time, he sought only her pleasure and it pleased him how well she responded and welcomed his touch, his desire rising to meet hers. "You are truly beautiful, my lady."

Her hands, spread wide, covered his chest. The light flicker of her nails against his flesh sent bolts of desire winging through his body. He nearly quaked as those same nails scraped down his torso, pausing at his waist.

He gripped the loose folds of her gown then lifted it over her head and he stood frozen, staring at the bounty of her body. The gown floated to the grass behind her unheeded. With a learning touch, he traced her from her shoulders, down her front, caressing and pinching lightly at her breasts and nipples as she wavered on rubbery legs. Her lids sank, hiding the blinding light of passion in her eyes. With her hands in his, he guided her down to the thick blanket of spring grass that encircled the lake. "Please, my lady, tell me this is no dream this night."

Her hand rose and caressed his face. "This is no dream, warrior. Your body, your heart called to mine."

"Edmon. I beg of you."

She sighed, pleasure and happiness in the sound. "Edmon, my darling Edmon."

And he bent over her from her side to caress and seduce her lips once more.

Selene felt no chill from the spring air, felt nothing but the heated look of desire in her lover's eyes, the scorch of his body lying so close to hers. She arched as his lips moved from hers to the skin of her throat, suckling with gentle then hard draws against skin and nerves until she shook as though it were winter, not spring. She felt the heat between her legs and gloried in the feeling. She knew what it all meant and craved the sense of completion she felt rushing toward her. A whimper caught her by surprise then she realized it was herself in answer to the damp pulls of his mouth on the tip of her breast. He twirled his tongue like a slow cyclone around the heated nipple, drawing her flesh deeper and deeper into the tender suckle of his mouth. Her hands delved into the fullness of his hair and held on as he repeated the torture, lengthening her pleasure before moving to do the same to the other side of her chest.

"O, mighty..." She gasped at the first flicker of his fingers on the curls between her legs. He masterfully slid her thighs wider. He growled at the first sensation of slick heat when she felt the press of his hand. She offered herself to him completely, and he stole the pleasure like a thief, making her cry out with delirious abandonment.

"Sweet lady," he rasped as he kissed her stomach, his hand slipping between her labia to find the honey of her sex. The pressure started with little warning but built quickly as he rolled the bundle of nerves that had never enjoyed such treatment. She gripped at the grass in passionate wonder as he swirled a finger, then two within the heated folds of her hungry body, teasing her, pleasing her.

She nearly soared to the heavens when hot breath replaced the torment of his fingers on her flesh. A slow delving lick that ended with a rolling motion over her clit. She arched, crying, whimpering, and pleading for more. He obeyed, stroking her with artful licks and sipping kisses that made her clench from her toes to her womb. She became lost in the twirl of his tongue on heated flesh, the suckled draws on her clit that made her hips rise in answer for the sweet torture.

The sinful twitch of a finger slipped up and down her soaked body as he began to suckle harder on her clit, lashing her with his tongue to soothe sensitive flesh with a tender kiss. She felt the winding of her body, a spring coiling in on itself until it broke its confines and exploded from her.

She screamed as light and pleasure enveloped her in glorious sensation, her orgasm sending her over the cliffs of a view she had never tasted, nor touched.

Gasps for breath filled her lungs even as she fought to regain some semblance of her senses, but it was not to happen. Edmon had ripped his own robe free and knelt before her in pure male domination.

"Goddess mine, lady mine," he said as he lowered to cover her body. It was her first encounter in a sexual situation and Edmon could not have known. Yet he broke through her virginity with the gentlest of movements, filling her with slow strokes, letting her breathe as the new sensations bombarded her body, his jaw tight as he fought for control against his own desires. "So lovely, my lady."

His rock hard body pressed to hers and he held himself above her, slipping into her with strokes that sent shocks in all directions, singeing nerves at every turn. Passion raged inside of her, fed her movements as she lifted to meet his thrusts, encouraging him to move faster, take her deeper. And he did.

He thrust into her body, his hard length reaching so deeply that she clutched his shoulders to hold herself together as he possessed her. Her muscles clenched at him, her body shaking with the hunger of release when he arched and shouted, stiffening in her arms. The pulsation of his orgasm sent her sailing into the bright light of the heavens again. She rode the stars with her warrior holding her tightly, not moving, skin to skin until her world began to right itself.

Chapter Four

Her hair had uncoiled, earthen colored braids tossed in disregard surrounding her in the dark emerald grass. Her eyes were closed, a soft smile gracing her lips. She looked blissfully sated. He lay beside her, resting on a raised elbow to look at her all at once when he traced a thumb over her full bottom lip, just to know the texture. He leaned to nip at her ear and she shivered. "My lady," he breathed. "Are you cold?"
She shook her head. Lazily he drifted his hand between the perfect rise of her breasts, caressing the valley between. Softest skin. Just touching her made him feel eager again, made him want to be clasped inside her hot body.
"Why, my lady?"
"Why?" Her voice was not unlike the gentlest breeze in the morning, breathtaking and consuming.
"Why now, me...only these nights?" he asked quietly.
She lay in the calm silence, turning toward his hand as it meandered across her shoulder. "You reached for me, as you have done for many months. This moon I was able to answer. I will only have this time of the Flower Moon and time is not on my side."
He hid his frown. He had known before she had appeared tonight but he could not stop himself from asking. "You will not return?"
Sadness dampened her pleasure, her glow fading. "Once more, if you so wish. I did not mislead you, my warrior."

He leaned closer. "I know your name, my lady."
Startled eyes opened, a fear he had expected but had hoped against lay bright within the richest browns of her gaze.
"Fear not, Goddess. I will not bring the fury of the gods down on us. You did not mislead me." He stroked a soothing path from her ear to her breast, feeling the renewed shiver of delight on her skin. She relaxed with his touch and his words. Even with her so close to him, relaxed and sated, he felt despondent that she would not be returning. She had not misled him, but he had not expected to grow feelings for the woman next to him in such a short amount of time either.
She was beyond beautiful, more than passionate. She was a goddess he reminded himself, but it was hard to not think of her in his own terms, mortal. His.
He leaned close and brushed a tender kiss to her lips. He splayed a hand over her stomach, possessively. For tonight, and the next, she was his.
Edmon deepened the kiss, delving between pinked lips to caress her tongue into motion, tasting the flavors of his goddess. Heady wine, unlike any other. He moaned at the press of her hands in his hair, clutching him closer as desire rose swiftly between them. With unwavering patience, he brought her desire higher, caressing her stomach then slowly making his way to her breasts. Luscious firm peaks that tightened at the slightest touch of his fingers on her cherry pink nipples. The firmness of her flesh rolling within his palm created a mirroring ache, filling his shaft with a hunger that demanded a feast of pleasure. A feast her body could feed for the rest of the night.
Moving with sipping kisses from her lips, he traveled

down the side of her neck, licking lightly at the hollow of her throat. Short gasps slipped from her. He aroused her slowly, stoking the fire with tender caresses and lingering touches of his lips, tongue and fingers. Her nipples hardened more beneath his touch as he pulled and rolled them with delicate strength, bringing her waves of pleasure that rolled over her body constantly, until the only thing he wanted her to be aware of was his touch, feeling him as he pleased her. Her pleasure was paramount. Pleasing her he had found pleased him more than any other woman in his life. Her touch sent shocks and heat pulsing across his skin, lighting fires down his frame to his cock. He craved her as though he had not already tasted her, but forced himself to move slowly.

She writhed and moaned in the cool grass. The slick heat of her pussy called to him as he maneuvered lower, dropping kisses and soft bites of his teeth on sensitive skin at her delicate waist and hip. She trembled when he touched her center. Wet and glistening at her sex, she watched him from beneath hooded eyes, trusting him completely. He was determined to imprint his memory on her. If they never had these moments again, he would share them as the best in his life with his goddess.

Her juice glistened on the fine curls and skin around her pussy. He touched her and she moaned, arching into his questing touch. He licked his lips remembering the taste of her, so pure, so sweet. The slick wetness glistened in the starry light from overhead, each bright star sparkling off of the opalescence of her skin. Lowering, he spread her labia and tasted her. She cried out into the night at the first touch. Taut legs rubbed against his body, urging him closer, pleading. Careful of soreness to her body, he slid two fingers into her pussy slowly, working them gently back and forth until she was gasping, breathless with wanting. Increasing the tempo between his hand and his tongue, he fucked her, keeping her mindless in the ecstasy he was giving her.

Her inner muscles clamped down and he purposely rubbed against her clit, sending shocks cascading through her body. She exploded, the silk of her sweet juice coating his hand and her body.

"Are you ready, Goddess?" he asked after delivering a few gentle sucking kisses to her sex in gratitude for the beauty of her orgasm.

She nodded and moaned, arching off of the grass, seeking. He knelt and looped her legs over defined and battle hardened arms, which lay her open like a sacrifice for his entry. His head snapped back at the scorching feeling of sliding into her body again. Nothing had ever felt so good. There had never been a woman he had ever made love to. Save her. There never would be again. Oddly, he was not saddened, nor angered by the realization.

Breathy whimpers quickly turned into heated cries of passion as he moved within the tight channel of her heat, slick and taut with friction from every stroke. Soon his hands were clawed onto her hips and he drove into her, commanding thrusts that filled her and took all of him. His cock throbbed and with each breath, his balls tightened close to his body. Her head was thrown back in bliss, her face ripe with the pleasure she felt and it encouraged him to thrust harder, until he pounded into the sweet body of his goddess.

She bucked and met his thrusts, her legs pinned behind him until she tightened and he felt her pleasure again, clenched around his cock, milking him. He tipped back his head and bellowed, absorbed in the sensation of his own orgasm, spurting his seed into the depths of her body.

Chapter Five

"What have you done?"
She whirled with a startled tremor at the voice that had the power to shake the heavens and found Zeus. Angry, he was not a god you wanted to pick a fight against. And he was furious, glaring and frowning, with fire in his eyes.
Selene stood proudly, meeting that condemning stare. "It was my choice. There is no cause for anger, or alarm."
"He is mortal!" he accused.
She paced then stopped, not wanting to appear torn or undecided. Strength was something Zeus understood. "I know," she replied. "I was well aware of that fact." Although now she had no idea how to handle the newborn feelings she felt budding within herself. Time was irrelevant in her mind. Time was something that happened but could not affect her, so the idea of the speed of how things had occurred or how swiftly she had succumbed to his touch had no impact on her. The argument that he was mortal, though, that one had massive impact.
While she would not suffer the effects of time, Edmon could and would. Even as her emotions tumbled within her, she presented a calm and unruffled expression to the mighty Zeus.
Sunlight streaked with wild abandon between the columns, glinting off of stone and marble floors and

walls. A light breeze kept the surrounds of Olympus cool, even within all the brightness from Helios's sun-bright light. In the fall, mists would collect below the mountaintop giving the palace a mirage that it was floating on the clouds itself, but for now until summer it topped the mountain like a colossal monument to the gods, unseen from below and ostentatious in its own beauty. The splash of blue and green that were the tails of the many peacocks parading within the palace itself lent a bright contrast to the milk white stone. It was in itself, breathtaking, but now even in all the grandeur, it felt more like a prison knowing that she only had only one more night to share with Edmon.

"Selene," he growled. She heard the distinct restraint in the modulated boom of his voice.

She looked him in the eye, her expression calm. "I tempered my decision but could not stay away," she informed him. Zeus gave her a disbelieving look.

He stepped closer, as if studying her. "When you came to your time, you could not find a suitable suitor in all of Olympus? In all of the mighty among you?" He shook his head. "You cannot descend, he cannot ascend. He will be forever locked away from you. What draw could a mortal male have to make you not want what is yours for the asking?"

She swallowed then silently argued the truth unwilling to give Edmon up without a fight. Gentle she may be, but she was still a hunter, a woman and goddess of strength. "There must be a way." She refused to answer the rest, aware it would only bring on at least a heated discussion, at worst a true battled argument. Neither of which she desired to spar with Zeus.

Selene refused to be the one to remind the almighty Zeus of his own love affairs.

When she remained silent, he conceded defeat and left her to decide her own fate on the matter. He disappeared through one of the many halls that fed from the courtyard of the palace. Fountains and benches lay scattered on the stoned walks with stretches of fragrant grass that never faded or dried in between. Flowers scented the warm air, the trails of iridescent blue and green feathers following after the many peacocks.

She sat, perched on the edge of one such bench, staring blankly at the fall of water in one of the many fountains. A sea nymph holding an urn that spouted water for the seas below, the water in the basin, bestowing life and nourishment from the heavens to the underworld of Poseidon.

"I have a way, if you so chose."

Selene turned and found Persephone standing just beyond the bench. "Where is Hades?" Selene asked, unused to seeing one without the other. Her sister goddess must have just returned for her summer hiatus away from her husband.

Persephone raised a hand in unconcern. "Doing what he does best, welcoming those who deserve his special attention."

Selene smirked, sensing the playful teasing in the other woman's statement. Selene moved slightly down the long bench allowing her sister goddess room to sit beside her.

"You heard what we discussed?" she asked the raven haired beauty who had won Hades's cold heart, a heart that now only beat for his consort and love.

She nodded, showing no condemnation for Selene's predicament. "It is a hard situation to be in, knowing my love is unending, but to be allowed to have him, I must concede to my mother's wishes. He would never survive on Olympus a full season cycle. He needs the dark, the pain. He also needs me," she explained with no conceit. "As I need the love that he has to give."

Selene nodded, hearing the true emotion in the other goddess's impassioned words. "That is how I feel."

"Do you love him?" Persephone asked, her voice a tentative whisper in Selene's ear.

"I do believe I do," she replied in a whisper, fearful of who else may swoop in and disrupt the conversation, or who maybe listening.

"Love can transcend all."

Selene glanced to her side. "How?"

"Sacrifice," she answered simply. "No sacrifice is ignored."

Selene wrung her hands together, the only sign of her anguish.

"Not even Zeus can begrudge the efforts of self-sacrifice."

She nodded. "How? And to what form?"

Persephone cupped a calming palm over her hands, stilling their fretting. Selene accepted her kindness easily. Persephone was a very giving, kind hearted woman, which is probably what drew Hades to her so well. She was so much of what he was not.

"Join him."

Selene sucked in a shocked breath. "I cannot!" She wanted to cry it out to the four winds in injustice.

"Not in the mortal plane, and not on Olympus, but there are places you can, ways to bend the rules. Would a love worth having not be worth the sacrifice?"

Selene almost agreed out of pure selfishness, but the woman who made the suggestion would know far better than she of what she was describing. Persephone relinquished her husband for six months every year to keep the peace on Olympus even when the goddess craved the company of her husband lover. In turn Hades only visited when she could be by his side to temper the darkness that followed him ruthlessly.

Finally she nodded, knowing in her heart she could not go on without Edmon.

"Then there is nothing to stop you from having each other save yourself," Persephone murmured, pressing a warm kiss to her temple then rising and leaving her to ponder her options.

Sunset was quickly lengthening shadows when she looked up again at the magnificent courtyard. She did not fear her decision. She feared only that she may be wrong. Selene had no history of mortals, had no idea how their emotions ran.

Standing from her perch, she went in search of Persephone.

Chapter Six

Selene stood behind him. Edmon was unaware she had arrived. He crouched near the water's edge, contemplating the languid ripples on the surface, his head held in a cupped hand. The movement on the water distorted the subtle glowing round of the overhead moon. She nearly smiled knowing his latest thought was of her. She could not have ignored the silent beckoning of this warrior any sooner then she could have ignored the rise of the sun in the East.

It was not fair. She had railed against all the laws, all the rules that made her what she was and found no way to cure her ailment.

She loved him.

She could not bear to be without him, yet what choice did she have? The time of the Flower Moon was nearly over. Once the pale of dawn struck, she would forever be trapped on Olympus again.

Was this what Apollo had meant? The danger that could befall either of them for her actions? Selene feared she knew the answer. There was no escape, not for her, not for him. Her feelings were still new, raw, volatile. Did he feel for her? Did he know what they had done had reached inside of her and would never set her free?

Unless...

It was a risk she was willing to take.

A quiet sigh escaped her and he stood, turning to find her standing only a few feet from him. He took a step and she rushed into his opening arms. The silence surrounding them weighed heavily on her heart.

"Selene," he breathed her name and it struck her like the sun's strongest rays against her heart. It was the first time he had ever spoken her name, and it sounded angelic in his deep voice.

"My warrior," she managed, her throat raw from unshed tears. They did not have much time before Persephone's maidens and Hades' minions gathered. She could stop this if she felt even the slightest possibility that she was wrong.

Her heart denied even the possibility.

He lowered to press a warm kiss to her lips and she ran her hands up his arms to tangle into the richness of his hair. Emotions bombarded her and she reveled in their intensity. Those were the signs she awaited, the depth of her love for him.

Because it would need to withstand dying tonight.

"What is wrong, my lady?" he asked, concern flowing from him in waves, in his voice, in his eyes.

"I have come to offer myself."

He appeared perplexed, studying her. "I do not understand."

"You will." She cupped his cheeks, unable to stop the slow trickle of tears that fell from her eyes. "Know only that I love you and I do this willingly."

"Oh, sweet goddess. I love you, have loved you since that first kiss." The taste on his lips was passion when he claimed her, devouring her with that same passion.

Joy swelled within her breast. "Then I pray you understand and accept," she told him when he finally rose to release her, her lips tingling from the sheer power of his claiming. She tempted the Fates themselves and the wrath of Zeus if she were wrong.

A sudden light blazed and extinguished quickly

several yards away on a flat area beside the lake. Edmon swept her behind his body in a motion of pure protection.

"Have thee no fear, great warrior," Persephone said, sweeping the pure white cowl loose from her head. "Tonight your prayers will be answered."

Edmon gaped then watched as Selene walked from behind his frame, stopping only a few feet from the group to drop her gown to the ground, a thin sheath beneath that covered her lithe form, hiding nothing from the watcher. Ahead of her stood a marble altar that had not been there before. Her hair hung unbound down her back in a glorious sheet.

"What is this?" he demanded.

With the help of two maidens, Selene was laid out on the altar. Almost mocking the silence a thick moonbeam covered the marble completely, giving it an iridescent patina. Edmon swallowed so hard, he thought he would not be able to breathe as the warrior realized what hell-spawned horror he gazed upon. A dark figure approached from the shadows where he had been unseen until now, dressed in a charcoal robe and very little of his face apparent. He was tall and broad, similar to a javelin thrower. Deceptive strength.

Edmon rushed the altar and tried to push the other away from her, but yanked his hands away, as he felt a burn on his palms like he had touched hot coals. He was forced to squelch the pain within tight fists to not roar in pain taking a step away from the body in that robe.

"Do not touch me again, mortal," came the low spoken warning. "Unless you wish to join me before your time." He did not look at Edmon when he spoke, and he realized that was intentional. He did not want to look full on the man beneath the charcoal robe, he realized with a shudder. The other woman who had to be a goddess as well with her beautiful features walked to the other side of the slab.

"Once first blood is drawn, it cannot be stopped, as is the power of the dagger. You will bleed to death," the man spoke from beneath the hanging edge of his cowl. "Speak now before the first mark is made if you wish to stop."

"I do not wish to stop," she replied, strongly and calmly, looking upward into the night sky.

"Say your promise," the cloaked figure told her, withdrawing a wicked looking dagger from one of his sleeves. It had to be half the length of Edmon's forearm and curved like a serpent. The hilt broadened to the golden sculpted head of a snake with brilliant rubies for eyes.

"Selene!" he shouted, nearing her without touching the man holding the knife. A knife he did not want to see touch her delicate skin. "What is this?"

Her eyes were clear when she tilted to look at him. "I am sacrificing my place, my soul and my life. There is only one way I can be with you and I give it all."

"Selene. Please do not do this."

She frowned. "Do you not wish to be with me, to love me as I love you?"

"Yes! You know I do, but in this manner?"

"Have no fear, warrior," the other woman spoke, calm dulcet tones at odds with the raging fear he felt for his love. "All will be revealed, but time is of the essence. Once the ceremony begins, there will be only minutes and she will be incapable of any action. Know it in your deepest heart that you will do what must be done or she will not survive."

A glimmer of hope warred with his fears. "She will

live?"

The other woman nodded. "But have no doubts, have only the deepest love you carry for her in your heart. It is as it was spoken. The power of the dagger is irrefutable and she will die by blood loss as no cut made by its blade can be healed. Not even the body of an Olympian is safe from its blade."

"Then how am I to save her?"

"You will not," came the bass tones of the man again. "You will die with her and be reborn."

Chapter Seven

"No!" He reached for her. "Do not do this!" Scooping her up he cradled her against his chest, taking her away from the reach of that serpent's bite. "Selene, my precious lady, you do not need to do this." The man stepped back, sliding the evil looking dagger back up his sleeve.

"We only have tonight, my love," she whispered against his throat because he had curled around her body to protect her. "I will never return."

Hearing her say the words sliced through him as cleanly as the dagger itself.

"But you are giving up everything. Do you not wish to remain the goddess you are?"

She shook her head. "I will be the woman who loves you for eternity if this is done. Either take me now into your heart or leave for I will not remain to live without you on Olympus."

He shook hearing those words. She would die for him, or kill herself to not be without him. Edmon could not put into words the humbling feelings swarming through him.

He swallowed to clear the choked sensation clogging his throat, something he could not ever remember experiencing. "Take me."

"What?" The one word question was repeated three times over.

"Take me." He looked up to the woman who stood nearby. He still could not quite bring himself to look at the charcoal robed figure for too long. The two maidens who had helped her had vanished, and now there stood two more robed bodies in the shadows. "She cannot die." He realized how and with whom she had made the bargain and knew she was too pure for such a bargain.

Edmon, however, was far from pure. He had killed in the heat of battle, had treated men and women as though they were beneath him, no more than the lowest of slaves in the empire. It fit his station, but it did not make it acceptable. His soul would be worth far more.

What would he live for? More battles? More marches? Mindless sex with nameless women if he could bare the touch of one after the time of the Flower Moon with his goddess? This was the right choice, the only choice.

"You would take her place?" The chilling bass tones sent a shudder across Edmon's shoulders and he avoided looking in his direction.

"I would take her place, always," he replied, catching Selene's surprised gaze. "I love you, my sweet goddess. You are too sweet, pure and kind for what will happen. You do not deserve this pain, or the bargain made to create our balance."

"Edmon," she whimpered, large tears cascading down her face.

"I love you, Selene." He pressed a quick kiss to her lips, pouring his love and affection into her, letting her soul absorb every last second. "Take my heart into you and live with peace and joy." Her lips quivered beneath his.

"Are you sure, mortal? Once this is done, it cannot be undone, nor stopped. Be very sure for your life here will be gone."

Edmon caught Selene's gaze as the son of Hell explained. Two deep breaths later, he nodded. He clutched Selene to his chest, kissing her with all of his heart, then stretched out on the marble, taking her place on the altar. The slide of the dagger dragged on fabric and suddenly he was staring at his own death, and the face of the one who would forever hold his soul, and was frozen.

Chapter Eight

"I have seen enough," a grumbled, annoyed voice rose from one of the darkened robes standing at the side of the group.

Selene and Persephone both gasped, whirling at the lowered voice that still had the power to boom across land and sea.

Mighty hands lifted a dark cowl revealing the displeased if accepting countenance of Zeus, his golden wreath crowning his head. Sun streaked curls covered his head, dropping to his broad shoulders like a wild sheaf of wheat.

"Put the dagger away, Hades," he said, drawing near. "There will be no blood-letting this night."

"Zeus! I beg of you!" Selene cried. "Do not leave me a cold life to be the only way I can live from here forward."

He placed a hand on Selene's shoulder. "I am a man of honor, a god who can make the future you desire come to pass." He glanced at the frozen man on the altar. "If this is the one you desire. As before, there will be no way to undo the change. He will no longer be mortal on this earth."

"He is willing to take her place, to take on her pain."

Persephone quieted but did not bow or hang her head to the flare of anger in Zeus's gaze.

"Zeus, what do you want for this gift?" Selene asked, unafraid of the price.

He cupped her face, his hands large and warm on her

skin. "Be happy, daughter of Olympus." He bent and kissed her on the forehead then he turned to Hades. "The dagger," he said, holding out a hand. After only a brief hesitation, Hades laid the dagger in Zeus's hand. The hilt writhed with vicious snaps of the head and a startling hiss could be heard by all. He grimaced. "Fear not, blade of souls. You will be returned to your master soon." The forked tongue of the snake flicked out then withdrew, calming at his words.

He looked at Selene once more. "He will not be able to ascend. He will remain on this earth as an immortal, able to love and live with you. There can be no doubts." The gravity of the request was in the roughness of his voice.

"I have none," she whispered, joy within her at Zeus's munificence.

Zeus looked down at her one last time then turned to the marble altar where Edmon lay, breathing, but again unaware to the many gods in his presence. "Blade, grant me this wish," he intoned, speaking clearly as he stood over Edmon. He sliced the front of his robe from navel to shoulder, exposing the solid expanse of his prone torso. Then he placed the dagger on his chest, the tip barely beneath his throat. Each shallow breath brought the razor sharp point to just touch skin.

The golden god raised his hands toward heaven, when from a cloudless sky a lightning bolt struck the blade of the dagger. Selene stood unable to move, watching as the blade acted as a pathway, passing the lightning bolt throughout his body, causing her lover to jerk and twist. The dagger remained where it had been placed, unmoved. The surge of power flowed around Edmon's neck bright white and blue, then the pure power stopped and died against the side of his neck, where the imprint of the same dagger was now tattooed against his skin in startling detail.

Zeus lowered his arms, watching for a moment. "Should he ever die, his soul will belong to Hades, but for now, he is yours, sister." Zeus lifted the dagger, now silent and passed it back to Hades who caressed the blade with a slow touch then slid it back into his sleeve. "However..."

Selene clenched her hands before herself fearing the rules to this gift.

"He will only be able to see you when the sun has set, yet can walk as any man of Earth. He will live as he wishes, but he cannot return to the life he held, as he is no longer mortal. He will need to find his comfort again on this world."

She nodded. "I will ensure he understands and help him to find that comfort."

"Then may you both reach the eternal happiness you both seek." He nodded his head and vanished. Persephone and Hades both disappeared on less than a blink.

Selene put her palms on Edmon's face, cupping his jaw. "Wake my warrior. Wake and breathe, reborn."

A deep breath lifted his chest and his skin warmed beneath her touch.

DARK BOND

Eliza Gayle

Chapter One

"I know what you are and you deserve to die once and for all!" A hooded man screamed at him as Ezra stood transfixed next to him. Darken reached for his lover and pushed him far enough out of the way.

"Go and get some help. Call 911!" The vicious tone of his voice chilled his own blood. When Ezra didn't move, he yelled again. "Go now!"

From the corner of his eye he saw an arm with something gripped in the hand swing and arc down toward his chest. He tore his gaze from his lover and blocked the blow but not before the sharpened tip of the stake tore through his shirt and scraped at the skin of his chest.

Darken managed to jump up on a ledge giving him enough time to recoup his wits and check on Ezra, who was no longer sitting where he'd been pushed to the ground. *Thank God he listened to me for once.*

He and Ezra had been minding their own business and this prick had attacked them from nowhere, now he was pissed.

He flew down from his perch, his black coat billowing out behind him. Despite knowing what he was, the man showed no fear as he again made the first move and boldly attacked with reckless abandon; the kind of thing you saw when you watched someone being driven by vengeance or alcohol.

Darken drove his foot into the man's gut, sending him flying at least thirty feet. Not wanting to lose his momentum he ran after the man and pulled him up by the collar of his shirt.

"Who sent you?" He peeled his lips back in rage, baring his razor sharp fangs that he would happily use to rip out the man's throat, if he didn't stink so bad that is.

"I'm not telling you shit you piece of filth."

He smirked at the man. "Are you kidding me? Have you smelled yourself lately? If you're going to try and kill someone for no good reason the least you could do is take a shower and not suffocate me with the aroma cloaked around you." He crinkled his nose in distaste and slammed the man's head down onto the concrete hard enough to concuss him but not kill him.

Darken let go of the grimy clothing and stepped back, anxious to get away from here and the bad feeling he harbored in his gut. Something about this didn't feel right. He made his way back to where he'd tossed Ezra and pulled out his cell phone to call him when an ear splitting human scream split the night air.

He twisted around to his worst nightmare. The attacker had not only regained his equilibrium but he had grabbed a returning Ezra who he had tackled to the ground. But even more disturbing was the sight of the wooden stake driven into his chest.

Everything seemed to move in slow motion as the killer laughed at him and turned tail and ran, disappearing into the fog. Naturally Darken wanted to lay chase and rip the man's head from his body but he ran to where Ezra lay dying on the ground. Eyeing the wound, his heart shattered into pieces. No doubt the stake had pierced the heart in two, something no mortal or immortal for that matter could return from.

Darken looked down into the face he cradled in his hands. Blood trickled from his mouth and his eyes were glassed over. Ezra had been his mortal lover for three years and now he would die thanks to Darken's own curse. Some called it a gift, but most days it didn't feel that way. Especially when an attack on his life had just resulted in the death of his best friend. A man he didn't want to live without.

For the last six months he'd considered telling Ezra the truth, letting him decide if he had any interest in immortality. Not that it could automatically happen even if they both agreed to it. They still had to have permission from Nyx to do so, and over the centuries he'd learned she could be a gentle woman or a cruel bitch goddess depending on her mood and whether or not she was enjoying her current lovers.

"Damn you Ezra, why couldn't you have stayed out of it?" He bellowed in pain.

How could a simple act of walking downtown after a few hours of drinking and dancing result in something like this? Regret filled him as he remembered all the opportunities he could have come clean and given Ezra the choice that could have prevented this.

His cool fingers touched Ezra's face, wild grief ripping him apart with each breath. He couldn't let it happen this way, he had to do something.

"Nyx!" he screamed. "I summon thee...please hear my call for help and forgiveness." Wetness tracked down his face but he didn't care, he had to find a way to save Ezra.

"Darken, you dare to summon me? Have you turned suicidal?"

His body jerked at the sound of her voice behind him. It had been so long since he' heard it he thought he might have forgotten, but no, the smooth silk of it wrapped around him, bringing back a flood of memories he never wanted to remember.

"It's not me I call you for." He nodded to the body cradled in his arms. "It's his life that needs you, not mine."

"What do I care about your pet mortal? They die, get over it." She walked around him standing where he could see her if he wanted but he still refused to look up. Laying eyes on her would change everything between them and yet nothing at all. This close he couldn't avoid her scent though which was far more dangerous than her beauty. His fangs descended as he breathed in a deep noseful of her. His eyes flashed onto the black silk gown in his vision, the bare leg visible through a long slit in the skirt.

"Nyx please," he whispered his humiliation to her. The begging nearly choked him but he knew it was the only way. Too much time had passed for him to believe she might actually do something for him. Oh no this would be about her.

"I've no interest in him, he has nothing for me." Her hand reached out and grasped his chin, her power quaking through him at the touch. "Look at me Darken."

He allowed her to tilt his head upwards and he got his first glimpse of the woman he'd loved but not seen for over one hundred years. Her black hair waved around her face and fell in ringlets far beyond her shoulders, her skin so dark it looked like the midnight sky itself, but it was the silver eyes that shone down on him as iridescent as ever that captured him.

"Please Nyx, you are the only one who has the power to save him. Name your price and it's yours...anything." He never thought he'd turn to her again, not after everything they'd done to each other but Ezra meant everything to him now and he couldn't bear to see him die like this.

"Do you love this man? This...this mortal?"

"Does it matter?"

"No, I guess it doesn't really matter at all. But are you sure you can pay my price?"

He nodded. He knew what she would want. She would take him for herself for as long as she wanted him and he would never see Ezra again. The pain of that had already lodged in his heart and over time would spread until he was numb and no longer cared. As long as Ezra lived and was cared for until he could care for himself he would be happy.

"You're far too sure of my help, I don't like that. It makes me look weak." She let go of him and walked a few feet away. "No, that will not do. I think I will turn down your request."

"No!" Darken jumped up from his lover and rushed toward her back. "Tell me what you want me to do, what it will take to get this done."

"Tell me why you have forced yourself away from me for all this time." Her question startled him. He thought they'd been through this enough.

"Save Ezra and you and I can talk about this for as long as you want but his time to be turned is almost up."

She moved towards Ezra's lifeless body and peered down into his blank, staring eyes. "He is beautiful." Her gaze raked him from head to toe. "Did he fuck you better than I did? Is that why you can't bear him to die?"

"Dammit Nyx, don't be a bitch about this."

She laughed next to him. "Come on Darken you know better than that. This is not me being bitchy. That has yet to come darling."

"Jealousy then?"

"Curiosity maybe. I can almost picture the two of you together, naked and joined, you pounding that incredible cock of yours deep in his ass..." She licked her lips. "Are you sure you're willing to pay any price?"

"Yes." No hesitation. Whatever she dreamt up for him would be worth it for him.

"Fine. Do it."

He knelt next to Ezra and swept his gorgeous brown hair to the side baring his neck. How many times had he dreamt of this very thing? Every time they'd had sex he had to fight his impulses to feed on him. He knew how much it would enhance both their pleasure but he'd made a promise not to lie and for once in his life he'd made a pact to follow through with it.

"I'm so sorry Ezra, I hope you will forgive me someday," he whispered to his love before he pierced the skin smoothly and drank deeply. He moaned at the sweetness flooding his mouth. The rich, dark taste of Ezra...

"Oh my God, you haven't drank from him before have you?" Her voice lifted in amusement.

He didn't care. How could he? The feeding frenzy had kicked in and he focused on nothing but the glorious taste of his lover. His dick hardened and he longed for Ezra to feel the same things he did. The arousal...the pleasure.

When the blood ran dry he loosened his grip and released Ezra's neck. He stood and stumbled backwards, drunk on the effects of his indulgence.

"You have to hurry Darken." Nyx's words buzzed through enough to get him moving to her. He knelt down and passed his wrist to her lips. Her teeth sliced into his skin and he winced at the pain. She sucked hard and fast at the blood until he too began to feel light headed.

"Enough." He growled at her and jerked his wrist from her mouth, ripping his flesh from the bone.

"Aww, just when I was starting to have some fun." She flashed a wicked grin his way and he fought not to mouth off to her. He was too close to getting what he wanted to afford taking an unnecessary risk in pissing her off.

They both moved over to Ezra and Nyx sliced a cut in her own wrist with the long nails of her right hand and placed it over his mouth, letting the blood drip into his body.

"C'mon Ezra, drink it baby." The scent of her ancient blood was enough to knock Darken to his knees as the desire for a taste of his own coursed through him. He bent over willing his body under control not allowing himself to think about the times he'd partaken of both her blood and her body. He had to focus on Ezra and his will to live. He'd taken in a lot of blood but had yet to waken.

"Don't fret my pet. He'll be fine." She pushed her free hand over his smooth scalp, soothing him. His eyes slid closed at her touch as he leaned in toward her, aching for a closeness he'd done his best to shut out for the better part of a century. Now with her here touching him and giving her blood to his lover, his body trembled with a renewed need for it all.

"Darken, are you ready to pay the ultimate price?"

His head jerked up and they locked gazes. "You would take me now before he is trained or even informed? We can't leave him vulnerable like that."

Her soft laughter filled the air around them as a chill swept over him. "You thought you were sacrificing yourself to me?" She shook her head "No my pet, that was far too simple a price for you to pay. I don't want you...I want him...

Chapter Two

Spots wavered in front of Darken's eyes either from the blood loss or shock he couldn't be sure. She'd tricked him...why was he not surprised? He ground his teeth together and clenched his fists at his sides trying desperately not to lash out at her. He imagined his hands around her throat choking her as she begged for her release.

No not his Nyx. Not only couldn't he kill her but she would never beg for anything. They'd been through a lot and he'd suffered without her but this she would not take from him. Ezra was his and his alone.

"We had a deal."

"That's right we did and you said I could have anything I wanted if I would save him and that's exactly what I have done." He broke eye contact with her and looked down at Ezra. His eyes had closed and his face had softened. He was no longer dead but instead had slipped into a healing sleep.

"I need to get him home and away from here before someone starts to question what we are doing."

"You doubt my ability to protect our privacy?"

"No, of course not but he should be at home in his own bed when he wakes up. You know as well as I how hard this is going to be for him. He's a good man and it doesn't sit well with me that he didn't have a choice." Guilt tore at his insides as he did his best to convince himself that turning him was better than letting him just die.

"I'll take good care of him Darken. I took care of you didn't I?" She trailed her fingers along his neck and shoulders, caressing him.

Darken grabbed at her hand in a burst of strength and speed catching even her unaware. Her eyes bulged as he pushed her to the ground, pinning her under his much larger body.

Anger tore at him yet with her soft body underneath his old memories flooded back to him. Their naked bodies twined together, tongues tangling and the sensation of pushing his dick into the sweetest damn pussy he'd ever had.

"You don't want me to take him do you?" She whispered at his ear.

"Fuck no. I did this bargain with you so he could be free. He doesn't deserve to be your slave."

"Because being my slave is so goddamn awful?"

"That's not what I meant and you know it."

"Prove it then." She smiled baring her fangs, which did nothing to detract from her beauty. He'd always been attracted to the cruel side she could turn on at a moment's notice.

"What do you want? Are you offering a new bargain?" The scent of her arousal filled the air around them turning his semi erection into a full-blown hard on that throbbed against her belly.

"Such a smart man you've become," she whispered. "If you can make me come right now I'll take you both."

"No. Just me."

"Take it or leave it, but decide right now." Her words were forceful and determined. She was not a woman who could be swayed from a decision, this he knew. Perhaps if he used his body to satisfy both of their cruel needs then he could protect Ezra from that side of her. His dick twitched at the notion of the pain and pleasure they so enjoyed giving each other. Wrong or right never mattered when Nyx was around but protecting his love did, so he would take her bargain and hope that one day Ezra would forgive him for all of this.

He crushed his lips down on hers, forcing his tongue into her mouth in a rough and cruel kiss. Their tongues tangled and fought in the beginning of a sexual battle that would recapture his soul if he'd ever had one.

Nyx sighed into his mouth. Finally she would have her cruel lover back, the only man who could match her. After he'd disappeared from her life she'd indulged herself with every man she could find, refusing to drop her pride and follow this one. Even after they all failed and her body cried out for it's one, she still refused to give in and go to him. She was a goddess and no goddess begged for a man, not even her, especially not her.

Darken's fingers buried into her hair pulling the strands tight until she moaned and bucked her hips upward seeking more of him. It took every ounce of her restraint not to remove their clothing so she could feel his skin burn against hers but no he had a bargain to live up to and she had no intention of making it easy for him.

He tore his mouth from hers and grabbed her arms, she wanted to melt into him it had been so long since she'd felt the rough texture of his hands touch her body. With one hand he gripped her wrists, raising them above her head and pinning her to the ground.

"Have you missed me that much, Nyx? Missed the bruises I left on your body or the marks of my whip?" He rolled to the side and reached for her skirt, pushing it up and over her waist. "I can already smell how much you want this. What's wrong, couldn't you find anyone else strong enough to make you do the things you love to hate?" He ripped the silk covering from her pussy and inhaled a long deep breath. Despite the anger he insisted on expressing she saw the glint of lust in his eyes, watched his fangs lengthen at her smell. He could lie to himself all he wanted as long as she got what she wanted and right now she needed him.

"There have been plenty of men to take your place Darken. Men better at what you do." Lies all lies but she couldn't tell him the truth. He didn't need to know that she had quit taking male lovers and instead had only been with women for decades. All because of him.

A dark rage twisted his mouth into a feral grin. Yes, she'd pushed him to the point of no return. His hands loosened on her wrist and she found herself flipped and face first on the ground. A primal snarl sounded behind her when the first blow landed across her ass. The stinging pain traveled straight to her clit and her juices flowed from her pussy.

Over and over his hand landed blows across her ass until she squirmed mercilessly underneath him. Pleasure pounded through her until she thought she wouldn't hold back another second, but somehow she did. She needed to feel him inside her, fucking her like he used to before she would give in. It couldn't be this easy for him.

"You know the game Nyx, you know what you have to do." Rustling sounded behind her and she knew he'd freed his cock for her. Everything in her wanted to turn around and look, see what she'd been missing all this time but she couldn't, not this time. Cries tore from her mouth when his firm fingers ran through the sopping flesh between her legs, glancing across her clit.

"That's right my Goddess, cry for me." His rough words as much as the fingers sliding in and out of her drove her higher and closer than she could stand.

"No!" she gasped. "I won't do it, I won't beg you this time." His laughter rumbled over her, tightening her nipples to painful points of flesh aching for her man's touch.

His heat folded over her body as he bent across her, lodging the crown of his cock just inside her opening, stretching her. "Are you sure about that?" The whispered question stroked across her ear on a warm breath of air. Gooseflesh rose along her skin and her body trembled with the need for him to take her. The words hovered on her lips as she fought their escape. How could he turn her into this so quickly? Why did she need this from him all the way to her core?

"Darken, you cold hearted bastard."

"I can be." He moved his cock deeper another inch, the slightest rub against her nerves. "But not always. In fact most of the time I'm more than happy to give a lover what they want." He slid forward another fraction. "As long as they ask for it."

Her breath came in pants as sweat dripped from her skin. She didn't care anymore. This was the man she had waited a century for, the one she could now claim as hers as well as his current lover. Her head drooped below her shoulders as she suffered through her weakness. Her legs and arms shaking with the craving for him to take her now—fast. Still he didn't move, oh no, he waited for her and would until she gave in. It was always their way and it wouldn't change now.

The beast in her broke free then and she begged. "Fuck me Darken! Fuck me now!" His cock slammed into her, forcing its way through her tight channel until his body slammed against her ass. They both moved then, each riding the other, fast and rough with no thought to anything other than the pleasure rising between them. On the brink of her release she cried out and he answered by clamping his mouth down on the side of her neck, drinking from her.

Everything around them exploded into shards of lights and stars as he roared his own release deep inside her. A storm of sensation and excitement whipped around them until he fell from behind her. How long had it been since she'd felt sated after sex? Exhausted, she collapsed forward and buried her face in the familiar pillow.

"Where the hell are we?" His alarmed question brought her back and she flipped on the bed to look at him.

"We're home." He pushed backwards from the bed, his pants still tangled around his legs.

"Where is Ezra?" The fear in him jolted her as she realized again the extent of his feelings toward the other man.

"Don't worry, he's fine, I brought him too." She tempered her voice attempting to hide the bite of jealousy she felt. "I'll go to him before he wakes. He is mine now, as are you and as you know, I do try to take care of what belongs to me."

"This from the woman who just begged to be fucked."

"Don't push me like that Darken, you won't like the consequences."

"I'll stop for now just so long as you remember that you are not always the one in control despite what you might think."

She rolled her eyes. How could she have forgotten just how arrogant the man could be after sex? She'd have to do something about that and now that she knew how much he cared about her beautiful new vampire, she was going to have fun with them both.

Nyx couldn't wait to see the two of them together in bed. Surely Darken wasn't the only one who did the fucking in that relationship. Such images floating through her head started to heat her up again. Soon, very soon he would awaken and then the fun would begin.

Chapter Three

Darken looked out over the sea, searching for the horizon knowing he wouldn't find it. Nyx's hideaway was located on the edge of the world on the thin line between the mortal and immortal worlds. The sun didn't shine here, giving Nyx and her kind the freedom to keep any schedule they wanted. Here there would be no hiding from the sun or anything at all. This is what he would call a vampire safe zone.

He'd missed looking out from this balcony at the endless dark water and sparkling night sky. It never failed to take your breath away with its beauty. It was a shame all the years he and Nyx had wasted because of pride but had it not been for that time apart then he wouldn't have met Ezra and he would never regret any of the time they had shared, even if that was about to change.

Would Ezra find his way to forgiveness after this? He possessed a far more forgiving heart than either Darken or Nyx ever did but he couldn't be sure it would be enough this time. This was pretty damn big.

"Wow it's beautiful here. Wherever here is." Darken whirled at the voice to see Ezra awake and standing behind him. Taking in his appearance from the tousled dark hair, to the rumpled clothes he'd been wearing for more than thirty two hours now. His skin retained much of the golden hue from before but his eyes were different and the lips...the colors seemed richer and darker giving him an even more rakish appeal than before. Where he'd been handsome before he now seemed devilishly breathtaking. The night suited him very well.

Darken moved tentatively towards him, anxious to take him in his arms. "I have a lot to explain. I hope you'll give me a chance and listen."

A sexy smile broke out on Ezra's face. "Don't look so worried Darken, of course I will although some of it won't be necessary."

"What do you mean?"

Ezra grabbed his hand and brought it to his lips, the warm breath tickling his skin. "You really did believe I was that naïve didn't you?" He shook his head and dropped his hand. "You don't live with someone as long as we have and not learn things about each other. Despite your insistence on hiding from me, I've known you were a vampire for some time now."

Shock swamped him as that statement sunk in. He'd known? He'd been so careful, always covering his tracks. "But—but how?"

"He always did consider himself far smarter than he is Ezra." They both turned at the lyrical feminine voice. Nyx had joined them looking even more gorgeous than she had the night before in a green gown that hugged her body in all the right places before falling to the ground around her feet. "I'm Nyx by the way; I think Darken is too shocked to remember his manners right now."

"Who can blame him? I'm not even sure I can remember my own name right now."

Her laughter came deep and powerful, sending shivers down his spine. This all seemed far too civilized and calm considering the circumstances.

"Another sweet talker I see. How will I ever keep up with the two of you?"

"Keep up with us?"

"Aww sugar, hasn't Darken gotten to that part yet?" A smirking look passed between Nyx and Ezra that he didn't know what to make of. This all of a sudden felt entirely too surreal for his comfort.

"No, I haven't. He just woke up and I have yet to tell him anything."

"Well, other than me admitting I already knew that Darken was a vampire and I would guess that it's safe to say that you are too?"

"Not exactly Ezra. Our gorgeous hostess is far more than a simple vampire. May I introduce you to Goddess Nyx, creator and ruler of all things dark?"

"A goddess, now isn't that interesting?" His wide grin revealed a beautiful smile that Darken knew he would remember forever no matter what happened tonight.

"You don't know the half of it." He smartly retorted.

"Come now Darken, there is no call to be nasty here. In fact I think that eventually you will both come to enjoy being in my service."

"Service? What is that supposed to mean?" She stepped close to Ezra and traced down his chest with one of her long, painted nails.

"Exactly what it sounds like and anything I want it to be." She tipped her head up to gaze at Ezra and that spurt of jealousy he'd felt earlier returned. He wanted to keep the man all for himself. He wasn't sure he could bear sharing him with her.

"I think I'm ready for that explanation now." Ezra sounded breathless when he spoke. A condition that always got Darken hard as a rock, like now.

"You died last night Ezra. You got caught in the line of fire meant for me and died. Only I couldn't bear to lose you like that so I made the only decision I could at the time, I asked for Nyx to turn you."

"I'm a vampire now?" Ezra's question came out slow and thoughtful, making Darken cautious but hopeful about his thoughts.

"Yes, beautiful one. Your lover bargained with me to save you and I did. And now I have to say I'm really glad I did. The two of you make quite a pair."

"A bargain? Dare I ask?" Ezra didn't look at him when he asked but instead looked directly at Nyx for the answer.

"It's simple really. He was so desperate to keep you my dear that he promised me anything I wanted. I chose you."

"Me? You wanted me? I don't understand."

Nyx leaned forward and softly pressed her lips to Ezra's. Darken's body went rigid watching the contact between them as he struggled to keep his hands at his sides and not rip the two of them apart.

"After decades of only female lovers, I decided to take a chance on a man, or now in this case two men." She looked between them both and Darken recognized the building lust in her eyes. She wouldn't give Ezra much time to adjust to his new role. She was an impatient goddess, hell, they all were.

Ezra finally turned and looked at Darken standing next to him. "This is what you want?"

"I wanted you to live and I was willing to pay any price for that. I had no idea she would take you as well."

"Enough of that, I'm getting bored. Kiss me Ezra. Show me what a prize I have been given."

Ezra looked at him searching for something, a way out or permission? He couldn't read him very well tonight. There was hurt in his eyes but it wasn't the only thing there. His vampire hungers had awakened and he would quickly forget anything but sex and blood until he was sated.

"Don't think on it too hard Ezra or I may get offended. I can smell your hunger and whether it's for him or me doesn't really matter. Soon you will take whatever anyone will give you. Do you want to wait for that to happen or are you willing to honor your lovers bargain on his behalf?"

Ezra took her mouth then with a hunger that didn't surprise him. Nor did his moans that began immediately. Darken knew the heaven that was Nyx and her body all too well. His own hunger awakened and pissed him off because right here, right now he didn't want just Ezra, he wanted them both. He wanted to see how it would make him feel to watch his lover fuck the gorgeous goddess; the possibilities were endless for what could happen here. But would they all survive it?

Darken shook his head. Less than twenty-four hours back in her house and already he'd changed. After years of learning to control the blood and sex lust, she'd reduced him to it in the blink of an eye.

Nyx pulled free from Ezra and glared at Darken. "You need to learn to control the anger Darken, relax I'm not the enemy here."

He snarled in response. Not sure that was true at all. She could be as honest and faithful as they came if she wanted to. The trick was knowing if she wanted to.

"Take him Ezra." She motioned through the doors to the bed filling the center of the room. "Show me and him you still care for him and that everything will be fine with you."

Ezra didn't hesitate at all, he grabbed his hand and pushed him towards that bed. Her bed. He hadn't yet told Ezra how much time he'd already spent in that bed or the things he'd done while there. He shook his head clearing those thoughts, there would be plenty of time for that later. Right now he wanted to focus on his love and take what he could get before it all changed again.

At the bed, Darken automatically grabbed for Ezra with thoughts of pushing him down and taking control of the situation but at the last second he stilled. No, after what he'd just learned he needed Ezra to set the tone and the pace. Let the other man take control of both their pleasure. He was a new vampire, which would change his needs. Darken wanted to learn what this Ezra needed by allowing the other man to show him.

"Show me Ezra, take what you need from me this time." The man's eyes glowed bright with lust and he placed his hands on Darken's shoulders, pushing him to his knees.

In this position he had the perfect view of a straining hard on through Ezra's thin trousers. Unable to resist he reached for his waistband and jerked the button free. With a slow slide of the zipper the pants were loose enough that Darken slid his hands between the fabric to the smooth bare skin of his ass. Ezra rarely wore underwear, a situation that turned them both on when people in public noticed his mighty erection.

He pulled the pants down his lover's legs, releasing the hardened flesh from its flimsy confinement. Veins bulged along the darkened shaft and drops of pre come coated the crown. Darken flicked his tongue to lap up the salty fluid savoring the taste that exploded in his mouth. Opening further he sucked in as much of Ezra as he could take. Although his was not quite as large as Darken's cock, he wasn't a small man by any means.

Ezra threaded his hands into his hair and tugged him farther onto the thick shaft, forcing the crown to the back of his throat. Darken relaxed his throat taking as much as he could without gagging. His lover gave him no time to adjust to the feel of him in his mouth before he quickly withdrew and thrust back inside once again. The motions were repeated over and over as Ezra fucked his mouth with frenzied jerks of his hips. Moans fell from his lips as his motions continued until the telltale swelling of Ezra's cock alerted Darken to the oncoming release. He didn't spend a lot of time on his knees pleasing his lover; it was usually the other way around which didn't seem fair now considering how every lick and nibble seemed to drive Ezra crazy. He liked seeing him like this. Out of control and desperate to come.

"Fuck yes. You're making me come." Ezra roared into the silence of the room as the hot jets of sperm filled his mouth. Darken sucked harder and ruthlessly took in every drop without stopping or slowing. A newly made vampire had no use for gentle and slow these first days, instead craving a lot of rough and fast sex with his feedings.

"Do you have any idea how hot that made me to watch?" Darken froze at the whispers of Nyx at his ear. He'd forgotten she was even in the room. He slid from Ezra's still hard cock and looked at her.

"Wait until you see me fuck him then." He stood and tore his own clothes from his body as Ezra removed the rest of his as well. He needed to fuck so damn bad he ached with it.

"Ahh but not yet Darken. Not unless that's what he wants. Until his blood and sex lust are sated it's his choice." She looked between them both but it was Ezra's lust crazed gaze that caught his attention. She was right if he wanted to do the fucking tonight that would be his choice, despite the slight trembling in Darken's body from his own need. Being around Nyx had ripped his dark side free and he wasn't sure he could rein it again. Later when Ezra slept she would pay for this.

"You're taunting him Goddess. Why?" Ezra's question came as a surprise. In fact he didn't understand how he could think straight at the moment. The room was filled with the scent of Ezra's demands.

"He likes it when I do that, makes him hot. Look at him." And they both did. Two gazes swept over his body focusing on his dick, which pulsed in excitement hoping one of them would touch him before he lost control.

"You should remove your clothing as well." Ezra's statement to Nyx surprised him. He should have expected that he would be curious but still it startled him.

"Should I?" she reached up behind her neck and unfastened the one tie that held her clothing in place. With a wicked seductive smile to them both she let go and the dress fell from her body to pool at her feet like a dark shimmering pool of water at midnight. For several tense moments no one moved or said a thing as Darken fell mesmerized by her form. Her skin beckoned to him for a touch or a taste. The smooth color of dark chocolate gave it the look of satin and the even darker nipples were hardened tips begging to be bitten.

The smattering of curls covering her sex did nothing to hide her arousal. Her wet juices had trickled from her cunt, adding a glossy sheen to the tips of the curls. His fangs lengthened as he remembered feeding from her there. Not only the juices of her arousal but the tasty vein at the top of her thigh that nourished him well.

"On the bed, both of you. It's my turn to watch." Ezra demanded.

"I thought it was him you wanted to fuck?" Nyx seemed surprised by this turn of events.

"You said I could have what I wanted this time and right now I want to watch Darken fuck your sweet pussy that I can smell creaming all the way over here."

She shuddered with fury or desire Darken couldn't tell but true to her word she moved to the bed, laid out on her back and spread her legs wide giving them both the perfect view of her pretty little pussy.

"Ezra, are you sure about this?" Darken questioned without looking away from Nyx. He couldn't, not when she was offered up to them like this.

"I'm sure, although I will reserve the right to have her myself next time."

He laughed at that. They would see. He wasn't sure how far Nyx was planning to take this although right now she seemed as eager as they were.

Darken climbed on the bed and settled between her thighs breathing in deep letting her scent wash over him. His fingers moved through her drenched slit parting the lips on the way to her entrance. He hooked two fingers deep inside her until she cried out in pleasure. They twisted and turned glancing across every nerve ending he could find until satisfied she was desperate for more, his lips clamped around her clit sucking it into his mouth.

"Do you have any lube?" He heard Ezra question behind him. She whimpered something about the drawer as she fought against Darken's insistent caresses. Rustling sounds surrounded him as Ezra searched for what he wanted as his fingers picked up the pace, roughly moving in and out of her body.

"Darken, you bastard," she barely panted out. He was driving her wild and he knew it. Finger fucking and licking her every which way he could except the way she needed for her release. The release that he felt building in the tense clamps of her muscles around his fingers or the nails scratching at his shoulders.

When the ache in his own balls became too much he removed his fingers and tongue and flipped her quickly to her stomach. A squeak of protest sounded from her lips, which he ignored and pulled her onto her hands and knees. The sight of her little puckered ass hole made him yearn to fuck her there, he wet the head of his dick in her own juices and rubbed it against that smaller hole. Her body jerked in response and he smiled. Soon, very soon he would take it, after she begged of course. His cock sought the slick entrance to her pussy and slammed deep inside. She cried out and even he couldn't hold back a groan of ecstasy. The heat of her tight sheath shot through him straight to his balls which tightened against his body. He wouldn't last long at this rate.

"You can't come yet Darken." Ezra's words sounded behind him as his cool fingers found their way to his tight opening. Darken's body froze as his lover worked a single finger beyond the tight ring of muscle, sliding against those nerve endings that shot pure pleasure up his spine. When he added a second finger next to the first, Darken moved against them wanting even more.

"Tell him what you want Darken. Do it!" His eyes popped open at Nyx's urgent words and he saw the dark, satisfied smile on her face. Despite his control over her, she knew that Ezra now held him just as much in thrall. He pushed his dick further inside her and Ezra followed his move with a deeper stroke of his own.

"You know exactly what you want right now Darken, don't you? His fingers aren't enough are they? I want you to beg for his cock just like you make me beg for yours."

"Bitch." He bit out through gritted teeth.

Sweat popped out on his body as he stilled himself trying to calm the raging heat running through him. This was more than he'd bargained for.

He held still trying to control his movements and give Ezra what he asked for but when the little Goddess underneath him started to move and wiggle against him, he gave into the urge and surged farther into her heat until her nails clawed into the silk sheets, shredding them underneath her.

The honey coppered scent filled the room and Ezra's fingers stilled before sliding out. His lover behind him moaned and Darken didn't need to see his face to know that the scent of the blood now controlled him.

A big hand grabbed his shoulder at the same time the tip of his cock pressed against his asshole. The time for gentle and loving was over for them all as Ezra rammed his full length deep inside Darken. The burning pain of his force combined with the pleasure sizzling at his nerve endings drove him forward, stretched out across Nyx. He too needed to feed and the creamy skin underneath his mouth beckoned as he kissed and scraped her tender flesh.

"Bite him Ezra. Take everything you need from him now." Nyx's voice sounded harsh but Ezra did as she told him and his fangs pierced through Darken's shoulder to drink.

The wild pumping continued until Darken could no longer hold back and his teeth pierced the soft flesh of her neck. The blood flooded his mouth as his mind reeled with pleasure. He couldn't focus it was all too much as the sensations crawled along his body, his balls drawing up to his body before exploding his release. "Ahhhh" he cried out as his mouth popped free and their combined movements forced an explosion encompassing them all.

The few candles lighting the room guttered and flickered out as harsh male groans combined with a female scream. Emotions for the both of them poured over him followed closely by guilt as Ezra slipped from his body and tumbled to the bed beside them.

"Holy shit Darken, is it always like that?"

He rolled to his side, settling himself between Nyx and Ezra on the bed before answering. "No. While it's always been incredible, I can't remember anything quite like that before."

Ezra kissed Darken's shoulder where'd he'd bitten him, lathing the wound with his tongue and staunching the flow of blood. "Mmm"

Chapter Four

Hours later while both men slept, at least for now, Nyx watched their chests rise and fall in rhythm as they held each other. She found it surprising to discover just how deep a bond Darken had developed with Ezra. The domineering man she'd pined for all these years had gotten over her and found love with another. She expected to be jealous but found that wasn't the case, instead she felt the unfamiliar pangs of envy. *Her*. The Goddess of Night, wanted to crawl across their naked limbs tangled together and lie between them. The sweetness of Ezra along with the hard edge that was Darken seemed the perfect combination for a woman like her.

As in life her needs in love were complex and divided. For as much as every cell of her being craved control and order as she dictated, she also needed a man who would at the right times stand up to her and not back down. A man to show her how much of a woman she could be. That man was Darken.

Discovering Ezra's existence had not only shocked her but also filled her with more hope than she could remember in centuries. In their previous life together, she and Darken had fought viciously for control at times and ultimately she'd been forced to show him once and for all what a goddess could and would do to stay in charge.

She winced at the memory of his public humiliation and the searing look of betrayal he'd bestowed on her the last time she'd seen him. It may have been the right thing to do in order to maintain her dominant status to the real world, but she'd been unable to fight the haunting image of Darken looking at her with fire and agony. When he'd left her she'd let him go assuming that the day would come when he would swallow his pride and return to her side. Their union had been fated and eventually she would win.

She followed the lines of their naked bodies to the sleep softened expressions that tore at her heart. Instead she'd grown tired of waiting and decided to take matters into her own hands. So far things were working out, not even Darken could deny the sexual chemistry that bubbled constantly between the three of them. Now she only needed to convince him there was more.

Ezra stirred and rolled from underneath Darken's arms and came off the bed, walking toward her. She admired his muscular physique from his broad shoulders and chest to the tapered waist with a thin trail of hair that led to his semi erect cock. And what a glorious piece of flesh it was.

"You look worried Goddess."

"Why do you insist on calling me that even now? It's okay to call me Nyx you know, at least in private." She smiled at him.

Ezra stepped close and dipped his head to hers, his lips brushing against the edge of her ear. "I'd much rather refer to you as my Goddess. It suits you."

Chills shuddered down her body at his words causing her nipples to tighten and even a pulse in her clit. His deference to her was the perfect foil to Darken's harsh and unrelenting need for control.

"Is a little goddess worship appropriate around here?" Moisture dribbled from her sex when his lips pressed against her neck. The thought of this incredible man, the one who loved Darken as much as she did, playing worship to her body humbled her. Not to mention the need rising in her to take this man and use him for her pleasure. She couldn't remember the last time she'd felt like this for a man other than Darken. Was it possible there was more to the two of them than just a shared love?

"Are you teasing me Ezra? Because if you are I might have to punish you. It's not nice to tempt a goddess with a body like that and not really mean it."

"My body pleases you?" His mouth traveled lower raining kisses along her collar and the top swells of her breasts.

She wasn't going to answer him that would be far too easy. If he wanted to serve her then it would be her needs that would be satisfied and then she would see for sure if he really meant what he continued to hint at.

"Do you like women Ezra? Or is this all about Darken?"

"If you are asking me if I've been with women before the answer is yes. I'm a very open minded man and I spend my time with whoever catches my interest. Their sex doesn't matter. I love people."

"How very new age of you." Her voice betrayed her sarcasm in husky pants when she spoke. She needed to get control of this scenario.

"You belong on your knees Ezra." She pushed against his chest getting his lips off her breasts before he could touch her nipples. If she let him go much farther she wouldn't want him to stop. "That appeals to you doesn't it?"

"Anything for you my Goddess." She laughed deeply at his eager tone. Now he was mocking her.

"On your knees then." She spoke the words firmly but was unable to hide the smile on her face.

His fingers slid down the sides of her body as he did as she asked. She loved the look of him there and when she gently grabbed two handfuls of soft curly hair on his head she looked up to come face to face with Darken sitting on the bed watching them. Her hands and arms froze and her breath caught in her throat. Anger sparked in Darken's eyes and the scowl on his face gave her a quick warning as to the storm about to break free in the bedroom.

"What the hell is going on here?"

She wanted to tell him with soft words how they'd ended up like this but his ire goaded her and she couldn't resist an opportunity to teach him a little lesson.

"Your lover wishes to service me, something you should have learned how to do as eagerly." Ezra attempted to stand and say something and she gripped his hair tight and held him firmly on his knees in front of her. This was between her and Darken now and Ezra would have to learn he didn't need to come to the man's defense every time she pissed Darken off.

"Like hell." He shifted his legs to the side of the bed and headed her way. "I thought you were going to let him call the shots until he got a handle on his blood and sex lust?"

"He is calling the shots in a matter of speaking. He asked for this." She bent down to Ezra and pulled his head back so he looked into her eyes. "Didn't you my sweet?"

"Of course my Goddess."

"This is bullshit. Ezra get up off your knees and explain this to me." Darken approached them both, anger sparking from his green eyes.

"What? Can't stand to see your lover desire me? This was part of the bargain." She willed him to not come closer. Not yet.

Instead of getting up Ezra leaned forward and nuzzled her sex with his nose. He licked at her arousal swiping his tongue across her clit. Nyx gasped and bit her lip to hold back a moan but somehow managed to keep her eyes on Darken as Ezra ate at her pussy.

"He's caught up in the lust isn't he?" Darken's tone had softened as he realized what he thought was going on.

"Somewhat, yes." She answered through clenched teeth. Ezra had a wicked technique with his tongue that mimicked fucking and drove her close to an orgasm where she stood. Her knees buckled when he dipped a finger inside her stroking against the sensitive nerve endings.

Darken rushed forward to grab and steady her. "You both seem to be enjoying each other."

"What's not to enjoy? The man knows what the hell he is doing." She watched Darken's eyes turn black as his own lust rose up as well as his dick. She spied a glistening drop of pre come beaded on the crown and she longed to lick it for him, knowing his taste would drive her crazy. She knew the day would never come when she would be tired of them.

"Dammit woman what am I supposed to do when you look at me like that?"

"Like what?" She batted her lashes and feigned innocence, not an easy feat with Ezra finger fucking her mindless.

Darken moved around behind her, his naked body rubbing against hers until he had his steel hard cock nestled between the cheeks of her ass. "You're looking at me like a woman dying to be fucked. No, not just fucked. Taken..."

Of course he was right, but she wasn't quite ready to admit it. Ezra's tongue swirled around her clit again as his fingers pumped faster fueled by his own desire. She could smell his lust and need and soon he would feed from her and they would both tumble into that abyss of pleasure. She spiraled higher and higher with every graze of his tongue and teeth until her mind and body teetered on the edge.

"Yes...oh yes!" Ezra replaced his tongue with his thumb providing more pressure against her clit, but when his fangs grazed against the sensitive flesh of her inner thigh her body tensed in anticipation.

"Relax Nyx and just go with it. You know how much he needs this." Darken didn't have to convince her, she wanted it too. When Ezra's fangs pierced through the skin and he drank from her vein, the moan of pleasure from him pushed her over the edge. Black spots danced around the edge of her vision as wave after wave of intense pleasure crashed over her.

She barely noticed Darken's hands rough against her body, plucking at her nipples and slapping against her breasts. Everything he did no matter how painful only heightened her orgasm even throwing her into another one when she'd barely gotten past the first. Every pull of Ezra's mouth and every sting from Darken's hand felt like liquid fire against her skin until all the pleasure, all the pain combined to leave her breathless and lax in their arms.

Her brain considered that her body was being moved back on to the bed. That her arms and legs were being pulled in opposite directions but she couldn't bother to focus or care. The last thing she heard before slipping into unconsciousness was

Darken instructing Ezra to bind her hands and feet to the bed posts.

Chapter Five

"She is going to be really pissed when she wakes up." Darken looked over her nude body splayed out across the bed.

"Maybe, but one way or another I'm getting the truth out of her tonight once and for all." He trailed the red flogger he'd chosen from her goodie chest along the inside of her thigh testing to see if she was awake yet.

"What truth is that?" Ezra looked at him worriedly.

"I want to know why she is doing this. Why after all these years does she care to have either one of us in her bed?" He pushed his hands roughly through his hair. "Surely there are other men that are willing to push her like I do. Not everyone is afraid of her."

"But maybe it's not them that she loves." Ezra had whispered his thought but Darken heard him loud and clear.

"You are incredibly naïve to think that she would ever love, especially someone like me."

"What about you Darken? How long have you been in love with her?"

"Where did you get a crazy idea like that? These last two days have been all about lust not love."

"I'm not just talking about today or yesterday am I?" Ezra stared at him and he saw knowledge in those beautiful pools of blue. How could he know? He had never mentioned Nyx to any mortal.

"I don't understand."

"Tell him Ezra. We might as well get it out in the open and deal with it now." Both men turned at the sound of her muffled voice.

"Let me untie you first and we can do this together."

"No!" both Darken and Nyx yelled at Ezra who froze in mid movement.

"This is where he wants me and this is where I will stay until he says different." Darken swallowed hard at her gesture. He didn't know what they needed to tell him but he guessed he wouldn't like it but her willingness to lay there at his mercy while their revelation was revealed spoke volumes about how much she'd changed. Much more than words ever could.

"I have a confession to make," Ezra started.

"I'm not sure I want to know..."

"I met Nyx a few months ago." Darken's mouth dropped open in shock.

"You contacted him and didn't tell me? How could you? I never thought you could be such a coward."

"Darken, stop! You said you wanted to hear it so now you have to listen." Ezra's voice vibrated with anger and nerves. "The truth is that I contacted her, over and over actually. It took me a while to convince her to talk to me. She was still pretty pissed at you even after all that time."

Darken closed his eyes, not wanting to face either one of them at the moment. But he had to know how.

"How did you know? I mean how could you?"

Ezra laughed tightly. "You talk in your sleep Darken. Didn't you know that?"

He shook his head.

"Not every night just every night after having sex. Guess you sleep harder and let yourself go when you are exhausted enough." He moved closer to Nyx. "You missed her."

"N—"

"Don't even go there Darken. I listened to your dreams for years and I think I know your heart better than even you do. Despite that, or maybe because of it, I fell in love with you but as the dreams increased I knew that you would never be complete without her."

Darken didn't know what to say. He remembered the dreams vividly no matter what he did to try and wipe them from his memory. But his love for Ezra was genuine and he wouldn't have him denying him that.

"You doubt my love for you?" Darken's words came out far harsher than he intended and when Ezra winced he felt guilty.

"Actually not at all. I would know if you didn't mean it."

"So then why are we here? You set this whole thing up? Is that what you are trying to say?"

"Are you going to let me finish? Or just badger me to death?" It was Darken's turn to wince. He tamped down his anger and motioned with his hand for Ezra to continue. The least he could do was listen before he decided what he wanted to do about them.

"You kept a big piece of yourself hidden from me. I figured out the vampire part pretty quickly but decided to wait until you were ready to tell me. And then the dreams started and those have added to the secrets between us. So I set out to figure out what would work for you...How you could have everything you wanted and stop dreaming for more...So, here we are. The three of us."

Darken swallowed hard as he looked over the two of them. Ezra sat next to Nyx with his head bowed rubbing her arms and wrist in comfort. Did the man even realize how much he so obviously cared for her, which at least now made more sense? And her, the bane of his existence and the other true love of his life. They'd conspired together, which on one hand pissed him off to be in the dark, but on the other hand, he wasn't sure he could stay mad at either of them. Instead he wondered if what they were proposing could actually work.

Could the three of them live and love together?

"So what now? Do I accept your treachery and return to my old life alone?" He looked hard at Nyx. "I assume that after all this I do at least have that option now correct?"

She nodded despite the tears welling in her eyes. No, he was man enough to at least admit to himself that they owned him. He wanted to give this a real shot.

"I have to say I'm shocked you don't have anything to say here Nyx. You always used to have the last word in everything."

"I think our pride has kept us apart long enough. It comes down to you Darken. Ezra and I love you and we will do anything to keep you. We need you."

Darken inhaled deeply taking the relief inside. He let the long minutes drag out in silence as he considered how to tell them.

Just tell them.

"Then you shall have what you want because I belong to you both." He watched their expressions change as his words sank in. He smiled wickedly at them, loving their attention to his needs as well.

"But..." Darken picked up the flogger that had fallen to the floor earlier. "You both have to be punished.

"Promises, promises." She whispered while trying to hide a sly grin.

When Ezra dipped down and kissed one of her bare nipples before traveling to her mouth, Darken's cock pulsed with need to see them both like this. Not just with him but with each other. A true bond.

No, a dark bond...

THE SPOILS OF WAR

Kayleigh Jamison

The Debt

They come to see; they come that they themselves may be seen.
-Ovid, Ars Amatoria

London, 1815

The Duke of Wellington was not pleased to be roused in the middle of the night by a visit to his bedchamber. Clad only in his dressing gown and heavy red velvet robe, he sat in the large overstuffed chair by the fireplace, a tumbler of brandy in one hand and a smoking cheroot in the other. Irritation sketched across the hard, battle-weary lines of his face as he regarded his guest. "I wondered when you would come," he grumbled. The visit was not unexpected, nor was the hour. The first time he'd entertained the Greek god of war had been at a similar uncouth time five years before, though then he'd been in his tent, and not sleeping, too consumed with worry over the possibility of defeat at the hands of Napoleon. Of course, then he'd had a pistol and sword nearby; he wished he had them now, though he knew they'd have little effect upon a god. Prior experience had taught him that, as well.

"I've given you time to rest now that you're home," Ares replied calmly. His accent was subtle, unidentifiable, but distinct. "I upheld my end of our bargain. The little Frenchman is defeated, you have your victory, and your glory. Now I want my prize."

"You must, at long last, tell me what it is you desire," the general countered. *Victory for you, the spoils of war for me,* Ares had proposed. *You won't tell me precisely what you want,* Wellington had countered, *because you think I'm too desperate to care.* The god had smiled and simply replied, *yes.* And he'd been correct.

Ares shrugged his well-muscled shoulders. He was dressed oddly, as he'd been in that first meeting, a linen tunic barely visible beneath a silver and gold breastplate, with large black horses decorating the sculpted pectorals, flame and smoke curling from their nostrils. A cast brass and silver belt circled his waist, and thick leather pteruges hung from waist to knee. The ensemble was topped with a blood red cape, fastened around his shoulders with a gold, jewel-encrusted pendant the size of a fist. On his feet were sandals with straps that wrapped around his feet and ankles, leather styled with more gold. The outfit of a Roman warrior, one who preferred his Greek name. "A simple thing, given your influence and status. I want a woman."

"A woman?" Wellington repeated, blinking. "Bloody hell." Fully awake now, at last, he reached for the crystal decanter and poured a second drink. He'd expected money, jewels, power...but a woman? There had to be something comic about the great military strategist being reduced to matchmaker. At half past three in the morning, though, his Grace couldn't find it. "What sort of woman? A wife? Mistress? A whore?" Lord knew England had plenty of each.

"A companion," the god continued, pacing the length of the opulent bedchamber. "One of the most beautiful that your island has to offer, and of noble birth."

"And, ah...where shall I deliver this woman? How shall I choose her? I've no understanding of your personal...tastes."

Ares smiled. "I will be with you, of course. You need only point her out, and introduce us. The seducing will be my task, not to mention my pleasure. I require assistance inserting myself into your world, following your ridiculous customs."

"I should have known it would be a bloody woman." He'd seen many great men felled by the fairer sex.

"You should have. I am, after all, the god of war *and* manliness. It stands to reason that I enjoy fighting and fucking, preferably, though not necessarily, in that order."

"Well," the duke countered, "there are other ways to prove one's manliness than...fucking."

The god shot him an annoyed expression. "Yes, fighting. Do you not listen to me at all? It's taken me thousands of years to learn: Everything starts and ends with woman. It cannot be avoided."

Thoughts drifted to his own wife. Kitty tried his patience in a manner the whole army of England never had. *He* certainly would not choose a woman as his prize, but then, he was not a god, either. "Very well," he said at last. "When do we begin this grand search?"

"How about tonight?"

Wellington cast a forlorn glance at his tiny camp bed – identical to the one he'd used while at war; he couldn't seem to adjust to a normal bed. He'd never been one for dalliance, never needed much sleep, but if given a choice at the moment, he'd opt for a few more precious hours of slumber. "Protocols of the *ton* are strict and numerous. I'll present you as a foreign nobleman, so some missteps will be forgiven, but you have much to learn in a very short time. We'd best begin," he said wearily.

The Hunt

Every lover is a warrior...
-Ovid, Amores

Ares was not pleased. How in Hades did Englishmen wear this ridiculous garb day in and day out? His strong legs were encased in tight breeches and boots that made him feel uncomfortably restricted. The extravagantly tied cravat at his throat choked him, and the layers of coats were suffocating. Neither did he like the dark brown beaver hat jammed atop his head, mashing his trademark golden curls to his head in an unkempt mess. And gloves? He didn't even wear gloves to wield his sword, why were they necessary for strolling through the city?

"I look like a fool," he grumbled, stepping out of Wellington's carriage in front of a large, stately mansion in Mayfair.

"You look like a nobleman," the stalwart duke replied in his typical, dry fashion, donning his hat.

"How am I to seduce a woman in *this*?" Ares continued. Flexing his biceps, he'd discovered, was a tried and true tactic. He tugged at one sleeve with disgust.

Wellington snorted. "I thought the seducing was your task, not mine. I'm sure you'll make do. Mine was to make you presentable, and I have."

It was the god's turn to snort. Customs changed over the decades, he knew that all too well, but the trend over the last few centuries had been towards increasingly more clothing, and it was not a pattern he liked.

Particularly on women. Women, in his opinion, should always be naked, or as close to it as possible. But no, they were far too prudish these days for that. Most infuriating of all, almost none believed in *him*, anymore.

Once, he'd had great temples built in his honor. Humans had served his every whim, and families had traveled for weeks, even months, to present him with their daughters, in the hope that she would become his chosen, his Consort...until he grew bored and selected another.

Those times were over. His temple crumbled slowly into ruin and he had little choice but to sit in idle boredom on Mount Olympus and watch the world change, alone.

Until a foolish miniature Frenchman (no doubt compensating for something, the god believed) got it in his head to rule the world and Ares saw the perfect opportunity to indulge his penchant for bloodlust, followed by his need for carnality. Ah, fate. He'd never admit it, but the Moirae had their uses.

The battles *had* been good. The woman, he hoped, would be even better.

"Let's go," the duke commanded, a tone that said he was used to giving orders and having them followed without question.

Of course, so was Ares, but he'd long ago learned it was best to defer to the general who knew the lay of the land. With a nod and a grimace, he strolled beside Wellington up the wide stone steps and through the open double doors. The butler led them through a wide foyer and into the marbled ballroom, already full to capacity. After a brief, whispered conversation the butler stepped to the side and announced their names.

"His Grace the Duke of Wellington, and Lord Aristoun."

The cacophony of voices hushed and several hundred faces turned to regard the newcomers with open curiosity. Wellington, without doubt one of the most famous men in England, disliked the "frippery of social gatherings," and to see him tonight was a surprise. To see him with a handsome, mysterious foreigner had the crowd fairly vibrating with interest.

In terms of its composition, no less than two thirds of the crowd was made up of the fairer sex, both young and old, he noted, making a discreet scan of the room as he and his companion stepped over the threshold.

Ares was suddenly quite overwhelmed. "What's that expression? 'Bloody hell?'" he asked.

A woman nearby gasped and fanned herself vigorously.

"That is the one, yes," Wellington replied, "but not in polite company. You nearly gave Lady Moxley an apoplexy just now."

The god turned towards said lady, a stout, grey-haired woman with feathers protruding from her hair like a peacock's tail, and gave a short bow, followed by a devilish grin.

Music drifted across the room from a quartet of strings situated in the far left corner by the open balcony doors. Couples paired off and wandered into formation for a dance. Ares and Wellington strolled along the perimeter of the room, pausing now and again to murmur greetings and effect introductions. Remaining cool and aloof, the god continued to survey the crowd as discretely as he could manage. Beautiful women were everywhere, but none quite struck his fancy.

And then they turned a corner and he saw her. Leaning against a tall white column, a bored look on her face, the woman surveyed the crowd as if she'd rather be anywhere else. She was tall and slender, with jet black hair twisted into a series of knots and loops atop her head, a strand of pearls woven throughout and short ringlets framing her face. Skin pale and smooth, she had an oval-shaped face. Narrow eyebrows arched over slightly slanted brown eyes, a small thin nose, and peach-colored pouty lips. Her body was lean and fit, clad in a simple cream gown, dotted with red embroidered flowers and short puffed sleeves. The waistline was high, embellished with red cording, and a v-shaped neckline that rode low along the curves of her breasts. She wasn't a classic beauty, her features perhaps a bit too strong, body too slim, but Ares found himself captivated. He slowed his steps, and then stopped all together.

"My, my, who is that?"

"Lady Madeline Winters," the duke replied. "Eldest daughter of the Earl of Sedgewick. Quite a few men after that one, I'm told, and my wife claims she's made red hair fashionable this Season or some such nonsense."

Ares shook his head impatiently. "Not her." He'd barely noticed the raven beauty's companion; they stood together, heads slightly bent in conversation. "The other one."

Wellington frowned. "The gangly one?"

"I'd hardly call a woman with breasts to fill your palms gangly, General," the god replied *sotto voce*.

"Lady Serena Tolson. Her father was the Marquis of Bentley. He served with me on the continent. Took a ball in the head at Vitoria, which may or may not have been meant for me. I considered him a friend."

"Then you know her, and can introduce us?" Another stupid custom of the English, he'd learned; to speak to a woman, one required a mutual acquaintance to introduce them.

"I can, but I doubt you want that one, my friend."

Ares had already started moving in Serena's direction, but stopped and turned at the general's admonition. "Why the hell not?"

"Rumors…a great many of them, about the lady entertaining certain companions." A frustrated sigh. "Her mother died in childbirth, and the title passed to an uncle who has no interest in Serena's well-being, other than to put a roof over her head and food in her mouth. After Bentley's death, I made a point of checking in with her whenever I was in England, providing money when I could. Would that I had the ability to do so for all the families of my fallen men…" Wellington trailed off, then shook his head, as if clearing the regret from his mind. "Last season, she was pursued quite doggedly by a newly inherited Viscount, and I expected her to marry then be taken care of. When I returned from Waterloo I was told the young man had cried off, and that there were questions in regards to Serena's virtue. She refused to discuss the matter with me when I called. I distinctly recall you informing me that you require a *virgin*, did you not?"

"I do." Ares could no longer recall if this was due to personal preference, force of habit, or actual Olympian law (not that he followed them when they didn't suit his purposes), but his consorts were *always* virgins. Because of this, or perhaps because he was a god – again he wasn't sure which – Ares was able to spot a virgin on sight. He was also able to spot who was not, and the pretty Lady Madeline with whom everyone was so enamored, was not. "Who started these rumors?"

"Impossible to know. That's the way of rumors."

"Or lies, in this case. Your pretty ward still has her virtue." He grinned. "She's the one, General. Now, provide me with an introduction, and your task will be finished."

Wellington appeared ready to argue. Clearly, he hadn't expected Ares' choice to be a personal acquaintance.

"This is the price of your victory, *your Grace*."

At last, he sighed and nodded. "Then let us collect your prize."

The Spoils

Love is a kind of warfare.
-Ovid, Ars Amatoria

"He's staring at us."

Serena frowned at her best friend. "Who?"

"That handsome foreigner who came in with Wellington," Maddie replied, the tip of her tongue darting out to touch her top lip. "Lord Ari-something or other."

"He's staring at *you*, I'm sure," Serena replied.

"Oh, I wouldn't mind if he was; he's quite fetching. But no, his attention appears more directed at you, darling."

"Then gossip spreads even faster than I thought." She sniffed and turned to study a nearby plant, arms folded across her chest in a defiant, and scandalous, gesture. It was amazing how effective starting one little rumor could be. She'd only sought to wiggle her way out of marriage to a ridiculous, overbearing fop; and she had, but the price had been her reputation. She'd grown used to the disparaging stares after her father's death – *look at the poor orphan* – but it hadn't prepared her for just how venomous the *ton* could be. *Look at the poor orphan slut.* Only Maddie had stuck by her side, but then, Maddie was so blindingly beautiful, and rich, that she could do whatever she wanted without so much as the smallest blemish upon her reputation.

"Rena, have you even looked at him? You haven't, have you?" Maddie asked, ignoring as she always did the reference to Serena's scandal.

"No. I've better things to look at." The potted palm really wasn't so interesting as all that. Thirty seven – no, thirty eight – leaves. She hadn't paid much attention to the General and his guest, barely a passing glance. He was just another overstuffed aristocrat to her.

"Where do you think he's from?"

A shrug. "You could always go ask him."

"Or," her friend countered, wrapping slender fingers around Serena's upper arm, "stay here and ask him, since they are apparently heading this way."

"Damnit," she muttered, dropping her arms and straightening her spine. Of course the general would want to speak to her; he always did if they happened to be in the same place, at the same time. He fancied himself some sort of fatherly guardian. It took a considerable amount of willpower for Serena to not tell him he was *nothing* like her father, and never would be. Crude and opinionated though he'd been – a military man to the core, long before his brother had died and left him a title – the late Marquis had loved his daughter.

"Lady Serena, Lady Madeline," Wellington said in greeting, stopping a few feet from them and sketching a shallow bow. "A pleasant surprise to see you this evening."

"More surprising for us than you, I wager, your Grace," Maddie replied smoothly, dropping into a curtsy. "For we are often at such gatherings and you, often, are not."

"Your Grace," Serena acknowledged with her own curtsy and a slight bob of her head.

"Touché, my lady." Wellington gestured towards his companion. "Allow me to introduce Lord Aristoun. He also fought in the war. My lord, Lady Serena and Lady Madeline."

Aristoun bowed, and reached for her hand. "A pleasure, Lady Serena," he said, in a melodic, cultured accent.

Serena hesitated for a moment before slipping her fingers into his. When his lips made contact with her wrist, a light, tempting pressure, she focused her gaze upon him for the first time, and gasped.

For once, Maddie hadn't been exaggerating when she'd called the man fetching. In fact, she'd understated things. He was...*beautiful.* Hair comprised of tight golden ringlets, almost effeminate in their composition, fell hap hazardously about his head and draped his cheeks, framing a wide square jaw and cleft chin. He had a slender, aquiline nose, thin, defined lips, and deep set blue eyes below thick, golden brows. His skin was tanned a deep gold, and his body was muscular and solid, evidence that unlike so many men of noble birth he didn't shy away from physical labor, perhaps even relished it.

There was something regal and commanding about his presence, and something hypnotic in the way he smiled, revealing dimpled cheeks, as he caught her staring.

"I must confess, madam," he commented casually, only now releasing her hand, "I saw you from across the room and demanded an introduction."

Maddie elbowed her in the ribs and coughed delicately. Wellington's forehead creased with the beginnings of a frown, then he seemed to stop himself and blanked his expression.

"Where is it that you are from, my lord?" Serena asked, changing the subject.

"The continent."

"The continent is comprised of many countries," she replied.

He grinned, white teeth flashed devilishly. "Yes, it is."

Several moments of awkward silence passed. The quartet struck up a waltz. Lord Winslow appeared at Maddie's side to claim the dance she'd promised him. With a coy smile and a wink, her friend took the earl's proffered arm and moved off towards the dance floor.

"Wellington," a deep voice called from their left. A glance revealed the Duke of Rutland and several other gentlemen. "A word if you please. We'd like your thoughts on the latest proposals."

Wellington glanced from Lord Aristoun to Serena and back again. "Excuse me then, Aristoun, Serena." He shot the foreigner an undecipherable look, and then strolled away to talk politics.

"I suppose the gentlemanly thing to do would be ask you to dance, no?" Aristoun asked.

"I suppose," she nodded, "but I would decline. I dislike dancing."

This made him smile. "As do I. Shall we take a turn about the garden, then?"

"By ourselves?" Her own lips curled. "That would be positively scandalous, my lord."

"Is that a 'no'?"

One glance to her right revealed a crowd of older women watching them intently, a collective scowl on their features. The gossip hounds fairly frothed at the mouth in anticipation. "No," Serena said, placing her fingers on her elbow.

Together they strolled along the perimeter of the room and out the wide French doors to the balcony. His arm was warm and hard beneath her hand, the muscles flexing slightly. A handful of couples peppered the balcony in an attempt to escape the hot, stifling air of the ballroom. Had they stopped here, it would not have been outside the bounds of propriety, but they didn't stop. Aristoun navigated her down the curved staircase and into the quiet darkness of the garden. An owl hooted in the distance. A feminine giggle drifted towards them from the bushes, followed by a masculine chuckle.

They happened upon a small garden, walled in on three sides, thick ivy covering the stone. They were isolated. Alone. Serena was suddenly painfully aware of the strong male at her side, a man she'd met just moments before.

"So, why won't you tell me what country you're from?" she asked, breaking the silence, attempting to push away her unease.

"I'm not from a country," he replied.

"That's nonsense. Everyone is from *somewhere*."

"My home is very different from yours." Moonlight glinted off his golden curls, and white teeth flashed. "Lush and beautiful. Everything is strange here."

"How so?"

"We don't wear quite so many...clothes."

"What do you wear?"

Aristoun chuckled. "Would you like to see? Close your eyes."

His tone was soft, seductive, but commanding. She obeyed. Her heart slammed in her chest, and a moment passed.

"Now open them."

Serena complied, and immediately clamped a hand over her mouth to stifle the shriek. Gone were the tight-fitting, aristocratic clothes. Now he wore a suit of armor – *Roman* armor. His legs and arms were bare, thickly muscled, bunching with raw power. And his eyes had changed as well. No longer blue, they appeared red in the pale moonlight, the color of fire.

"Bloody hell," she whispered, torn between attraction and fear. "Who are you?" She took an involuntary step forward, then a conscious one back. "*What* are you?"

"Sweet thing," he said patiently, countering her retreat with an advancement of his own, "I'm Ares. And I am a god."

She turned to flee, to run back to the balcony where things made sense...and slammed into the warm, solid surface of his chest. She hadn't seen or heard him move, it was as if he'd simply materialized directly in her path. Serena tried to back away but his arms slipped around her waist, locking her firmly against him. His armor had disappeared, leaving nothing but the thin fabric of her gown and underclothes between his flesh and hers.

From a distance, she had merely thought that the god's eyes were the color of fire, but upon closer inspection she could see that they were, in fact, *on* fire; tiny, swirling flames leapt within his irises, dancing around his pupils in a hypnotic rhythm. She knew that Ares was associated with the element of fire, but none of her reading had told her that the relationship was quite so literal.

"I helped the General defeat Napoleon. Gave him victory, power, fame. And all I want in return," one of his strong fingers traced down her cheek, "is you."

"Let me go." Serena's mind spun. A god. It wasn't possible. And yet, no other explanation made sense.

"No."

She squirmed, tried to free her leg in order to kick him. Square between the legs, as her father had taught her. *In any situation*, he'd told her, *a swift jab to the bullocks will do.*

Ares sensed what she planned to do, and tightened his grip in a silent, unmistakable warning. "You play with fire, my precious virgin," he warned. His head dipped closer, and she relaxed.

"Do I?" she asked absently, distracted by his ever-changing eyes.

"You do." His face was stern and hard, but as he lowered his mouth to hers his expression softened.

The kiss was intense and demanding, but at the same time surprisingly gentle. His lips were smooth and feather soft, a contrast to the firmness of his body, the strength of his arms holding her in a vice-like grip. Ares' tongue snaked out, teasing at the seam of her lips and she stiffened, momentarily startled by his actions. He was undeterred, running his hands up her spine to tangle in her hair, yanking it free of its coiffeur and sending a rain of pins down upon her shoulders; grasping the base of her neck he angled her face to better plunder her mouth. After another brief hesitation, she gave in, parting her lips and granting him entrance. Her hands settled on his biceps, fingers spreading to caress the silky skin and the taut musculature beneath. He surged forward, plunging his tongue into her mouth and tracing the line of her teeth, teasing, exploring. Warmth washed over her, and she whimpered.

The instant she surrendered to his assault he moved, lowering them both to the ground without breaking the kiss.

The god pulled away and gazed at her, eyes blazing. "Beautiful," he murmured, brushing a few errant strands of hair from her face. "My virgin sacrifice."

"I'm not a sacrifice," she gasped, twisting beneath him, relishing the heavy weight of his hard, muscular body above her.

"No, you're a gift. A prize," Ares countered, one strong hand skimming across her stomach, brushing over her breasts. A tiny trail of sweat broke out on her skin wherever he touched her, leaving a scorching trail in the wake of his fingertips.

Serena reveled in the god's attention. Spread beneath him on the grass she felt his description had been appropriate; she was, indeed, his virgin sacrifice. She prayed that her naiveté wouldn't be off putting, and did her best to reciprocate, tracing the corded muscles of his arms and skimming her palms over his back. She felt a bit awkward, but her reaction to him, at least, certainly came natural enough.

His large hands roamed her body, sliding down to her thighs and tugging up her gown, exposing her legs, then her stomach. She was completely helpless, but at the same time, freer and more in control than ever before. Ares was merciless in his assault; he wouldn't stop stroking, teasing, torturing. She didn't want him to. The heat ignited by his touch seemed to pool low in her abdomen and she felt a shocking spread of moisture between her thighs.

He planted light, airy kisses across her face, covering her cheeks and eyelids, then her lips, and lower, along the column of her neck. In a flash of savagery, he gripped her gown's neckline and tore it from her, ripping the thin fabric. Then her corset and slip disappeared in the same way as his armor. Naked and vulnerable before him, he studied her, his gaze an inferno.

"Your breasts are flawless, little mortal," he commented, covering one of the round globes with his hand, lifting the soft flesh and testing its weight. "Do you see? A perfect fit; as if made for me."

She did see, watched as he dipped his head and kissed her there, drawing the pert tip into his mouth, flooding her with warmth once again. Serena moaned, long and low in her throat, pulse racing, threading her fingers through his hair as if to draw him closer.

His hand slipped down her stomach and between her legs, which she instinctively parted for him. He stroked her thighs almost absently, always stopping just short of where she truly wanted him to touch her. His arousal pressed against her side, rock hard and insistent. He was all firmness and muscle, she softness and curves. And he was right, despite their contrasts, they fit. Her instincts screamed at her. Inexperienced though she was, she knew that there was more to the act of lovemaking than this.

"My lord," she gasped, "can we not fit...more?"

He laughed, sending delicious vibrations through her. Finally, his fingers brushed against her sex, a teasing sweep, through her slick folds before settling on her thigh once more. That devilish tongue continued to tease her, sliding around the hard pearl of her nipple, the occasional graze of his teeth making her squirm in delight. "We can. And we will. But not yet, I want to have my fill of you."

Serena whimpered, frustrated that he could appear so maddeningly patient when she was spiraling so far out of control. Her hips lifted, seeking contact, but he pulled just out of reach with another chuckle. She decided to mimic his game, and ran her hands down his arms, then slipped around to peruse his chest, and the lines of his abdomen. The planes of his body formed a sharp 'vee' at the crest of his hips, and she lavished her attention there, tracing the groove with trembling fingers. His muscles jumped under her touch, and she felt him smile against her breast.

"Clever minx. Touch me," he urged, taking her hand in his and guiding it to his rigid length. Uncertain, she wrapped her fingers around him, barely circling his girth. He was much larger than she'd anticipated, the long, pink shaft curving upwards towards his stomach from amidst a thatch of blond, wiry curls. He groaned, a harsh, guttural sound and she tried to pull away, startled. He held her firm, aiding in her exploration.

Serena stroked him, growing bolder, tightening her grip on his erection. She loved the feel of him, velvety soft and hard like marble at the same time. He reciprocated by returning his hand to her sex, one elegantly crafted finger sliding into her wet center.

"Oh!" she cried, squeezing him tighter, which spurred him to reward her further, withdrawing only to push forward once more.

"Do you like that, precious?" he asked, nuzzling her shoulder.

She could only moan in response.

"You'll like this as well, I promise." Ares slid down her body and settled between her thighs. With two fingers he spread her wide to his fiery gaze, and grinned up at her. "Close your eyes."

She did as she was told, resting her palms on his shoulders. The first sweep of his tongue sent sparks of pleasure through her and she cried out, bucking her hips. He traced the outer lips of her sex with his tongue, sliding up one side, and then down the other.

"You taste like ambrosia," the god said, voice thick with lust. "Honeyed and sweet."

Ares pushed the tip of his tongue inside her slick heat before moving to the ultra-sensitive sliver of flesh at the apex. Her trembling was continuous now, the sensations he was creating had become her entire world, the tiny bud where his tongue danced the center of her being. She felt one finger enter her and begin gently probing her passage, then a second. She screamed when his fingers hooked upwards.

One more pass of his tongue and she saw stars. Waves of heat and pleasure washed over her and she succumbed to the tide, dimly aware she was sobbing, clawing at his back. For one precious moment her mind blanked, and she could only feel.

Serena was dimly aware of Ares' weight settling over her, the stiffness of his erection nudging against her sensitive flesh, seeking entrance.

"Now?" he murmured against her ear. Though it was phrased as a question, there was a clear note of dominance in his voice.

"Yes, now," she agreed hazily, wrapping her arms around his thick neck.

Her lover surged forward, sheathing himself with one fluid thrust. The muscles beneath her hands jerked as he held himself still, and she adjusted to his length buried within her. Was it strange that she felt no pain? She knew it was supposed to. But no, it didn't hurt; instead all she felt was wonderfully, deliciously full. A desperate, keening wail slipped past her lips and she wrapped her legs around the small of his back.

A perfect fit, she thought. His heat raced through her, her skin burned where they were joined.

The god groaned, murmured something to her in a language she didn't understand. Capturing her lips in a searing kiss, he began to move, slowly at first, in and out. The friction he created sent her climbing towards release once more, and once again she lost herself. Gradually he picked up speed.

His body grew hotter still, scorching her from the inside out. Serena closed her eyes and surrendered to the sensations. She burned alongside him, around him, and was consumed by the flame.

The Conquest

The gods have their own rules.
-Ovid, Metamorphoses

Ares tried to be gentle with her, tried not to unleash his full strength as he thrust into her, but Serena's tiny, mewling cries fueled his desire, and pried away the grip on his control. By Zeus, she was intoxicating. The way her skin darkened as the flush of pleasure rushed upwards from her neck to color her cheeks, the way she struggled valiantly to keep her eyes open, watching him through the thick sweep of her lashes, the look of delight and surprise as he'd filled her to capacity, nudging against her womb. She was tight and hot around him, like liquid fire, perfect as no mortal had any right being. Somehow, her fumbling, inexpert touch felt more divine than even the most skilled of his past lovers. Had he been deceived? Was she a goddess after all?

"Harder," she gasped as she clung to him. The sensation of her delicate nails raking down his back made his groan. "More, my lord, please!"

He loved that she surprised him. Her courage was a potent aphrodisiac, and he did not view her surrendering to him as weakness, but as further evidence of her strength. Gripping her hips, he reared back so that he was almost kneeling upright. He withdrew until he'd nearly left her body, paused, and then, gritting his teeth, surged forward. The pace he set was blistering, brutal, animalistic. The rhythmic cadence of flesh against flesh echoed off the walls of the small garden. Through the haze of lust he was dimly concerned about hurting her, but then her sex began to flutter around his length, signaling her climax.

Serena's head was flung back, tossing from side to side amidst a dark halo of onyx tresses. Her eyes squeezed shut, mouth frozen in a perfect "O," she screamed, raw and visceral, her own battle cry. Her breasts shuddered with each lunge of his hips, their rosy tips begging for contact, and he obliged, leaning forward to trap one between his teeth. He didn't slow his movements, didn't pause to coax her through her orgasm – couldn't have even if he'd wanted to.

His thrusts were frenzied, the inexorable drive for completion almost like the cloud of rage that would descend upon him in battle, obliterating all rational thought. With one last push he found release, roaring in triumph as he bathed her womb in the molten lava of his seed. Gathering her limp, panting frame against his chest he rolled onto his back, then simply held her until both their tremors had subsided.

"I don't know what magic you have wrought over me tonight," Serena sighed, nestling further into his arms, "but I feel so marvelously free and happy."

Ares laughed and affectionately ran a hand through her silky hair. "No magic, little mortal. A bit of skill, perhaps, but no magic at all." It wasn't entirely true, he acknowledged internally – he'd dulled her senses for a moment, when he had broken her maidenhead – but as he'd been in no mood to go slow with her, it had been the best course of action. All the endless years he'd spent searching for his perfect mate and here she was, an innocent. A mortal.

She felt so fragile in his arms suddenly, so...human. He cradled her closer. Music drifted on the breeze faintly, carried from the ballroom while the party raged on.

"So," she spoke finally, voice hesitant. "You fought years of war for one night with...me?"

"Not one night," Ares replied. "Many."

Serena stilled. "You plan to stay in England?"

"No. I plan to take you with me. To Olympus. Or will you try to say there's still something here for you?"

"There isn't, but...do I have a choice?"

No, he wanted to say. But he had to give her a choice; another of his traditions that may have been a rule, or may have been a preference. "Yes, you have a choice. But know that you'll always be mine, whatever you decide." And she would be. No mortal man would satisfy her now.

"I don't want to just be some whore," she said.

"You will be my Consort. My companion; the only one."

"Will I be able to return here, once in a while? I may not be overly fond of it, but it's still my home."

Ares nodded. "Of course. We shall both visit, Lord and Lady Aristoun."

Serena sighed and nuzzled his neck with her cheek. "Do we leave now?"

The god lifted her slim waist and settled her atop him, slim thighs straddling his groin. "Not yet," he growled, before claiming her mouth in a hungry, promising kiss.

♈ TEASE PUBLISHING LLC
Quality Women's Fiction and Literature
www.teasepublishingllc.com

With something for everyone, Tease Publishing is a publisher committed to bringing readers quality works of both fiction and literature sure to keep you coming back for more!

Tease Publishing is a GREEN company, utilizing POD (print-on-demand) printing and E books so there is no waste and no unneeded stress on the environment.

Shop Tease books online at All Romance E books and Amazon.com and in print at bookstores around the world.

To receive special promo, goodies and up to the minute information on all our authors and events! To join the email list: Email marketing@teasepublishingllc.com with "Mailing List" in the subject

To join the snail mail list: Email the above email or send your address to :

Snail Mailing club
Tease Publishing LLC
P.O.Box 234
Swansboro N.C.
28584-0234